Dark Water

Dark Ship

Dark Horse

Dark Shadows

Dark Paradise

Dark Fury

Dark Shadows

© 2019 Evan Graver

www.evangraver.com

All rights reserved. No part of this publication may be reproduced, distributed, or transmitted in any forms or by any means, including photocopying, recording, or other electronic, or mechanical methods, without the prior written permission of the publisher, except in the case of brief quotations embodied in critical reviews and certain noncommercial uses permitted by copyright law.

ISBN-10: 1-7338866-3-X

ISBN-13: 978-1-7338866-3-5

This is a work of fiction. Any resemblance to actual people, places, or institutions is entirely coincidental. Any resemblance to any person, living or dead, business, companies, events, or locales is entirely coincidental.

Printed and bound in the United States of America

First Printed March 2018

Published by Third Reef Publishing, LLC

Hollywood, Florida

www.thirdreefpublishing.com

DARK SHADOWS

A Ryan Weller Thriller

EVAN GRAVER

CHAPTER ONE

Phillipe Fernandez swung down from the semi-truck and glanced around the crowded dock space. Shipping containers stood in long rows, stacked four high all along the waterfront of the Luis A. Ayala Colón San Juan Terminal. Phillipe consulted his paperwork and checked the number of the container against the manifest. Satisfied he had the right container, he stowed the paperwork on the seat of his truck and pulled on a pair of leather gloves, then walked around the container, which sat on a trailer chassis. He took comfort in the routine. It made this job much easier. The repetitive actions calmed him as he tried to control his heart rate through his breathing. Blood thundered in his ears, eyes darting around furtively.

Phillipe knew many of the workers at both the Colón Terminal on the mainland and the Isla Grande Terminal on the Isla Grande isthmus, the two facilities forming the San Juan Port Authority. Standing on the shore of either facility, a worker could look across the sparkling Bay of San Juan and see the giant gantry cranes of the other. The Colón facility was twice the size of Isla Grande.

The web of freeways right outside the Colón's gates would allow Phillipe to make a quick escape.

He kicked the tires on the trailer and peered through the small holes in container corner castings to see if the twist locks securing it to the trailer were engaged. Satisfied the container was secured to the chassis, he backed his tractor under the trailer until the fifth wheel locked onto the trailer pin. Then, climbing out of the cabin, he held onto the chrome grab bar on the side of his aging red Kenworth T800B day cab and swung himself back to the tractor's rear frame. He shoved in a lever to lock the trailer king pin into the fifth wheel, then plugged in the various air lines and harnesses.

This had become Phillipe's standard routine, ever since he'd lied about his age to get his commercial license at sixteen. Driving trucks was his dream job.

After Hurricane Maria had struck the island in 2017, he'd been one of the first drivers to show up for work. He understood the vital importance of distributing the supplies being shipped in from the United States. There had been more containers at the port facilities than he'd ever seen before. Some companies couldn't access their normal shipments because of the relief supplies flooding into the country. During those desperate weeks and months after the hurricanes, he'd contended with diesel shortages, proposed driver labor strikes, and the lack of electricity and food.

Phillipe dropped to the ground and used the hand crank to raise the trailer's landing gear and when fully retracted, locked it in place. He took more deep breaths while walking back to the truck cab. The breathing exercises calmed him before he had to face the scrutiny of the security guards. He swung into the seat and checked his dash to ensure everything was functioning properly. Then he shoved the gear shifter into first and idled through the yard before stopping at the gate.

Phillipe rolled down the window and handed over his paperwork to the guard. He felt like his heart would beat out of his chest. Sweat peppered the back of his neck and trickled down his back. How many times had he done this in the past few months? His skin still crawled like someone had eyes on him and they knew his secret.

"*Buenos dias*, Phillipe," the guard named Emanuel said in greeting.

"*¿Como estas?*" *How are you?* Phillipe asked, his tongue thick in his dry mouth.

"*Bien, ¿y tú?*" *Good, and you?* Emanuel replied.

Phillipe grinned, fighting back his anxiety. "*Bien, bien.*" He'd been dealing with the guard for years, and while they joked like old friends, Phillipe didn't think Emanuel would look the other way when it came to stealing containers. Phillipe's conscious screamed at him to stop his crimes, but the devil on his other shoulder urged him to continue. He needed money for his family.

Emanuel handed the manifest back and returned to his guard booth. He reached inside, and Phillipe drew a deep breath. Was he calling port security? Or the State Police, what the Puerto Ricans called *La Uniformada*? Did Emanuel know he was stealing the container?

Open the gate, Phillipe willed silently.

The gate swung up, and Phillipe let out the breath he'd been holding while easing off the clutch. The truck rolled forward, wheels pressing down the spike strip embedded into the black top. The tiger teeth clinked and rattled as they popped down and up when each tire rolled over them. Phillipe watched his rearview mirrors to see when the trailer cleared the gate.

He turned onto the on-ramp for John F. Kennedy

Expressway and sped away from the port. He'd cleared the biggest hurdle. Now he needed to snake his way over the mountains to the south side of the island and deposit his cargo container at the Rafael Cordero Santiago Port of Americas in Ponce. After dropping the trailer, he would haul another load back to San Juan.

Such was his life as a bandit. He collected a manifest from his contacts and hauled a trailer to a different port or dropped it somewhere on the island. To him, it made little difference where the containers went or what they held, as long as he received the thick white envelopes full of cash.

Phillipe smiled as he downshifted for the long climb up through the mountains, his favorite part of the drive. From the top, he could see the ocean stretching to the horizon, an endless rolling mass of blue. Tomorrow, he'd do it all over again.

CHAPTER TWO

Shawn Lindowel pulled a hand-rolled Don Collins cigar from his shirt pocket and lit it with a match. He stared down the expansive fairway of the fourteenth green of the Bahia Beach Golf Course. This was his favorite hole at his favorite course in Puerto Rico. He loved to break out the driver and swing big. He liked to believe his fifty pounds of extra girth helped him flow through the swing and drive the ball deep down the fairway.

"Think you can clear the water and land it on the green?" Dan Foose asked.

Shawn ran a hand through his sandy blond hair. "Nah, I've tried it before, and I can't make it. That's like five hundred yards."

Dan, Shawn's business partner, was a slim man whose brown hair was close-cropped to ease the pain of losing the battle with male pattern baldness. "Let it eat, big dog."

Shawn balanced his cigar on the edge of the golf cart and extracted his Callaway driver from the bag. Stepping into the tee box, he planted a ball and tee and took his stance over them, wiggling the club and grinding his feet into the turf. In the silence, he could hear the ocean crashing onto the beach. An iguana eyed him with curiosity. Then he wound up and smacked the tiny ball two hundred and twenty-six yards.

"Hooked it," Dan said, holding a hand up to shade his eyes as he watched the white orb soar through the air.

"Don't gloat," Shawn replied, still in his follow-through stance and tracking the ball.

The ball landed in the tall grass beside the lake edging the fairway.

"You're in the rough," Dan said.

Shawn grunted and stepped back to the cart, slid his club into the bag, and picked up his cigar. He drew deeply on it and watched Dan take his time to line up his shot. "Any day now, princess."

"Shut your pie hole," Dan said, staring at the ball and taking a few practice swings. He set his feet and drove the ball just shy of two hundred yards.

"Nice shot," Shawn said.

"A rare compliment, but I'll take it."

Shawn sat down in the cart's passenger seat. "Let's go chase our balls."

Dan slid into the driver's seat, but just as he put his foot on the pedal, Shawn's cell phone rang. "This better be good," Shawn said to the caller as he answered the phone.

"Mr. Lindowel, this is Erik Salazar. I'm at the port to pick up the container for Dark Water Research, and it's not here. I had the port check their records and they found a forged manifest showing the container went out last night."

Shawn punched the roof of the golf cart. This was the fifth container stolen from the port in the last two weeks. DWR wasn't the only company losing containers. The shipping companies built cargo losses into their models, but this blatant theft right from the docks was unacceptable.

Shawn let out a long breath to control himself. "Thanks for letting me know."

"*¡No te preocupes!*" *Don't worry!*

Shawn ended the call without responding and muttered, "But I am worried about it."

Containers were turning up missing at all nine ports on the island. During the glut of shipping after the hurricanes, the thieves had stolen everything they could get their hands on for either resale or to distribute to the hardest hit areas while the governments argued with each other. Now that shipping had returned to normal, the thieves had become more creative in their approach. To Shawn, the thefts were another symptom of the problems plaguing the U.S. territory.

He remembered when it wasn't like this. When he'd first come to Puerto Rico on a golf vacation following his divorce in 2001, the island was thriving. He'd fallen in love with the slower pace of life and the lush green mountains surrounded by a color wheel of watery blues. Instead of going back to the freezing temperatures of Wisconsin and the business he ran with his father, he'd stayed on the island. He loved his dad, but they rarely saw eye to eye, and the constant pressure to perform to impossible standards had driven him to drink and cost him his marriage. His drinking had slowed after his move to the island, but he still got hammered. He knew his alcoholism was affecting his health, but he couldn't pass up the delicious rum.

He'd seen his buddies off at the airport and made a friendly bet with them about how long it would be before he was back shuffling paperwork for dear old Dad. Shawn vowed he'd never go back, and he'd prove to his father, his friends, and to his ex-wife that he could make it on his own.

With his background in shipping, Crowley Marine had hired him to work at their terminal on Isla Grande. After a few years of midlevel management, he was running the whole

Crowley terminal. Then a few years later, he left to start L&F Logistics with Dan. His income had dropped, but he was his own boss, and if things worked as planned, they would sell out and retire to the golf course for good.

The 2008 American recession and the two devastating hurricanes in 2017 had put a crimp in his plans, pushing back retirement by a good ten years. But the island was making a slow comeback. The Puerto Rican government had pushed through reform bills to reignite the stagnant economy and were in talks with Washington on how to mitigate their debt. A spark of enthusiasm was burning for the reforms, which would push Puerto Rico toward becoming the Singapore of the Caribbean. If that were to happen, it would line Shawn and Dan's pockets with cash.

Until then, they needed to find a way to combat the cargo losses and end the freight claim lawsuits being filed by cargo owners for the non-delivery of their shipments. L&F Logistics and several other cargo carriers had been jointly sued for lost profits.

Dan let off the throttle and the cart rolled to a stop. He left Shawn sitting in the cart as he went to get his ball. Shawn puffed on his cigar. Dan wasn't a great golfer. He could hit the long ball, but his short game left room for improvement. Shawn watched as his partner centered himself and drove the ball a meager one-hundred yards. He was on his way to shooting well below par.

Dan returned to the cart and shoved his club into his bag, muttering unintelligible expletives.

Shawn took another draw on the cigar. With his buoyant mood now gone, he didn't care about finishing the round. He had a phone call to make, and he was dreading it. He pulled the cigar from his lips. "Let's call it a day."

"We only have four more holes," Dan protested.

"You and I both know who will win this round, and I've lost my enthusiasm for the game."

"The missing container?"

Shawn nodded and rubbed the bridge of his nose. "That makes three DWR containers they've stolen."

"We need to call them."

"Unfortunately."

Dan raised a brow. "You serious about quitting?"

"Let's go to the club house," Shawn said. "I need a drink."

Dan shook his head and drove the cart to where Shawn's ball was nestled in the rough. He picked it up without getting out of the cart and then continued down the fairway to where his own ball rested in the grass between the sand trap and the green. "I had a decent lie for once."

Shawn grinned. "You still won't beat me."

"Probably not." Dan shrugged. "I don't know why I bother playing with you."

"You're a glutton for punishment."

"A freaking sadist is more like it," Dan grumbled. "I'm always getting my ass kicked, first at golf and now at sporting clays."

Shawn smirked. Several years ago, Dan had introduced Shawn to shooting sporting clays, and Shawn knew it irked him that he was a better shot.

At the spacious club house, the two men took seats at one of the restaurant's outside tables and ordered locally made rum and their usual lunch. After Shawn had belted down the first drink, he pulled out his phone. The waiter brought another shot, and Shawn kicked it back before dialing Greg Olsen, DWR's owner and logistics manager on the island.

When Greg answered, Shawn introduced himself. He had met Greg only once before, when he'd dropped by Shawn's office to discuss the first missing container.

"Don't tell me we've lost another shipment," Greg said.

The waiter had returned with the bottle of rum. Shawn cleared his throat and pointed at the shot glass. He wanted to feel the warmth of the liquor sliding down his esophagus and spreading across his belly. Once the waiter filled the glass, Shawn motioned for him to leave the bottle, then shooed him away with a gesture. "You're not the only one losing containers. There's been a rash of thefts since the hurricanes."

"Are they targeting us or is it random?"

"So far, it seems random. My theory is that they're getting a look at the manifests and picking what containers they want. We know they're forging manifests to get the containers out of the port facilities. From there, I suspect they're changing the container numbers and creating new manifests to ship them off island. The police have also found repainted containers."

"This puts a crimp in our deadline, Shawn."

"I know, Mr. Olsen," Shawn said. "We can try to source the supplies locally."

"I'll probably do that. Getting a new container shipped here will take too much time."

"I'll do what I can to expedite it." Shawn spun the shot glass on the table. Three shots were a warmup for him. He could kill the bottle over the afternoon.

"I knew I should have loaded a supply vessel with everything we needed," Greg said. "I was trying to use just-in-time shipping to minimize costs and better allocate DWR's resources."

"I understand, Mr. Olsen, and I promised you I would do everything in my power to keep this from happening, but it's beyond me now. We should ask the police to investigate."

"With all the missing containers, aren't they investigating them already?"

"Not that I know of," Shawn said. He would have kept

track of such an investigation—not just for DWR, but for all the shipping companies he dealt with.

"When are you back at the office?"

"Monday."

"Good. I'll come by in the morning."

"See you then." Shawn hung up and laid the phone on the table. He poured a shot and spun the glass. He'd been fifteen when he'd had his first beer, and he couldn't remember a day since when he hadn't had at least one drink. His stomach rubbed the edge of the table, preventing him from getting closer. Too many carbs had packed on the pounds. Shawn drank the rum. Its fire flared in his belly, tamping down the withering sarcasm he wanted to hurl at his partner. The waiter arrived with their food, and they dove in. Shawn used it to avoid the topic at hand.

The golf course manager, Andrea, approached the table. Shawn looked up at the young woman. He was in no mood for her bubbly cheerfulness. He somehow resented her for being so young and beautiful and already a manager of a golf resort. She wore her normal uniform of a golf skirt and polo shirt bearing the club's logo on the left breast pocket.

Andrea paused under the shade of the umbrella. With a smile, she said, "*Buenas tardes, señores.*" *Good afternoon.*

Dan smiled back. "*Buenas tardes.*"

Shawn ignored her.

Andrea inclined her head. Her forceful stare made Shawn glance up. With a sweetness that made Shawn want to puke, she asked, "*¿Cómo estás?*" *How are you?*

How was he? He stared at his sandwich and mumbled, "*La piña está agria.*" *Times are tough.*

CHAPTER THREE

Ryan Weller leaned on his shovel and watched the excavator dredge its bucket through the mud, roots, and water of the old canal before depositing the overburden in the back of a truck. Shirtless like most of the Haitians he was working with, sweat ran down his broad, tan back. At six feet tall, he stood a good six inches above his average Haitian contemporary. He wore khaki cargo shorts and desert tan combat boots. To keep his head cool he'd trimmed his shaggy brown hair back to a "number three all over." He dragged the back of his hand across his forehead and looked at the sweat puddled on his skin.

The men around him chatted in Creole, eager to return to their farming. The canal, when opened, would provide irrigation to their fields from the Grande Rivière du Nord. He watched the people mill about. Their jubilant attitude was infectious. Even though many of them suffered from abject poverty, they were a joyous people. The simple things in life made them happy. For them, getting water to their crops was one of the best things to happen to them in a long time.

A month ago, Ryan and his crew on the salvage vessel *Peggy Lynn* had recovered twenty-five-million dollars in gold from a sunken freighter. Haitian warlord Joulie Lafitte had provided them with protection, and in exchange, they'd returned half of the gold to her. The gold had been payment for an arms transaction between Joulie's former fiancé, Toussaint Bajeux, and international arms dealer Jim Kilroy. Both men were now dead, and Joulie was putting her portion of the gold to use by helping the locals rebuild from the damaging hurricanes of Maria and Irma.

Joulie's residence was in Cap-Haïtien, and she controlled large portions of the island state's northern peninsula. To date, she had built a facility that converted plastics to fuel oil, rebuilt houses and schools, endowed grants to the local colleges, planted orchards and scores of trees to help combat deforestation. She employed hundreds of people to scour the beaches, riverbanks, and city streets to collect plastic trash to feed the fuel oil plant. Men removed sunken vessels from Cap-Haïtien and Fort-Liberté Bay before dismantling them on the beaches. She'd ordered derelict homes torn down, the usable material salvaged for future projects, and the debris burned or discarded.

Thousands of vehicles crowded the junkyards around Cap-Haïtien. An obscure Haitian law allowed for the importation of vehicles, regardless of operational status or age. The shippers, often family members in the U.S. or local businessmen, packed the vehicles with everything from canned goods to car parts to bicycles and clothing before sending them to Haiti. For many, it was a cheap way to transport goods into the country.

The Haitians stripped all the valuable parts from any vehicles that didn't run before abandoning them in the streets and woods on the outskirts of the city. Joulie hired a towing company to transport the broken vehicles to a crusher she'd set up near the fuel plant. Then she sold the crushed vehicles and other scrap to a Chinese recycling company, which shipped the metal overseas. Not only was she providing jobs, Joulie was making money cleaning up the country. She put the money back into rebuilding the economy, like this canal project.

Ryan watched as a young boy leaped off a mound of dirt into the canal. His parents scolded him, and he climbed from the water, coated with mud. Despite the reprimand, he grinned from ear to ear, and Ryan laughed.

James, another young boy ran up to Ryan. "*Meyse* Ryan, mambo Joulie wants to speak with you."

Ryan smiled down at the kid who'd been his shadow since he'd arrived at the dig site three days ago. "Yeah? What's she want to talk about?"

James held his hands out, palms up, and shrugged. Then he pointed toward the tent used for a headquarters. "She call on the telephone."

"All right, chief, let's go."

James raced ahead of Ryan, who handed his shovel to one of the other workers and made his way across the field to the tent.

The boy had taken to sleeping outside Ryan's tent until Ryan had caught him, and James had explained that his parents had died, and he lived with his uncle. Ryan had set up a cot for him in his tent. James carried messages between the foreman, Jonas Ineus, and Ryan. Having learned English in school and by watching television, he acted as an interpreter when Ryan had trouble understanding the Creole language or the heavy accents. The workers were deferential to Ryan. They knew the *nèg blan*—white man—had a special relationship with the *mambo*—vodou priestess—who financed their projects.

Jonas pointed at the satellite phone sitting on a desk and left the tent.

He picked up the phone and sat in the canvas chair. "This is Ryan."

"Hello, *mennaj mwen*." *My lover*.

Her sultry purr was intoxicating, even over the sat phone. He pictured the mahogany-skinned woman with jet-black hair falling in waves to her mid-back. Her blue eyes were a genetic anomaly that she claimed were a gift from the loa. They'd also blessed her with above average height and a commanding presence which she'd cultivated with a bit of ruthless aggression to take Toussaint's place. Ryan had seen her be both the caring visionary and a cold-blooded bitch.

"What's up?"

"Your boss called for you."

"I know." He grinned. "What can I do for you, boss?"

Joulie giggled. "No, *mennaj*." Her tone became more serious. "Your other boss, Greg Olsen."

Ryan nodded, watching the excavator through the tent flaps. "What'd he want?"

"He didn't tell me. He just said to have you call him. You left your satellite phone at *Roi* Christophe." The King Christophe had once been a summer home for Henri Christophe in the 1800s. Now it was a hotel in the heart of "the Cap," as the locals called their city, and Joulie's home.

"Yes, I did." Ryan smirked. He'd done it on purpose. Despite the abject poverty and the supposed security risks, he enjoyed helping with the infrastructure projects Joulie was implementing. It was a nice break from his normal underwater salvage and troubleshooting gig. If Greg couldn't reach him, Ryan didn't have to go back to work. "How's everything in Port-au-Prince?"

Joulie sighed. "Not so well. Have you not heard?"

"Heard what?"

"The people of Port-au-Prince are rioting in the street and demanding Prime Minister Lafontant and President Moïse step down. President Moïse tried to institute a fifty-percent price increase on both diesel and gasoline, higher for kerosene, all to balance a budget." She sighed again, sharper this time. "The people are angry because a liter of petrol would cost seven dollars. How can my people afford fuel when they make less than three dollars a day? What started as protests has turned into looting and burning stores. They've put up roadblocks and have killed several people. We're trapped in the hotel."

"Are you all right?"

"I'm fine."

Ryan recognized the weariness in her voice, both from the strain of being trapped and from the desperation she felt for her country. "Why are they burning the stores? They're only hurting themselves."

"They say they have nothing left, so burning the stores doesn't change their lives, but in many respects, it doesn't. At the same time ...." She let out another long sigh. "Those stores provide the goods they need to survive."

Joulie paused and spoke to someone else, her muffled voice impossible to make out. Then, she came back on the line.

"David Pinchina is coming to get our delegation. Jean-Claude Duval needs to get back to the Cap to help stabilize things there."

Ryan had met Cap-Haïtien's mayor and thought he was doing a fair job under Joulie's tutelage. "Are they rioting there, too?" he asked.

"Yes. The fuel hike would affect the whole country."

Ryan watched the excavator work, water streaming from each bucket of mud it dragged out of the canal. Little waterfalls cascaded from holes in the truck bed as it drained and ran in rivulets back to the canal. A line from an old Desert Rose Band song sprang into Ryan's mind. *One step forward and two steps back / nobody gets very far like that.* It could be the country's theme song.

Joulie interrupted his thoughts, her frustration palpable over the phone. "I'm afraid our mission to lobby Parliament and the UN for money for a desalinization plant and a wastewater treatment facility is a failure."

"I thought President Moïse's Change Caravan was trying to address those issues."

"He was. As you can see, it hasn't gone well."

"I think you should do what we talked about and build a Civilian Conservation Corps. Like Roosevelt did during the Great Depression."

Joulie sighed. They'd been over this before. The idea was that the population would get training in a variety of skills, and the country's infrastructure would receive a much-needed facelift. "I am trying. It is difficult to win over the minds in Port-au-Prince. The government is not always cooperative. I thought we might find common ground ... maybe after they sort the fuel crisis out."

"When will you be back?" Ryan asked.

"David is landing the helicopter on the roof in a few minutes. I need to finish packing."

"All right. Greg probably wants me to do some troubleshooting."

"I felt the same. The loa will bless you."

Ryan smiled. Joulie often consulted the many vodou gods of her religion, believing they assisted the God of the Catholic Church. "I'll call you after I find out what's going on."

"Please do," Joulie said. "You will need to arrange for alternate transportation off the island. All the airlines have stopped flights in and out."

"Can David fly me down?"

"I think we can arrange it. We'll stop to pick you up. It would not be safe for a lone white man to drive through the city. I must go. I will see you soon."

"*Wi*, madam." They said goodbye and disconnected.

He stretched his legs out and crossed them at the ankles. The country had experienced an illusionary feeling of peace. Underneath the beautiful Caribbean exterior lay a current of resistance and unease. It had been that way since the Spaniards had first arrived on the island, named it Hispaniola, and enslaved its residents. Ryan reached into a cooler and pulled out a bottle of water.

He wondered what the crew of the *Peggy Lynn* was doing. After they'd received a cash payment from Joulie for the gold salvaged from the sunken freighter, *Santo Domingo*, they'd scattered. The *Peggy Lynn* herself was in dry docks in San Juan, Puerto Rico, for a refit of both her engines and running gear.

Travis Wisnewski, *Peggy Lynn*'s trained commercial diver, and his girlfriend, Stacey Coleman, had flown back to the States to visit their respective parents and continue to cement their relationship. Don Williams, the boat's mechanical engineer, had gone back to Texas City to spend time with his girlfriend, Ashlee Calvo, a computer technician at DWR. Captain Dennis Law, *Peggy Lynn*'s owner, and his octogenarian first mate, Emery Ducane, had elected to stay in San Juan to oversee the refit.

Ryan had stayed in Cap-Haïtien with the beautiful warlord. He'd been sharing her bed since he'd first come to the country to retrieve the gold. He'd given her his share of his salvage profits to invest in infrastructure projects with a promised return. Not only was he doing something worthwhile with his money, he was able to keep his profits and dividends hidden from the prying eyes of government tax collectors.

Although, he had doubts now about seeing a return. He was thankful he didn't need the money. He'd squirreled away over a million dollars after he and his then-partner at DWR, Mango Hulsey, had split a bag of cash they'd taken off a gunrunning ship in the Gulf of Mexico. He considered it hazardous duty pay after having his sailboat shot out from under him and enduring two long days floating in the open ocean before being picked up by a Mexican fishing vessel.

In Haiti, Ryan was acting as a day laborer and construction consultant. He'd grown up working for his father's construction company and had tried to make it his life's work after a ten-year stint in the U.S. Navy as an explosive ordnance disposal technician, but he'd missed the adventurous life he'd led, sailing around the world when he was eighteen, then working with the military's elite bomb squads. When Greg Olsen had offered him a position at DWR as their Homeland Security liaison, Ryan had jumped at the chance to get back into the action.

The first mission to hunt down pirates in the Gulf of Mexico had resulted in Ryan seizing the gunrunning ship and killing the leader of the Aztlán Cartel. Jose Luis Orozco, the cartel's new leader, had placed a two-million-dollar bounty on Ryan's head. Undeterred, Ryan tracked down the international gun dealer, Jim Kilroy, who had sold weapons to the Aztlán Cartel.

Kilroy had coerced Ryan and Mango into transporting a shipload of weapons to Toussaint Bajeux in Haiti, but a rival warlord sank the shipment along with Toussaint's gold payment. Ryan and Mango had gone down with the ship, swimming to shore using rebreather diving equipment. His mission had been unsanctioned by his Homeland handler, which had led to Ryan's unofficial disassociation with both DWR and Homeland. Mango and his wife had sailed off on their sailboat, and Ryan had hidden in the Florida Keys, teaching scuba diving.

But the gold had called to him, and he'd convinced Captain Dennis to use his vessel to help salvage it. Now, Ryan was an independent contract troubleshooter for DWR and in a complicated relationship with Joulie.

Ryan drained the last of the water in the bottle and tossed it into a nearby recycling bin. He wished he had a cigarette. Two weeks ago, he'd smoked the last of his American Camel Blues and had vowed to quit. He wasn't sure if he was glad that he had stopped or if he just missed the repetitive action of bringing his hand to his mouth.

He dialed Greg Olsen and put the satellite phone to his ear. When Greg answered, Ryan asked, "How's life in Puerto Rico?"

"Better than yours, I can tell you that."

"Is it?"

"Air conditioning and ice-cold beer. I hear you're sweating in some old tent in the middle of nowhere while the natives burn down their country."

"Pretty much," Ryan said.

"Get your ass to San Juan. We have a job."

"What's going on?"

"Someone is stealing cargo containers from the terminals," Greg said. "Three DWR containers have disappeared in the last two weeks."

Ryan sat forward, intrigued. "An inside job?"

"I don't think so. We're using a local company with a good reputation. How soon can you get here?"

"I'm not sure. David Pinchina might have to fly me down. The airlines have stopped all flights in and out of Haiti."

"We're scheduled to meet with the shipping company execs on Monday morning. That'll give you three days to get here."

"What day is it?"

"Friday," Greg said. "Have you been in the bush that long?"

"We're digging an irrigation canal."

"Sounds romantic. Now get a move on. I'll see you in a few."

"Aye, aye, Skipper," Ryan said and hung up the phone. With a sigh, he shoved himself out of the chair and walked out of the tent.

James came running up, drenched to the skin. His wet, baggy shorts outlined the thinness of his legs and his bare chest heaved with excitement. Pointing at the canal and a group of boys sliding down the muddy bank, he exclaimed, "We made a slide."

Ryan smiled. The boy had a huge grin on his face, like most children worldwide despite their circumstances. They enjoyed the simple pleasures in life before what Ryan liked to call Adult Worry Syndrome set in. "Glad you're having fun."

"*Wi*." James grinned. "Do you want to jump in?"

Ryan laughed. "No, I've got to get going."

James stuck out his bottom lip and hung his head.

Ryan squatted beside him. "Don't worry, kid. I'll be back before they finish this project."

The boy nodded solemnly. "Can I come with you?"

"Afraid not, buddy. I have to go to Puerto Rico. Did you know they lost all their power after the hurricane?"

James shook his head. How could he know? The boy didn't have access to newspapers and what television he did watch consisted of soccer matches.

"They have problems with their food and electricity just like you guys do. I'll help them for a little bit and then I'll be back."

One of the nearby men yelled at James. Ryan caught a few words, some of them not too kind. The man laughed, and James ran into the woods. Ryan wanted to run after him and tell him everything would be okay, but he didn't. He couldn't make such a promise.

Ryan walked down to where Jonas Ineus stood with a group of men beside the now silent excavator. They were staring into the trench and discussing something in rapid Creole. Ryan motioned the foreman away from the group.

When Jonas walked over, he said, "They are arguing whether to dig another canal to a small village nearby."

"Tell them to finish dredging the existing canal, and then talk about making changes."

"Yes, sir," Jonas said.

"I have to go to Puerto Rico, but I should be back in two weeks. Joulie expects the canal to be completed by then." He'd lied to James. He didn't know when he'd return to this tiny village, if ever. He was being called back to his life in a world much different from this simple way of existence.

Jonas bobbed his head. "It will be."

"Good," Ryan said.

"When will you go?"

"Soon. Joulie is coming to pick me up."

Jonas moved closer to him and lowered his voice. "I would recommend you stay in your tent until she arrives. The people are rioting against the government's increase in fuel prices. There is much anger and there are men here who want to take it out on you."

"I had nothing to do with it."

"This, I know. They only see you as a wealthy white man

who represents the evils of the UN and the United States, you understand?"

"Yeah, I get it," Ryan said, glancing around.

"Good. Go quickly, now, to the tent. Remember what I showed you there?"

Ryan nodded. There was a rust-pitted Beretta M9 in a footlocker.

The foreman said, "Keep it handy."

CHAPTER FOUR

The excavator started as Ryan walked to the tent. He kept a wary eye on the armed guards hired to protect the dig site. There were six, rotating in shifts of two, each bearing either an AK-47 or a pump-action shotgun and a side arm. Several had sheathed machetes dangling from their belts. One guard sat on the catwalk of the excavator's cab, gun laying across his knees. The other smoked a cigarette near the tents.

Inside the tent, Ryan opened his backpack and pulled out his Walther PPQ 9mm. There was a round locked in the chamber and fifteen more snub-nose hollow points in the magazine. Out of habit, he press-checked the slide just enough to see the cartridge. He slipped the inside of the belt holster between his shorts and underwear, inserted the pistol, and pulled his shirt over the butt. In his right pocket was a tactical folding knife. He was preparing to run if things went loud, but he hoped the loonies left him alone. He was here to help people, not hurt them.

Just as he finished zipping his bag closed, he heard angry shouts outside. The noise of the excavator's engine died, and the shouting grew louder. Cautiously, he peeled back the tent flap to peek outside.

A mob of men, bared to the waist and shiny with sweat, crowded around the excavator. Several carried rifles and shotguns while others brandished thick clubs or garden implements.

Jonas climbed up to the cab of the excavator and beseeched the crowd in Creole. Ryan picked up parts of the man's speech. He railed against the government for raising fuel prices but insisted that Joulie and Ryan were helping them by digging the canal.

A rustling at the rear of the tent startled him. Ryan swung around, left hand sweeping his shirt away, right hand pulling the Walther. He trained the gun on the moving canvas.

James poked his grinning head underneath.

The grin disappeared when James saw the gun pointed at him. He scrambled backward.

"Stop," Ryan hissed.

James froze, but when Ryan holstered the pistol, he wiggled forward. Ryan ran to him, grabbed him under the armpits, pulled him under the tent wall, and stood him on his feet in one swift motion.

He knelt by the boy. "What's going on?"

"They ..." James's voice quivered.

"They can't see you or hear you. Whisper if you want."

"The men are angry about the fuel prices and want to know who is paying for the digger. They think you are. You are a rich man, *non?*"

"No," Ryan said. "Everyone knows mambo Joulie is paying for the excavator."

"They think you are using her. That's what the man said before I ran away." Tears welled at the corners of his eyes.

"It's okay." Ryan put a hand on the boy's shoulder.

James wiped tears from his cheeks with the back of his

hand, but the comforted look on his face changed to one of terror.

"What is it?" Ryan asked. He understood a moment later: The crowd was surging toward the tent, chanting his name. "Go, James. Run and hide."

"Please don't leave me," he whispered. His lower lip quivered, and Ryan hoped the boy didn't have a sobbing meltdown on the earthen floor of the tent.

"Run—go now," Ryan pleaded.

James shook his head and stood his ground.

Ryan rose to his feet. He had to protect this brave little boy and keep him safe from the angry crowd. He wanted to know what the crowd was chanting, to understand their grievances, but Ryan knew a mob ran on fear. It would be difficult to rationalize with them.

Right outside the tent flap, Jonas's voice boomed above the crowd. "*Sispann!*" *Stop!*

The crowd did not listen. Their chanting filled the tent with a noise so loud it caused James to cover his little ears. Ryan reached for the reassuring grip of the pistol as the tent began to shake. If they were coming for him, he'd take a few of the bastards with him.

He smelled smoke before spying the flame licking at the rear corner of the tent's canvas. He shouldered into his backpack and drew James to him, squatting again as he placed both hands on the boy's shoulders.

"We're in trouble, buddy. If they come in, I'll hold them off. You're young, kid, but you need to get away. Go to the Roi Christophe in Cap-Haïtien. It's a hotel."

The boy nodded.

"Find mambo Joulie and tell her I sent you. Tell her ..." He tried to think of the right words to get Joulie to take the boy in. "Tell her you worked for me and tell her that she has a scar on the back of her thigh. Right here." He pointed at the spot just under the buttocks on his right leg. "She got it when she was a little girl, climbing through the rubble of a landslide to find her parents. She fell and sliced it open on a piece of glass. Tell her I told you and I said she is to take care of you."

Tears left trails through the dust on James's face. Snot bubbled from his left nostril, but he nodded. Outside, the crowd grew louder. The flame had spread up the walls, opening a hole in the wall.

When Ryan glanced up, the angry faces of the mob stared back.

Ryan shook the boy's shoulders to bring his eyes back from the gnawing flames. "Repeat it to me."

"Go to the Roi Christophe. Tell mambo Joulie she has a scar, here." James pointed. "She cut her leg on glass when her parents died in an earthquake."

"Exactly." Ryan stood, gripped James's shoulder, and steered him toward the burning hole. He held the Walther out in front of him.

CHAPTER FIVE

Joulie Lafitte stared out the window of the dark green Bell 212 helicopter, a civilian version of the Vietnam-era Huey. Below, a crowd encircled a smoking tent. Flames fed on the sides, curling away the canvas. A slight wind lifted ash and still smoldering pieces of tent into the air and swirled them into the thick, black smoke pouring off the fully engulfed excavator. The wind from the helicopter's rotors fanned the flames of both the tent and excavator.

"Can you land near the tent?" she asked the pilot, David Pinchina.

"*Wi*," he said, angling the machine toward the open field on the far side of the flaming tent.

Her throat burned with bile and her heart lurched when she saw Ryan. He'd stepped out of the burning hole, pushing a small boy with one hand and swinging a pistol back and forth with the other. The crowd did not part. Men with guns pressed the crowd closer to them.

Ryan pulled the boy tight to him and pointed the gun at the head of a man holding a shotgun at port arms. The man tried to stumble backward, but the roaring crowd pushed him forward. Ryan put his pistol's muzzle between the smaller man's eyes. The man dropped his gun and spread his arms. He moved backward, parting the crowd.

Joulie's whole body thrummed with her heartbeat. She felt lightheaded and clammy. Seeing her lover fight with her people was tearing her apart.

"I'm going to set it down right on the crowd," David said calmly into the headset.

Joulie looked up at him and nodded.

"Throw open the door as soon as I'm down. Don't let anyone on but Ryan and the kid."

"Okay," Joulie replied.

"He must mean something to Ryan. Looks like he's protecting him." David turned back to the controls and lowered the aircraft toward the crowd, bringing it to hover a mere ten feet off the ground. Smoke roiled in the rotor wash. Sand, grass, and loose debris pelted the mob. They scattered and ran for cover as the tent blew over and flapped along the ground.

Joulie placed her hand on the door handle, ready to slide it open. Just as the skids touched the ground, a hole appeared in the door's plexiglass window, and a crack formed between the hole and the bottom of the window's steel frame.

She fell back, eyes fixed on the hole. Her breath caught in her chest. No air came in through her windpipe despite the automatic flexing of her jaws.

"Open the door!" David screamed at her.

She couldn't make her limbs move. Everything was in a haze except the bullet hole.

"Open the door, Joulie! Open the door!"

The helicopter lurched a foot off the ground. For Joulie, the relief of leaving the danger buoyed her spirit, but the skids settled back onto the ground, flexing under the weight of the helicopter.

A hand clamped on her arm and shook her. Looking up, she saw David twisted around in the seat. He released her arm and put his hand on the flight controls. Behind her, someone pounded on the starboard door. The door behind Joulie rattled and shook on its track as people tried to jerk it open. She was thankful David had instructed her to lock it.

Adrenaline shot, raw and hot, into her veins. She had killed men, looked them in the eyes and watched them die, but being trapped in the helicopter while the crowd surrounded them had triggered an irrational terror.

With a new determination, she scrambled forward on the slick steel floor, reaching for the door handle. Before she could grab it, the door slid open and a small black boy tumbled into the cabin, followed by a familiar white man.

David threw full power to the twin jet engines, which shrieked in protest. Thunder roared off the rotors. The air flow rocked and buffeted the airframe. Dust and dirt whipped the air. Lost in the machinery's scream was the *pop, pop, pop* of small arms fire and the cries of the crowd. Several rioters jumped onto the skids. Ryan fought them off as they tried to crawl through the open door.

Suddenly, the helicopter shot into the air. Joulie's stomach, raw from the bile and adrenaline, seemed to slide down to her knees as centrifugal force plastered her to the floor. She saw two wide-eyed men clinging to the door frame. She glanced at Jean-Claude Duval, Cap-Haïtien's mayor, but he was ashen faced and remained belted to the seat beside her, fear palpable in his rigid body.

One rioter lost his grip and wheeled his arms to keep his balance on the skid. Ryan lunged for the man and grabbed his hand. The man hung in midair; the only thing connecting him to the helicopter was the tenuous grasp Ryan had on his wrist.

She sat up and the little boy stumbled into her lap, his

bare chest pressed against her. She attempted to cover his eyes, but he pushed her away. She tried to cover them again, but he crawled out of her lap.

Strangely, in his absence, she felt cold and alone.

"We've got a problem," David said. His dry voice didn't belie the seriousness of the issue.

CHAPTER SIX

Ryan's upper body hung out of the helicopter's passenger compartment; feet hooked around a passenger seat brace. Out of the corner of his eye, he saw the smoke trailing from the engine compartment. There was little he could do about it even if his hand wasn't locked around the dangling man's wrist.

Ryan looked into the man's dark eyes. He was no longer the fearsome rioter, pillaging and looting. He was a frightened man about to die, and Ryan couldn't hold on to him forever. His grip was weakening. Sweat slicked his cramping and spasming muscles. Ryan squeezed his legs tighter around the brace and reached down to grab the man's wrist with both his hands. He tried to pull up, but the man was a dead weight.

Without warning, the rioter slipped through his weakening grasp, flailing his arms and legs as he fell. Ryan stared after him until he disappeared into the trees. Dropping his head to the cool metal deck, he closed his eyes. He wished he'd looked away and wondered if he could ever forget the image of the man falling, the protuberance of his eyes, the inaudible scream escaping from his gaping mouth.

The other rioter who still clung to the outside of the helicopter edged along the skid and climbed into the cabin. He stepped over Ryan and sank into a seat beside James. When he caught sight of Joulie, his fear of the warlord replaced his fear of falling off the aircraft.

When he rolled over, Ryan noticed the man staring at the vodou priestess. Even crumpled on the floor, the woman looked radiant. Her eyes glared daggers back at the unwelcome interloper. Beside her was Jean-Claude Duval, a balding, reed thin man dressed in a rumpled black suit, who averted his gaze as well. He dabbed at the sweat glistening on his high forehead with a white handkerchief.

Ryan scrambled to his feet and slid the door closed, partially muting the wind and rotor noise. A whistle filled the void as wind rushed over the bullet hole. He extended a hand to Joulie and helped her to her feet, then donned a headset.

David strained to maintain control of the dying bird. Warning lights flashed across the control panels.

"What can I help with?" Ryan asked.

"I need a second pair of hands up here," David said.

Ryan climbed over the center console and settled into the left-hand seat.

"You ever flown a helicopter?" David asked through gritted teeth. The whine of the turbines had changed. Someone had perforated one with gun fire.

"I've had a few lessons," Ryan said, scanning the dashboard clusters and warning lights. He pointed at the blinking indicator for the port engine. "Want me to shut that off?"

"Yes." David glanced out the side window and then at the ground ahead, his eyes continuously scanning the dash, horizon, sky, and ground.

Ryan punched the button with the tip of his right index finger. The engine indicator light and several others winked out.

"Are we going to be okay?" Joulie asked.

Ryan glanced over his shoulder. She was standing between the two pilot seats, hands and knees braced against their steel backs. Behind her, James had a headset on and was seat-belted in beside their unknown passenger, who looked like he was about to shit his pants. James used his hands to push the earmuffs tight against the sides of his head, beaming a million-watt smile. He gave a thumbs-up when he saw Ryan looking at him.

The kid's calmer than the rest of us, Ryan thought as he turned back to the console. They were losing altitude. He took a minute to buckle his harness. Turning to the priestess, he said, "Better strap yourself in."

She met his eyes. He raised his eyebrows and motioned toward the back with a jerk of his head. Joulie stared at him for a moment longer before she pushed away and sat between James and their uninvited guest, buckling her seat belt.

David said, "We're not going to make it to the airport."

"Roger that," Ryan said. The drive from the outskirts of Cap-Haïtien to the canal worksite took about thirty minutes. Flying time was much less, and David had the helicopter angled to the northwest on a direct route to the Bell's hangar at the airport, but with a damaged engine, the bird was struggling to complete the journey.

They flashed over Route Nationale 3, a long ribbon of black tarmac stretching arrow-straight through a patchwork of green and brown fields interspersed with trees.

At least we have a clear landing, Ryan rationalized.

A massive banging reverberated through the airframe. The whole helicopter shuddered. Hydraulic fluid sprayed across the cabin and ran down the back walls. The rioter took the brunt of the pressurized liquid, and it soaked his pants and shirt. Joulie's clothes were wet with the purplish fluid, too.

Through the windscreen, Ryan could see the individual rotor blades as they spun in a slower and slower arc.

"We're going in," David shouted. He disengaged the clutch between the main gearbox and the rotors to allow the blades to freewheel, raised the nose, and lowered collective pitch to allow the upward thrust of the airflow to spin the rotors, so they auto-rotated into the field. David continued to manipulate the controls as the ground rushed up at them.

The Bell 212 smacked hard into the unforgiving earth, snapping off the starboard skid. Corn stalks and dirt flew as the rotor blades dug deep trenches into the earth before shattering into thousands of carbon fiber shards that pelted the helicopter's aluminum skin. A three-foot-long sliver punched through the windscreen like a javelin and embedded itself in the rear wall just inches from the rioter's face.

Upon impact, David had automatically begun to shut off switches and punch buttons. He seemed unfazed by the aircraft sliding forward on its belly, the drag of its port side skid slowly turning it to the left, tilling the soil and mowing down stalks of corn.

They came to a grinding halt. In the silence following the wreck, everyone sat stunned for a second, then Ryan and David scrambled out the doors.

Ryan jumped to the ground and ripped at the rear compartment door. The crash had buckled the airframe and jammed the door. He braced his feet for added leverage. He glanced up and saw Joulie through the window, helping to push. It wouldn't budge more than a few inches.

"Go through the front." Ryan pointed.

James was already scrambling out through the pilot's door. Ryan smiled. Leave it to the kid to figure it out.

Joulie tumbled out a moment later and wrapped her arms around Ryan. She pressed her face into his chest, and he held her close, one hand around her waist and the other on the back of her head. He saw their uninvited guest poke his head out of the Bell and glance around. His roving gaze froze on Ryan and Joulie.

"We need to get away from here," David said, coming around the nose of the crumpled helicopter. "There's a fuel leak."

He motioned for the other Haitian to come out and told him in Creole about the danger. The man leaped from the helicopter and ran away without looking back, disappearing into the corn. Jean-Claude Duval was the last man out of the damaged aircraft.

"Let's go," Ryan said.

Joulie steadied herself on her feet and extended her hand to James. The boy glanced up at Ryan before taking her hand. Ryan swore he saw a look of glee on the kid's face.

They hurried away from the helicopter. David led the way toward a house they'd seen from the air before crashing. Ryan recalled seeing the small cluster of white houses near a barn and a pond. He provided rear security for the group; thankful he still had his Walther holstered on his hip.

"How are things in Port-au-Prince?" Ryan asked.

"They are horrible," Joulie replied sadly.

David picked up when Joulie did not continue. "All the cars in front of the hotel were on fire. I had a hard time spotting the landing on the roof."

"Did you see rioters in other areas?" Ryan asked.

David said, "I got a call telling me the rioters had shut down the Cap airport and they're burning rubbish and tires in the streets. They seem to be in the major metropolitan areas, except for your friends."

"I thought Moïse was pro-business and free trade," Ryan said. "What's he doing tampering with gas prices?" Sharp hairs on the corn leaves brushed against his arms and made him itch. He bladed his body in a failed attempt to avoid the leaves.

David sighed. "The Banana Man is all about himself. When he ran Agritrans, he seized twenty-three hundred acres, displaced about three hundred farmers, and bulldozed their homes just so he could declare it a free trade zone and export bananas."

Jean-Claude regained his voice with the comfort of the topic, saying, "He raised prices because the International Monetary Fund demanded it as part of a deal for low-interest loans and grants. I was all for the deal but told him the gas prices shouldn't increase. Now we're paying the price."

Ryan was about to comment on Jean-Claude's unintended pun when a muffled *whoomph* filled the air as the helicopter's fuel tank ignited. A second later, an explosion shattered the stillness.

The blast wave washed through the corn, ruffling the leaves and bending the stalks. Ryan felt the shock pass through his body and rattle his brain. A staggering pain exploded behind his eyes, and he fell to his knees, hands pressed against the sides of his head.

Just before he clamped his eyes shut, he saw Joulie, David, and James sprawled on the ground. Colors exploded and pinwheeled behind his eyelids. Heat radiated off his back from the fireball rising from the helicopter. He stayed bent over, holding his throbbing head. His brain had been rattled more than once by blast overpressures during his Navy EOD days. The helicopter's explosion had produced a post-traumatic response.

Warm hands touched his shoulders. "Are you okay?" Joulie whispered.

Ryan opened his eyes to see her kneeling in front of him. He nodded, feeling the pain lessen in his skull. He glanced up, feeling a little sheepish about the concerned looks David,

Joulie, and James were giving him. She helped him to his feet, and he turned to look at the cloud of black smoke staining the blue sky.

A moment later, he faced the direction they'd been traveling. "Let's roll."

David continued to lead the way until they broke out of the corn, into a tangle of overgrown weeds and brush surrounding several cement block houses covered in peeling white paint. The bottom rows of blocks were mud splattered from rain running off the gutterless tin roofs. The only gutter Ryan saw led to a large plastic barrel on stilts. A faded red hose trailed from the barrel to a small garden of beans, squash, sweet potatoes, and weird-looking plants he'd learned were cassava.

As they approached, a man and woman looked up from weeding the garden. Several small children stopped playing to stare. David greeted them in Creole and introduced the group, giving special privilege to Joulie.

The farm woman bowed slightly and spoke to Joulie. Joulie smiled and nodded, accompanying the woman toward one of the small houses.

David interpreted for Ryan. "They're going to the woman's shrine. It's not every day she gets to pray with a mambo."

Ryan nodded, continuing to survey the area. He was the only white man, and he could feel the villagers' eyes on him. Still, he continued with his situational awareness assessment. "What about a vehicle to get to the Cap?"

"He says they don't have one," David said, indicating the farmer. "If we go further up the road, the neighbor has a truck."

Ryan nodded. He felt edgy, out of place, and wanted to get moving. He remembered the satellite phone he'd shoved into his backpack before escaping the tent. It would stay there until they'd left the farm. He couldn't explain his unease. The last time he'd had this feeling, the Taliban had ambushed his EOD team in Afghanistan.

James shuffled closer to Ryan and looked up at him. Ryan grinned, but the boy didn't return the gesture. Even James sensed something was off.

Time passed slowly as they stood at the edge of the garden. The man continued his work; the soft sounds of his pointed hoe chopping through the soil filled the air. After thirty minutes, Joulie and the woman emerged from the house. They walked arm in arm, engaged in deep conversation. At the garden, the woman hugged Joulie and thanked her for praying with her before picking up her hoe.

The crash survivors moved to the road and started toward Cap-Haïtien.

A hundred yards down the road, Ryan said, "Joulie, I have a sat phone. Is there someone we can call to pick us up?"

She stopped and stared at him, a look of disbelief on her face. "Why didn't you say this before? We could have waited at the house." She pointed at the place they'd just left.

"Because it was creepy," Ryan said. "My Spidey sense was on high alert."

James asked, "What's Spidey sense?"

"I meant something didn't feel right."

James nodded and kicked a pebble, not understanding the comic book reference.

Ryan handed the phone to Joulie, who called Stanley Lambre, her chief of security. Stanley told her to stay where they were, and he would pick them up. They continued to walk along the narrow road to not only shorten the distance for the driver but to give them something to do. Not a single vehicle passed them going either way.

Thirty minutes later, Stanley pulled up in a black SUV. The muscular black man hopped out and stood guard until everyone was in the vehicle before getting back into the driver's seat and speeding toward Cap-Haïtien.

Their first stop was the mayor's home. One of Stanley's men had called and said a mob had formed outside the mayor's office. They were demanding the mayor call on the president and the prime minister to resign and remove the new fuel taxes. Stanley called the police and informed them of the mayor's arrival. They'd surrounded Jean-Claude's house by the time Stanley pulled the SUV into the driveway.

After leaving the mayor at his home, Stanley drove them across town to Hotel Roi Christophe. Small fires burned throughout the city. Smoke clouds hung in the languid air, smearing the green mountains and darkening the sky.

Ryan took James to the hotel's restaurant and found the head waiter, Henri. He instructed Henri to get James whatever he wanted and to put it on his tab.

"Meyse," Henri said with displeasure, leaning in close, "he has no shirt."

Ryan glanced down at the youth with his heaving, concave chest. James stared back, fear and anger in his eyes. He squeezed them shut but a tear leaked out and streaked down his face, the wet trail glistening in the dining room lights. Ryan wondered why he cried now when he'd been such a brave trooper during the helicopter crash. *Was it embarrassment?*

Ryan pulled off his sweaty, dirt-stained shirt and laid it on James's shoulder. He stood and fixed Henri with his angry gaze and growled, "You will get this boy some food and do it now." To James, he mumbled, "I'll join you in a minute. I have to get a new shirt."

The boy smiled.

Henri looked distraught as he ushered James across the room. James pulled Ryan's shirt over his head. He smiled again. Kids amazed him.

He turned and jogged upstairs, taking the steps two at a time to Joulie's room.

She was coming out of the shower when he walked in. Ryan tried to step past her to use the shower himself, but she placed a hand on his chest. Her fingertips trailed over his skin as the towel slipped from around her breasts, and for the moment, Ryan forgot about the rest of the world.

CHAPTER SEVEN

Ryan and Joulie dressed and joined James for dinner. When they sat down in the almost deserted dining room, Henri approached, carrying their usual drinks and another basket of French fries for James.

"How do you two know each other?" Joulie asked Ryan.

James was too busy stuffing fries into his mouth to respond, so Ryan said, "James was my interpreter. Did you try those with ketchup?" he added.

The boy shook his head. Ryan grabbed the nearby bottle and squirted a small puddle on the plate. James dragged a fry through it before stuffing it into his mouth. His eyebrows shot up, and he grinned with ketchup-stained teeth. Ryan and Joulie laughed.

After dinner, Joulie excused herself to go to her office, located in a separate building on the hotel grounds. As the ruling warlord, she needed to meet with her security and informants about the riots and how they affected the provinces she controlled.

Ryan took James up to the room and explained how the shower worked. The boy laughed and giggled under the hot water. Ryan wasn't sure if the boy used the soap on every part of his body, but he sure smelled a lot better when he came out. A day of helicopter crashes and playing in the mud didn't leave anyone smelling like roses. Henri had scrounged up some clothes for James and the boy pulled his new tighty whities over his still wet legs, followed by shorts and a T-shirt with a New York Giant's logo. *At least it's not the Cleveland Clowns*, Ryan thought.

"Can I watch some TV?" James asked.

Ryan shrugged. Joulie's suite had a separate living room, and Ryan dug out sheets and blankets from an armoire to make a bed on the sofa. James crawled under the covers and Ryan clicked on the television. The soft blue glow illuminated the dark room.

He felt responsible for the boy, but he had no clue what to do now. James had gone to live with relatives after his parents had died from cholera. Since the start of the canal project, James had stuck to Ryan's side. He'd returned to warn Ryan about the mob. That would make him an outsider for siding with a white man over his countrymen. Allowing James to go back to his relatives was the right thing to do, but he and Joulie could provide a far better life for him.

"Can you read?" Ryan asked.

James yawned. "A little."

They both fell asleep watching a soccer match.

Joulie woke Ryan with a shake. He rubbed his eyes and glanced over at James. He had the sheet pulled up to his chin. The light from the TV highlighted his angelic sleeping face.

Ryan shut the television off on his way out of the room. He pulled off his clothes and climbed into bed beside Joulie, who lay on her side with her back to him. He cuddled against her, surprised to find she had on shorts and a shirt when she normally slept nude.

"We have a guest," she chided when Ryan ran a hand up the smooth skin of her thigh.

"He's asleep," Ryan whispered, kissing her neck.

"Speaking of guests," Joulie said, rolling to face him, "what's the plan for the boy?"

"We can get him into school. He's smart and needs a good education."

"So do the rest of the children of Haiti."

"You can take the cost of his books and uniforms out of my investment."

"But what am *I* going to do with him?"

Ryan lay on his back and put his hands behind his head. He'd hoped she would volunteer to take him in. "You can provide a good home."

"Why don't you take him on your boat? Make him a cabin boy."

Undeterred by her sarcasm, Ryan said, "He needs a home. His parents are dead. He was living with whatever uncle would take him in for the night."

"I'm not an orphanage. Did you not think of the family you took him away from? If he is an orphan, he is probably a *restavek*."

Ryan knew the country of Haiti was rife with child slaves. The parents or other relatives would give the children to wealthier family members who they believed would take better care of the children. The children were often forced to do menial household chores and other tasks the adults didn't want to do. Many times, the children were physically or sexually abused, even sold to human traffickers who shipped them to other countries.

Ryan turned to face her, propping himself up on one elbow. "You want to help your people, here's a prime opportunity. James needs a home and to go to school. You can help end this horrible system, starting with him."

"I'll see if I can find a family who will take him in."

"You want to make him a restavek again? Where's your motherly instinct?" He gazed into her blue eyes.

Joulie sighed and turned her back to him. "I don't want to be a mother."

Her flat rejection of motherhood genuinely surprised him. Ryan lay flat and put his hands behind his head again. He didn't want to turn the kid over to someone he didn't know. He had believed Joulie would take him in.

"Besides," she said, "you're leaving, and I don't know if you'll come back."

There it is, Ryan thought, *the heart of the matter*. He was leaving. In another month, *Peggy Lynn* would be out of dry dock and he would go to sea with her crew, doing whatever DWR needed and getting into adventures of their own. There was Spanish gold to find and old shipwrecks to explore. Living on the boat was no life for the boy, especially with the dangers they faced. He couldn't put a child in jeopardy. The others had made a choice to face danger. James would just be along for the ride. He needed a home, stability, and an education.

Ryan closed his eyes. Maybe saving James was his own biological clock telling him he needed to settle down.

CHAPTER EIGHT

At noon the next day, Ryan stood on the new helicopter landing pad inside Port Cap-Haïtien. The United States Aid for International Development fund was hard at work spending the sixty-five-million dollars they'd allocated for modernizing the port facility. Early that morning, Ryan had called Greg and explained about the helicopter crash.

Greg had pulled a few strings to get clearance for a helicopter to land at Port Cap-Haïtien. The flight would also evacuate two American engineers and three construction supervisors working at the port during its multimillion-dollar upgrade.

When the men heard the helicopter, they moved from the shadow of a small building and clustered around Ryan. He shaded his eyes against the brilliant sunshine to watch the incoming helicopter skim the muddy blue waters of Cap-Haïtien Bay.

When the Bell 407GXi helicopter came over the pad, Ryan used arm signals to aid the pilot in landing. He grinned when he saw the logo emblazoned on the side of the dark-blue bird. Max Webber ran Punta Cana Adventure Charters and had ferried Mango and Jennifer Hulsey from Guadeloupe to the Dominican Republic and back when Ryan had needed help during his showdown with Jim Kilroy. Ryan had accompanied them on the return flight, and Max had regaled him with stories about shuttling tourists and doing contract work for the DR National Police—who he described as a bunch of keystone cops compared to the *Bundespolizei*—Federal Police —of his native Germany, the organization Max had worked for before coming to Punta Cana.

As soon as the skids hit the deck, Ryan ran under the rotor arch and tugged open the door. He tossed his duffle bag behind the seats and signaled the rest of the men to board. They piled into the rear compartment, and Ryan took the copilot's seat.

Max powered the bird off the landing pad and turned north. Ryan pulled on a headset and glanced around the 407's high-tech dashboard. It made the interior of David's old 212 look spartan in comparison. He took a second to glance at Max, a stocky blond man with neatly coifed hair and pale blue eyes behind aviator shades.

Max stayed close to the water as they flew north. When he spoke, he had a thick accent. "I didn't clear into Haitian airspace. I'll stay close to the water to keep off the radar until we're out of the country."

Ryan nodded. Even if the commercial flights had still been operating, the airspace would be uncluttered, as there were only two or three flights per day in and out of the airport. Ryan looked out the window at the water flashing beneath them, then glanced at the altimeter. They were less than fifty feet above the ocean's surface, traveling at one-hundred-and-twenty miles per hour.

Max grinned when he saw Ryan staring at the airspeed indicator. From the previous flight, Ryan knew the Bell had a top speed just over one hundred and sixty.

In a straight line on a map, Cap-Haïtien sat two hundred and sixty-four miles from Punta Cana, a two-and-a-half-hour flight in the 407. With Max scuttling north, it would take much longer. To Ryan's surprise, about a mile out to sea, Max banked the helicopter and angled back toward land to make a straight line for the resort city on the eastern most tip of Hispaniola.

"We'll drop off our pax, refuel, and then fly to San Juan," Max informed him.

Ryan nodded and settled back into the comfortable leather seat. This was the plushest helicopter he'd ever been in. The thrum of the engine and rotor blades lulled him toward sleep. In the thick haze between sleep and wakefulness, he thought about how he'd left things with Joulie.

They'd argued a second time about what to do with James, and the matter had been left unresolved. He had tried to be conciliatory to her, but she'd rebuffed him and stormed out of the suite. When he'd gone to the office to see her, Stanley had told him she wasn't receiving visitors.

He'd left a frightened James in the suite, promising him he would return.

CHAPTER NINE

L&F Logistics occupied a corner office on the second floor of the old Trans Caribbean Airways Building in downtown San Juan. The four-story building had shops on the bottom floor and apartments on the top two where green plants spilled over the balcony walls. Ryan held the door open for Greg to push his wheelchair through, then let the door closed behind him, grateful for the air conditioning washing over his sweaty brow.

It was only nine a.m., and already, the heat was almost intolerable. He found it strange that just two days ago he'd been living in a tent and working in the foothills of the Massif du Nord mountain range with no problems. Now at sea level, the hot weather was causing a headache. Or was it the rum from last night?

They took the elevator to the second floor and followed the signs to L&F's lobby area. A secretary with sleek black hair and big brown eyes set into an oval face sat behind a walnut-and-black granite counter. She smiled radiantly and asked, "¿*Tienes una cita?*" *Do you have an appointment?*

Ryan returned her smile. "*Sí, nos estamos reunión con señor Lindowel.*" *Yes, we have a meeting with Mr. Lindowel.*

"In English, *por favor.*" Greg's pronunciation of Spanish for *please* came out with a hard A.

The secretary smirked with disapproval.

Greg continued without noticing. "I'm Greg Olsen and this is my associate, Ryan Weller."

"Mr. Lindowel is expecting you." She stood and stepped around the counter. She wore a silky blue blouse and a short white skirt that hugged her full hips so snuggly that Ryan wondered how she managed to get in and out of it. Her hip sway seemed exaggerated by her high heels as she led them down a short hallway to an unmarked office door. The door was open, but the secretary knocked and waited for acknowledgement.

The man behind the desk was heavyset with thick, unruly blond hair, a wide smile, and laughing eyes. The man's jovial attitude made Ryan smile, but he disliked the tactical situation the man had placed himself in by sitting with his back to the window. It would be too easy for a sniper to pick him off.

He dismissed the thought as quickly as it came. This dude was in shipping; he didn't operate in the murky underworld where he had to worry about being assassinated.

"Marcela," the man said, "can you get these gentlemen some coffee?"

The secretary disappeared into a room farther down the hall.

"Come on in, guys," he said, rising from his chair.

Ryan went in first and pushed a chair into the corner of the room. Greg wheeled into the empty spot.

Greg said, "Good to see you again, Shawn."

Ryan shook the shipping executive's hand. "Nice to meet you, Mr. Lindowel."

"Please, call me Shawn. Mr. Lindowel is my father."

"Okay, Shawn, let's get right to it," Ryan said. "What's going on with the containers?"

Before Shawn could answer, Marcela returned with a tray of coffee and doughnuts. She set it beside an assortment of rum bottles on top of a small bookcase. Ryan debated whether he wanted coffee or more rum to cure his hangover.

Marcela poured the coffee, serving Shawn first. She fixed cups for Ryan and Greg, offering cream and sugar, which they both declined.

"You know," Greg said before taking a sip, "my associate has a habit of ordering coffee black, like his soul."

Shawn laughed and wiped coffee from his chin.

Ryan shook his head and rolled his eyes. It was a line he used often, but today he needed something a little extra. He walked over to the bookcase and examined the bottles of rum, found one he liked and, with a grin at Marcela, poured a shot into his coffee. He took a sip of his concoction and judged it passable. Maybe the crusty old captain of *Peggy Lynn* was rubbing off on him. Dennis Law liked his coffee with Jim Beam.

Shawn leaned back, his portly weight straining the limits of the chair's design. "Three of your containers have disappeared in the last two weeks. I don't think the thieves are targeting you. It's a problem that's been on the rise since the hurricane. We had a massive influx of goods during the weeks following the storm, and the thieves had a heyday. They'd steal a container from one port, change the numbers or the shipping manifest, and move it to another port for shipment off island."

"They don't use the cargo?" Greg asked.

Shawn picked up an unlit cigar and rolled it in his fingers. "Right after the storm, they were stealing food, clothes—you name it—and distributing it. The cops would find empty containers alongside the road. I think they turned a blind eye. Whatever was helping the people was all right by them."

"Are they still turning a blind eye?" Greg asked.

Shawn shrugged. "I don't know."

"What about DWR's containers?" Ryan asked.

"Yours haven't been found, but that doesn't mean they're not still on the island," Shawn said. "What was in them?"

Greg answered, "Construction supplies to rebuild the ports."

DWR had wrangled contracts to rebuild or renovate several of Puerto Rico's hurricane-damaged port facilities. As a worldwide conglomerate, the company provided a wide range of ship husbandry, oil rig maintenance, underwater construction, infrastructure rehabilitation and design, inspection, maintenance, and technical services for all aspects of the commercial diving industry.

Shawn nodded and sipped his coffee. Ryan got the impression the man would rather be two-fisting rum shots. He glanced around the office. Most of the pictures hung on the wall were of Shawn on the golf course with various other men, some Ryan recognized but couldn't place. A bag of golf clubs stood in one corner and a putter leaned against the bookshelf. Several golf balls littered the plush carpet. The office window overlooked Juan Ponce de Leon Avenue, and between two tall buildings, Ryan could see the blue waters of Laguna del Condado.

"Do you have a way of tracking your containers?" Shawn asked.

"No, we haven't had the need to implement a tracking program," Greg said. "We've always relied on the shipping company to provide tracking and documentation."

Shawn shifted in his seat. "I would suggest you put GPS trackers on them."

Greg nodded. "I spoke to my COO about implementing such a program."

"Good," Shawn replied. "Maybe we can track these bastards if they steal another container."

Ryan sipped his drink, enjoying the taste of rum mingled with the locally grown coffee. "What about the other containers? Did they have trackers?"

"Some did, and the cops found them. The authorities confiscated the ones shipped off island when they reached their new ports. The ones here on the island were empty."

Ryan continued, "Where did they find the containers on the island?"

"Up in the hills. I'll have Marcela get the locations for you."

"Did the police speak to you about the containers?"

"Yes." Shawn nodded. "As the local contact point, I take responsibility for the containers and do my best to find out what happened to them. Container theft is a billion-dollar industry."

"Is that so?" Ryan raised a brow. "What's your kickback from the stolen containers?"

Shawn exploded from his chair, heaving his bulk up at an astonishing speed. "Get out!"

Greg held out his hands. "Calm down, Shawn. He's just punching your buttons to see how you'd react."

Shawn glowered at Ryan. "Take your best shot, but I guaran-damn-tee you I am not stealing cargo containers. We run a legitimate business here." He thumped his fist on the desk to punctuate the point.

"Fine," Ryan said. "How many containers have they stolen from your business?"

"Ten."

"How many from other companies?"

"We don't have an exact count." Shawn straightened his

suit jacket and sat down. "Most of what I've learned is through gossip, because the other shipping companies won't give me precise numbers. My best estimate is seventy-five in the last six months."

"Seventy-five?" Greg repeated.

"Considering over two hundred containers a day move through just the San Juan Port Authority alone, that number is pretty low. There are nine port facilities in PR."

Greg looked at Ryan. "Anything else?"

"I don't think so," he replied. "Just the locations."

"I'll have Marcela give them to you on the way out," Shawn said.

Both men shook hands with the shipping company executive and headed out, getting the files from Marcela on the way.

Ryan packed Greg's wheelchair into the back of a gray Jeep Wrangler Unlimited he'd rented at the airport after Max had dropped him off. Greg found the small doors hard to squeeze through with his atrophied legs, but he liked the comfort of the Jeep's seats. Both men knew they would need the four-wheel drive to get around on some of the muddy and unrepaired roads.

"Punch in the coordinates for the first container," Ryan said, sliding into the driver's seat.

"Already done." Greg set the portable GPS unit on the dash and watched it calculate the route.

"Ready?"

Greg sighed and rubbed his face. "Is it too early for a beer?"

"Never," Ryan said.

CHAPTER TEN

Their first stop was near the town of Utuado, one of the hardest hit areas. Heavy flooding and mudslides had isolated the already rural town even further. As they drove, the signs of destruction were still evident. Someone had pushed fallen trees off the road. Their brown, dead leaves marred the otherwise green hillsides. They saw men cutting the trees and stacking wood in neat rows. In other places, large sections of earth had broken away, carrying trees, houses, and patches of road downhill. Crews had hastily repaired missing sections of pavement with dirt and gravel.

Despite the destruction, the drive was still beautiful. Route 10 bisected the island on a north/south route between Arecibo on the Atlantic and Ponce on the Caribbean. It climbed over mountains, giving sweeping views of the surrounding hills and the deep blue waters of the two oceans. Tall stands of native teak and West Indian mahogany covered the hillsides, interspersed with green vegetation sprouting from reddish-brown earth. Flowering bushes lined the road, and they could see an occasional glimpse of Rio Viví's rocky waters on their left.

"According to the GPS, the cops found the empty trailer on the Y-bridge in the center of town." Greg pointed as they turned onto Utuado's main thoroughfare. The Y-bridge crossed the two branches of the Viví where they met to become one.

"At least they brought it someplace where it would do the most good," Ryan said. He could see homes with blue tarps spread across their gables standing beside other houses missing roofs.

"Don't go getting all weepy over someone playing Robin Hood."

Ryan fanned his face with his hand like a movie star diva. "I'm ... I'm tearing up."

"Shut up."

Steering the Jeep into a parking lot near the Y-bridge, Ryan said, "How about something to eat?"

"Or a beer," Greg replied.

"You better lay off the beer—you're getting a belly."

"Screw you, Weller."

"Be nice, or I'll leave your ass in the car."

Greg held up his middle finger.

Ryan laughed and got out. He started across the parking lot toward the restaurant without getting Greg's chair. At the door, he paused and looked back.

Greg mock-laughed before yelling, "Remember who signs your paycheck!"

Ryan turned and went inside. He went to the counter and ordered two cold Medalla Lights, then stood in the window so Greg could see him take long, exaggerated drinks from the bottle. After a minute or so, he opened the door, held the beer up, and pointed at it. "Come on, gimpy. Get your ass over here."

Greg flipped him off.

Ryan walked out the door, carrying both beers and

chuckling. Their bond went deeper than the mere brotherhood forged in the fires of combat. Ryan had been a petty officer first class and Greg a lieutenant when they'd first met. The needs of the Navy had placed them together in EOD Mobile Unit Two at Joint Expeditionary Base Little Creek in Virginia. Ryan had taken over the role of a chief petty officer and worked alongside Greg in the administration and training of their team. During that time, they had become fast friends, finding they had a lot in common and a similar sense of humor. In the teams, the separation between enlisted and officer, which preserved the chain of leadership and authority, often blurred, thus leaving the men on a more familiar basis. It was that friendship and understanding that had led to Greg offering Ryan a job at DWR.

Ryan never saw a need to treat Greg any differently because of his injury. He was still the same strong, capable leader, only his legs didn't work. If Greg made jokes about his "useless" legs, then Ryan knew he could, too. It was a license to screw with him, which Greg always reciprocated.

He handed the beer to Greg, went around to the back of the Jeep, and pulled out the wheelchair. He reassembled it and pushed it up to the passenger door, where Greg dropped into it.

"Helluva way to treat your boss."

"I told you not to mess with me," Ryan shot back.

"If I didn't like you so much, I'd fire you."

"Didn't you do that already?"

Greg pushed with one hand toward the restaurant door, alternating which handheld the beer and which hand shoved a wheel to keep himself going in a straight line.

"You want me to carry that for you?" Ryan offered.

"Um ... no." Greg hugged the beer protectively to his chest.

Ryan waited for Greg to wheel in front of him, then gave him a shove with his foot.

Halfway to the door, the chair's front castor caught in a crack in the asphalt. The immediate stop caused Greg's wheelchair to tip up on its front tires. Instinctively, he threw his arms back to stop his forward momentum. Beer sloshed from the bottle onto his hand. He teetered there, on the edge of losing his balance and falling out of the chair.

"Dammit," he muttered, more pissed he'd spilled the beer than the fact that he was about to fall on his face.

Ryan grimaced and raced forward to catch his friend, but before he could reach him, gravity pulled Greg back onto his rear wheels.

Greg changed beer hands and shook the liquid off his right. He looked pointedly at Ryan and said, "Let's not do that again."

"Sorry, buddy."

Everyone in the restaurant stared, aghast, at the two men through the picture windows. A waiter held the door open and asked, "Is everything okay, *señor*?"

"Fine," Greg said. "Can we get a table?"

"*Sí. Sí.*" The waiter pointed at a table beside the window and hustled to pull a chair away for Greg.

Ryan slid into a chair and they ordered two more beers and a pizza. Through the big window, they watched cars cruise past.

When the waiter delivered the beer, Ryan turned and looked up at him. "There was a trailer full of supplies dropped off here about a month after the hurricane passed through. Do you know anything about it?"

The man's smile disappeared. He spread his hands. "*Señor*," he implored.

"I know it was a great help to the community. I'm glad you received it, but can you tell me who brought it?"

The waiter spread his arms to the heavens. "*Ángeles.*"

Greg snorted.

Pressing his fingertips to his chest, the shop owner said in English: "*Señor*, I am Pedro, the owner of this restaurant." Then he switched to Spanish. "I would like to say I knew those men, but I do not. They are heroes. They brought help when others could not. But I saw them. They wore masks and carried guns. When the bridges were out, and the flood waters were up, they came. Not FEMA, not the military, but the bandits. They bring us food and water."

Greg glanced at Ryan for a translation.

"He says the Robin Hoods wore masks and are heroes."

Pedro glanced between the two *gringos*. "Why do you ask?"

"We're trying to find the men who brought the container," Ryan said.

"What did their truck look like?" Greg asked.

Pedro shrugged, arms out, palms up. "*Gigante*, *negro.*"

"Big and black," Ryan translated.

"I am sorry, *señores*, I must return to work." Pedro retreated to the kitchen, wringing his apron.

Ryan looked out the window at the passing traffic and took a sip of beer. "Black semi-truck and masked bandits."

"Narrows it down, doesn't it?" Greg said.

"To a needle in a haystack."

CHAPTER ELEVEN

Pedro wiped his hands on his apron as he walked to the kitchen. The Yankees were asking strange questions about the trailer he had helped unload outside his store. He'd also helped to unload other trailers. *Los banditos* had brought not only food, water, and medical supplies, but hope to a town many assumed the world had forgotten, cut off by swollen creeks, damaged roads, and a collapsed bridge. They'd strung a cable from the riverbank to the half of the bridge still standing and used a shopping cart on a set of pullies to shuttle desperately needed provisions over the flood waters.

He walked through the kitchen and out the back door. The door swung shut with a rusty squeak, and Pedro pulled a cell phone from his pocket. He dialed a number in his contacts and held the phone to his ear.

"*Hola*," the gruff voice of Diego Hernández said as they spoke in Spanish.

"This is Pedro Ortiz. There are men in my store asking about the containers you brought to Utuado."

"Why?"

"They are trying to find you. They asked if I knew who you were and what your truck looked like."

"And what do these men look like?" Diego asked.

"One is tall, muscular, with brown hair. The other is in a wheelchair. I think they are brothers. They look very much alike."

"What are they driving?"

"They are in a gray four-door Jeep."

"*Bueno*, Pedro. You have done well to call me." Diego ended the call before Pedro could say more.

Pedro put the phone back in his pocket and returned to his job. He carried a hot pizza to the table of the two Yankees. They quickly dug in while he gathered their empty beer bottles. Pretending to clean tables, he hovered just within earshot, listening to their conversation.

When they finished the pizza, the one who could walk went out to the Jeep and returned with a tan file folder. He opened it on the table and spread out several sheets of paper. Pedro yearned to read what they said. Without even thinking, he eased closer and rose on tiptoes to see while polishing an already clean table.

He felt the man in the wheelchair staring at him, and, for an instant, locked eyes with him. Pedro's heart felt like it skipped a beat as he glanced away.

CHAPTER TWELVE

Ryan continued to shuffle through the papers while Greg stared at Pedro. Pedro shoved his cleaning rag into his pocket and scurried to the kitchen.

"Your little buddy was trying to read over your shoulder," Greg said.

Ryan glanced over his shoulder, but Pedro had moved behind the bar. He closed the file and took a sip of water. "Next stop is Ponce."

"Well, we can drive all over the island and look at these sites, but I don't think we'll get anything out of it but an epic road trip," Greg said. "Especially if people think these guys are angels."

"Let's do it anyway," Ryan insisted.

"It would be fun, but I think it will be a waste of time."

"You got that from reading Marcela's handwriting?"

"No," Greg said.

Ryan looked around for Pedro. "Where'd he go?"

"He ran off when I caught him spying."

"We could call him Peeping Pedro."

Greg rolled his eyes. "Next you'll ask me what Puerto

Ricans call dinner. Do they go out for Puerto Rican or just call it something else?"

"Valid questions."

"The more valid question is, why am I drinking water and not beer? Pedro!"

"Stay focused, Greg," Ryan said.

"I am. You're chauffeuring me around the island, so I might as well enjoy myself."

Ryan knew it was no use fighting with him. Greg had used alcohol to help cope with the loss of his legs ever since an IED had detonated under his Humvee in Afghanistan. Ryan had been in the same convoy and had carried Greg out of the carnage. He could still see his hands slicked with blood from the shrapnel wounds to his lieutenant's back.

Ryan brought himself back to the present and felt like having a beer to wash away the atrocious memories. When Pedro approached, Greg ordered a Presidente, a Dominican Republic beer. Ryan asked for two waters.

"Don't be a pussy," Greg chided.

"I have to drive you home."

"Three beers won't give you a buzz. I know how much you can drink. I've seen you shit-faced on more than one occasion."

"Yeah, well, this ain't going to be one of them," Ryan said.

"Then lay off me."

"Aye, aye, sir." There was no hiding the derision in Ryan's voice.

Greg flipped him the bird.

Pedro delivered the drinks, and Greg ordered one for the road. Ryan wondered how much the man drank every day. It also didn't help that they were on the largest rum producing island in the world. It hadn't last night. His head still ached.

Ryan cracked open his water and drank half while watching Greg chug the Presidente. He gathered his papers and stuffed them into the folder. When Greg's last beer arrived, he paid the tab, and they went out to the Jeep.

"I like this arrangement," Greg said. "I drink and pay, and you drive."

"To think I quit smoking for this."

"Now, that shit will kill ya."

"I wish I had one now," Ryan moaned, longing to feel nicotine coursing through his veins.

"*Señor*," Pedro called from the pizzeria door. "Would you like a cigar? Grown in Puerto Rico."

"*Muchas gracias*," Ryan said. He walked over to Pedro, who held a small wooden humidor. He extracted a cigar and sniffed it before handing Pedro a crumpled ten-dollar bill. He lit it with the matches Pedro provided. Once he had it going, he returned to the Jeep.

"I told you Peeping Pedro was spying on us," Greg muttered.

"If you get to drink then I get to smoke a cigar." Ryan shoved the wheelchair into the back of the Jeep. "Punch the next destination into the GPS."

Ryan climbed into the driver's seat and chirped the tires as he pulled out of the parking lot. He drove back to Route 10 and turned left.

South of Utuado, the road switched back and forth in hairpin curves during its snaking rise out of the valley. The top-heavy SUV forced Ryan to slow down through the corners. With the windows down and the cigar in his hand, he relaxed into the leather seat to enjoy the drive.

"This isn't so bad," Ryan said.

"It would be better without that stinky in the car." Greg waved his hand to dispel the smoke even though most of it had blown out the open windows.

Just as they rounded a ninety-degree bend, Ryan caught a glimpse of movement out of the corner of his eye. Someone was standing in the road. He jammed on the brakes and grabbed for the steering wheel with both hands. The cigar fell from his fingers and landed on his thigh, causing him to jerk his leg back. He brushed off the hot ash and tried to locate the cigar rolling on the floorboard.

"Look out," Greg screamed.

Ryan glanced up to see two men aiming black automatic rifles at them. The guns spat fire. Bullets raked the front of the Jeep. The windshield cracked into a spider's web and then shattered. Safety glass flew, sparkling and glinting in the sunlight as it showered Greg and Ryan.

Ducking behind the steering wheel and dash, Ryan mashed the accelerator, aiming straight for the gunmen. He had nowhere else to go. Trees lined the edge of the road, and the ground rose straight up on the left and fell sharply away on the right. He hoped he could drive through the gunfire and take out at least one man with his front bumper.

A third machine gun, somewhere to their left, began to fire. The Jeep trembled as the heavy rounds punched through its skin. With a loud bang, the front tire exploded, jerking the vehicle hard right. The front end dipped onto the narrow shoulder. Loose dirt gave way under the weight of the tires, and the Jeep continued to slide off the side of the road between two trees.

"Oh, shit," Ryan said as something wrenched the steering wheel from his grasp.

Nose down, the Jeep careened off trees and boulders. Brush scraped along the metal sides, shrieking like fingernails on a chalkboard. At the bottom of the ravine was a small creek littered with boulders. Bouncing and swaying, the Jeep charged downhill as though it had a mind of its own. Ryan applied brakes and tried to steer the wounded vehicle.

It seemed opposite of everything he thought would help, but he mashed the accelerator. The back wheels gained purchase and forced the front end to the right, away from the largest rocks, but he could not regain complete control before the Jeep rolled head-on into a boulder field. Rocks ripped parts from the undercarriage. The front wheels dropped into a crevice, and the front bumper slammed into another rock. Airbags burst in their faces. Both men pitched forward, their bodies hanging by their seatbelts.

CHAPTER THIRTEEN

Ryan's head lulled from side to side. His body tilted forward, seatbelt slicing across his chest and hips. He didn't want to open his eyes and see the carnage of their rental or deal with the assailants and their automatic weapons. He wanted to remain still. If he didn't move, it wouldn't hurt.

The sound of men shouting in Spanish made his eyes snap open, and a wave of pain surged through his body. His head throbbed, and his chest ached. He knew there would be a massive bruise across his ribs, shoulder, and abdomen from the restraint. He glanced around the battered Jeep. The dented hood arched up at an odd angle and smoke rose from beneath it. Parts of the dash hung by electrical wires, and the white air bags looked like deflated balloons. A fine powder covered the dash and center console.

Glancing over at Greg, he knew his partner needed help. He appeared unconscious.

Ryan reached for the seatbelt release. It wouldn't unlock. He jerked at the belt and pressed the button at the same time. It still wouldn't give.

His next move was to reach for the orange handled CRKT folding knife in his pocket. He didn't even have to open it to use the seatbelt cutter on the thumb flip. The taut webbing gave easily as he sliced through it. He braced his legs and left arm to prevent himself from falling into the steering wheel. When he tried the door handle, it snapped off in his hand. He punched the knife's tanto point up through the fabric top and sliced it open.

"What's a cut in the roof compared to the rest of the damage?" he muttered as he shoved the knife back in his pocket. He reached over and shook Greg. "Wake up, lazy bones, we got tangos on our six."

Greg remained still. He had a small cut on his forehead and blood covered his cheek.

Ryan climbed out the hole in the roof. Swinging his legs around, he slid onto the mutilated hood, then hopped down onto a boulder. He took a moment to process the scene. The Jeep rested with its rear wheels in the air several yards past the bank of the creek. He'd need to hop from boulder to boulder to reach the path the Jeep had created through the underbrush. It amazed Ryan that the Jeep hadn't rolled over as it careened down the near vertical hill.

He braced himself on two boulders and glanced down at the water rushing around their base. Extracting Greg would be tricky. Worse yet, they were in the open, with little protection from the bad actors advancing down the hill.

Greg groaned, and Ryan moved around to the passenger door. Greg used the balls of his palms to rub his eyes.

"You okay?" Ryan asked.

The shouts were closer now. Through the trees, he saw three men sidestepping down the hill.

"I can't feel my legs," Greg moaned.

Ryan glanced from the leapfrogging enemy to his friend.

Greg had a grin on his face, but the words made Ryan's brain reel. He felt himself wavering on his feet. Every sound seemed amplified. A gunshot rang through the trees. Whatever joke Greg had intended had thrust Ryan right back to the day in Afghanistan when Greg had first said those exact words to him. Then, like now, Greg had ridden in the passenger seat.

The parallels were too great. Ryan held up his hands. His mind told him they were covered in blood, and he screamed.

DAMMIT, Greg thought. He reached through the window, grabbed Ryan by the shirt, and shook him. "Snap out of it!" he shouted. "Get me out of here."

Ryan's glazed eyes were wide open, the pupil's tiny pinpricks. His chest heaved in rapid, shallow breaths. Greg had never seen Ryan like this, and it frightened him. The man was almost unflappable. His own body tingled with fright. There were men coming to kill them, and Ryan had just lost his mind. He continued to shake his friend, who merely held his hands in front of his face, fingers spread wide, and stared at them while screaming.

He kept one hand on Ryan, using the other to brace himself against the dash to keep from sliding down the slippery leather seat into the footwell.

Damn these useless legs.

He squeezed his muscles, trying to force his mind to make connections in the damaged spinal cord. What cruel joke had God played on Man by making the spine the only body part that attacked itself when it began to heal? Tensing his muscles did no good. He kept sliding inexorably into the footwell.

A bullet slammed into the Jeep's tailgate. Another shattered what was left of the windshield. Despite what the movies said, the Jeep's thin metal skin was useless as a shield. Only the heavy metal of the engine block would protect them. Ryan needed to get his act together, right now, but all he was doing was blasting Greg's eardrums with shrieks of panic.

"I need you, buddy," Greg cajoled. "Come on, get it together."

Ryan did not respond. He began wiping his hands on his pants, threatening to break Greg's tenuous grasp on the shirt.

Not knowing what else to do, Greg reverted back to being an officer. Through gritted teeth, he shouted, "Petty Officer Weller, get me out of here, now!" and jerked Ryan toward the Jeep as hard as he could.

Ryan's forehead smacked into the top bar of the door.

———

RYAN PULLED AWAY and rubbed his forehead. "What the hell was that for?"

"You were having a panic attack. Get me out of here." Greg shoved at the door, trying to open it.

Gunfire raked the rocks and Jeep body. Ryan dropped to his stomach and felt his foot slip off the top of the boulder and land in the water, soaking the tan combat boot and sock on his right foot.

"Son of a bitch," he barked.

"Get me out of here!" Greg cried again, ramming his shoulder into the door.

Ryan pulled his foot up while looking under the back tires of the Jeep, which were several inches off the ground. The three shooters were advancing, one firing while the other reloaded and the third provided cover.

Ryan pulled his Walther from the holster and aimed at Shooter One's head. He could smell gasoline. The flame belching from the barrel of his pistol could ignite the fumes. It was a chance he'd have to take—a bullet or a burn.

Without waiting to discover the source of the leak, he pulled the trigger and knocked Shooter One down. He moved his sight picture to Cover and fired another round. He didn't wait to see the reaction, moving to the third man who was just shouldering his rifle. Ryan pulled the trigger again.

Shooter Two fell while Ryan swung the pistol back to Shooter One, who lay prostrate with his bloody head pointed downhill. Ryan popped a round into him. Back to Cover, who was climbing to his feet. Ryan punched a round into the man's abdomen. Shooter Two was down but received a second shot to ensure he stayed that way.

Ryan jumped to his feet and ran upslope toward Cover, who lay on the ground, clutching his stomach and moaning. Ryan's last shot had sliced horizontally across Cover's abdomen. His intestines had leaked out between his fingers, their shiny, purple casings covered with dirt and leaves. The man didn't have long to live.

"*¿Quién eres tú?*" *Who are you?* Ryan asked.

"*Fantasmas.*" *Ghosts*, he bragged through ragged breaths.

"More like gangbangers," Ryan said, pushing the sleeve of the man's T-shirt up. Instead of the tattooed artwork of one of the island's gangs, he found a U.S. Army Ranger tab inked across the skin. "Rangers?"

Ryan glanced at his face, but the ranger was dead.

With a practiced quickness, Ryan rummaged through the man's pockets and found a cell phone. He snapped a picture of the dead man's face with it, then moved to the other two men and did the same. He put their phones and money in his cargo pockets, dropped the magazines from their rifles, and threw them into the creek. Then he broke the guns apart. He left a pistol on Cover's chest.

When he looked up, he saw Greg twisted in the Jeep's passenger seat, watching his every move. Ryan trotted down to the Jeep. The smell of gasoline had grown stronger. He pried open the stuck door with a thick, dead limb scavenged from the creek bed.

Greg had left the seatbelt on, and his arms trembled from holding himself in place. "I can't do this much longer."

Ryan looked up and down the creek, then the hill. "The best thing to do is get you up the hill. The question is, do you want to wait here while I hike your chair up, or should I carry you up and then get the chair?" While Greg pondered the question, Ryan said, "If you weren't so damn lazy, you'd just walk up the hill."

"Yeah, that's why I use a wheelchair." Greg pressed his finger to his lips. "It's a scam."

Ryan grinned. "I know. Now get your ass up the hill."

"First, I need to get out of the Jeep, in case it catches fire. Then the chair goes up."

Ryan sawed through the tough fibers of the seatbelt while Greg braced his body. When the belt let go, he crumpled into the footwell.

"All right, come on." Ryan leaned into the Jeep. He slipped an arm under Greg's knees and wrapped the other around his shoulder.

Greg put his arm around Ryan's neck as Ryan slid him out with a grunt and got his balance.

"Don't get any ideas, pal," Ryan said.

Greg raised his voice an octave to imitate an old lady. "How about a kiss on the cheek for the nice boy?"

"Forget it." Ryan laughed and then concentrated on crossing the rocks.

All the jokes aside, Ryan knew Greg hated being helpless.

The loss of his independence had to be hard, and while Ryan tried to understand and had gotten into the wheelchair himself, it would never be the same as what Greg experienced. Ryan could always stand up and walk away while Greg was left to drag himself along by his hands. Ryan had seen him low-crawl, and it was painful to watch. He'd also helped Greg onto a dive boat by holding Greg's legs in the air while Greg used his hands to walk down the gangplank.

It made Ryan want to cry, but he knew, as he carried his friend to safety, he had to be strong for him. There was no quitting now, otherwise Greg would be stuck at the bottom of this hill until he died. Maybe he could drag himself out, but Ryan wasn't going to let him try.

After Ryan had set Greg down by a tree, Greg said, "Grab that little cushion off the seat. I don't want to get a sore on my ass."

Ryan traversed the rocks again and came back with the cushion and a bottle of water. While Greg got himself situated on the air-filled cushion, Ryan walked over to the dead men. When he came back, he placed a Beretta M9 pistol in Greg's hand. "Here, hang on to this. Don't shoot yourself."

Greg rolled his eyes as Ryan went back to the Jeep and liberated the wheelchair. He carried all the pieces across the rocks before putting it together. The hill was steep, but Ryan used tree branches and saplings to help pull himself up the near-vertical slope. He had to either carry the chair or push it ahead of him and block it with his legs or hands to keep it from rolling back down the hill. He couldn't afford to damage it. Greg didn't have a backup.

Thirty hard minutes later, he stood on the edge of the road. A blister had formed on the heel of his right foot from the wet sock. His sweat-soaked shirt clung to his skin. Below the hem of his shorts, his bare legs were scraped and scratched. Just getting the twenty-five-pound titanium chair up the hill had been a real workout. It was going to be hell getting Greg out.

Hands on his knees, sucking deep breaths, Ryan surveyed the road, the embankment, and the hill beyond. Brass shell casings twinkled in the sunlight on the black pavement. Brown tree trunks stood sentinel, their green branches shading jutting rocks and sheltering chirping birds. Somewhere high up, a woodpecker drilled for bugs. Behind the dead leaves of a fallen tree, Ryan saw a glint of metal.

Standing straight and interlacing his fingers on top of his head, he walked across the road, his heavy breathing interrupting the surreal jungle sounds.

After a short battle through the brush, he found two Honda dirt bikes leaning on kick stands. *Perfect*, he thought, *that's going to really help me.* He saw the way the bikes had entered the camouflage and returned with the wheelchair.

Both bikes had saddlebags. One set was a modern ballistic nylon version of the Old Western bags and the others were aluminum hard cases. He popped the hard cases open. Inside the right-hand one was a set of tools, a coil of rope, and a handgun. The left contained a raincoat and several bungee cords. The ballistic nylon saddlebags contained the same items, plus a small first aid kit, a roll of 550 paracord and a pair of leather gloves.

"So much for Rangers being Boy Scouts."

He stuffed the rope, bungee cords, and tools into the nylon saddlebags and headed back down the hill. This time, he used the saplings and branches to ease his way down. At the bottom, he trotted over to where Greg sat propped against the tree, legs straight out in front of him.

"You good?" Ryan asked.

"Yeah." Greg threw the water bottle to Ryan.

Ryan snagged it from the air and took several long gulps from it. Seriously dehydrated from the strain of climbing the hill and the previous night of drinking, his body craved the water and he longed to drain the bottle, but he knew he would need it even more after he'd hiked Greg out.

He capped the bottle and tossed it down beside Greg. "Let's get you out of here."

"I was thinking about that," Greg said. "We can use something off the Jeep and make either a drag or a travois."

"Great minds think alike." Ryan walked over to the Jeep. He glanced at Greg, who was watching him intently. He knew Greg felt helpless in these situations. Take away his wheelchair and he became immobile. They'd talked about this before, often over tequila and cigarettes.

Damn, I could use a cigarette.

Ryan stripped off the Jeep's top and folded it up. Then he tossed the floormats to Greg. "What do you think?"

"We can string this top between two poles and put the floormats on the bottom to protect my butt." He held up the rope. "This will make a nice harness."

Ryan lay down beside Greg. "I could use a nap."

"I don't want to sound selfish or anything, because I know you're doing all the work, but I'd like to get the hell out of here."

Ryan sat up and scanned the forest floor and creek banks for some poles. He found two and carried them back to the work area where he lopped branches off with his folding knife while Greg prepared the Jeep top to lace to the poles.

Another hour of work, and they were satisfied with their creation. Greg lifted with his hands and Ryan pulled out the cushion and put it on the floormats. Then Greg, using his arms for legs while Ryan held his feet up, waddled his body over to the cushion. When he was happy with his positioning, Ryan shouldered the makeshift harness.

The rope bit deep into his skin. His hands sweated in the leather gloves, but he was glad they took the abuse, as his hands were already rough from the first climb. His thighs burned, and his calves felt like hot knives were slicing through them with each step. The man on the travois was an extra one hundred and ninety pounds trying to drag him back to the creek. Just the thought of the cool waters made him want to turn back and dive in.

Yet, he persevered. It was the only way to get Greg out of the ravine and back to the road. He ached all over. Muscles he hadn't used in a long time screamed at him. Sweat drenched his clothes and coursed down his skin. He felt like he was back at EOD school, running laps up and down the giant sand hill outside the schoolhouse. The physical training had been exhaustive. Those were easy days compared to the strain Ryan felt now, but there was a difference. EOD school was personal glory. This was to rescue his friend. Ryan stuffed the exhaustion, the pain, the thirst, and the thousand other nagging complaints down inside and focused on cresting the ridge.

When he had Greg tucked into the downed tree beside the motorcycles, Ryan fell to his knees and collapsed onto his side. He closed his eyes. Exhaustion had set it. Dehydration caused a pounding headache, and nausea threatened to bring up the lunch left in his stomach. He knew the symptoms of heat exhaustion. He needed water.

"Here, Ryan," Greg said, holding the bottle out. "Take this."

Ryan opened his eyes and stared at the plastic bottle Greg that held out. He wanted to reach for it, but everything hurt. Cramps rippled up his legs. He pointed his toes and stifled a scream. His hands shot to his head, pressing against his temples to mute the agony of lightning bolts stabbing through his brain.

"You need the water," Greg said.

Ryan grabbed the bottle and slowly sipped the warm

liquid, holding it in his mouth for his body to absorb. He ached all over and his blood pounded in his skull. He concentrated on his breathing. In for a three count, out for a four count. Controlling his breathing was a way of controlling his heart rate. With any luck, he would shut all the way down and sleep. He didn't care about cargo thieves right now, but they were thinking about him.

CHAPTER FOURTEEN

Greg watched his friend's chest rise and fall in slow, even breaths. Every so often, Ryan would raise the water bottle to his lips and take a small sip. It was the best way to rehydrate other than an IV bolus of saline solution. Greg felt absolutely helpless. The man had made two trips up and down the steep mountain just for him. Not because it was his job, but because Ryan had been genuinely concerned about his safety and welfare.

The people Greg called friends and those who he had served with in the military often amazed him. They embraced the chaos, the creativity, and the comradery. They were fiercely independent, loyal, and decisive, able to separate the crucial from the irrelevant and produce order. What made these men and women willing to sacrifice their lives for others?

He couldn't explain it in himself. Words failed to describe those feelings. Even though he could no longer function as he once had, he still strove to meet those standards welded inside him, forged by his family and his service. It was his job, both as a former Naval officer and now as a business owner, to ensure the welfare of his people. It was a commitment honored by his deceased father, Allen, and his grandfather, Clifford, who had both run Dark Water Research after its founding by Homer Olsen during World War Two. The company and the Olsen family had a history of service and hiring those who had served.

Greg had offered Ryan a position at DWR just before Ryan had left the Navy. Ryan had refused, going back to work construction with his father. Greg had thought he was wasting his skills being a mundane carpenter. After Greg's father had died in a terrorist attack on the Texas Governor's Mansion, Greg had sent Clifford to recruit Ryan again. The octogenarian had convinced him to join up.

It was all water under the bridge. Now they needed to press on. From his pocket, he produced his cell phone. He had to get help for his friend and fast before the heat exhaustion became a more serious heat stroke. Ryan needed fluids. To get them, Greg had to find a way off the mountain. His phone hadn't worked at the bottom of the ravine and the tall trees were still blocking the signal.

"Hand me those cell phones. I want to look at them."

Ryan moved with deliberate slowness, without opening his eyes, and extracted them from his pockets.

Greg laid them out in a row on the ground beside him. He lifted his butt into the air to relieve the pressure and looked over the phones. All three had black rubber cases and one had a cracked screen. He adjusted himself on the cushion again and peeled off the phone's rubber skins. They were cheap silver-and-black prepaid units. Most of the calls were made and received from the same contacts. Following the call logs allowed Greg to recognize the coordination of the attack. He scrolled through the pictures on each phone. The first picture on each phone was a photo of the dead man's face from whom Ryan had relieved the phone. When they were back to civilization, he'd send the photos to Floyd Landis, DWR's contact at Homeland Security, and have him run the mugshots through the criminal and civil databases. Scrolling further through the pictures, he saw smiling and happy men. Then he found the Ranger tattoo Ryan had photographed.

"That's interesting."

None of the phones had any signal, which meant to Greg that the men had prearranged this location.

He heard a vehicle laboring up the hill, then zoom by without even slowing. Greg pulled his chair over and got onto all fours. He placed his arms on the cushion, pulling the chair under his chest. Then he pushed up and forward, dragging his limp hips onto the cushion. Once he had his chest over the seat back, he rolled to the side, forcing his butt around and onto the cushion. Finally seated upright, he untwisted his pants and squared his feet on the footrest.

He nudged Ryan with his footrest. "I'm going for a beer, want to come?" The man hadn't moved since handing over the phones.

"I'm good," Ryan croaked.

"That's what I thought," Greg muttered. Then louder, he said, "Drink the water. I'm going to get help."

Ryan put the bottle to his lips and sipped.

The hill was too steep for him to push up. He picked up the pair of gloves Ryan had discarded and slipped them on to help alleviate the constant friction of holding the metal push rims to control his speed.

Greg took one last look around, wished he could hop on the dirt bike, and made sure he had his cell phone. Then he pushed out of the brush and headed downhill.

It didn't take long for the friction to build up heat in the leather. Greg had to alternate braking hands and even take short breaks to let the gloves cool down. The speed also caused the front wheels of the chair to wobble. He ended up balancing on the rear wheels in one long wheelie while racing down the hill. He eyed each crack in the pavement with concern. If he lost his balance and the small castor wheels hit a crack or a stone, the chair would come to a sudden stop and launch him into space. He'd done that before, skinning his knees, ripping his pants, and gouging skin from his palms while rolling across the unforgiving pavement.

Fifteen minutes later, he was at the bottom of the hill and pushing up a slight rise toward a small farm on the west side of the road. The heat was making him sweat, and the back of the gloves were damp from the perspiration he'd wiped from his forehead. And he was thirsty. He couldn't imagine how Ryan was feeling.

He stopped on the road shoulder and checked his phone. It had three bars. He could call Rick Hayes, who was still recuperating from the torturous beating he'd received at the hands of Mexican drug cartel members in Haiti. Rick had stayed on *Dark Water* while Greg and Ryan had gone hunting for the cargo thieves. It would take Rick several hours to rent a car and drive to their location. Ryan didn't have that much time to spare. He needed medical attention fast. Greg thought it better to ask a local for help.

Still, they would need a ride back to San Juan. Greg dialed Rick's number.

"What's up, boss?"

"We were in an accident. Ryan had to hike me up a hill and has heat exhaustion, maybe stroke. I'm trying to get him a ride to a hospital in Utuado. I need you to come get us."

"Roger that. What happened?"

"We got ambushed by some road bandits. I think they're part of the group stealing cargo, but I'm not sure."

"I'll grab a helo and be right up. We'll drop warheads on foreheads."

"There's no place to land a helicopter. Besides, they're all dead."

"You guys have all the fun," Rick said. "I'll grab a car and meet you at the hospital."

"See you soon." Greg pocketed the phone, pushed out of the shade of a mahogany tree, and crested the rise.

Standing in a nearby dirt driveway were two young boys, staring at Greg as he rolled toward them, scattering a flock of chickens. Both boys had shaggy brown hair and bronze skin. The older boy, who Greg judged to be fifteen, wore a pair of red shorts, blue sneakers, and a soccer jersey. The younger boy, perhaps twelve, was barefoot. He wore dirt-stained white trousers and a blue T-shirt.

"*Hola, amigos*," Greg said with a big smile.

"*Buenos dias.*" *Good day*, the kids replied with a wave.

"*Habla inglés?*" *Do you speak English?* Greg asked.

The older boy said, "Yeah, what's up?"

"My friend and I were in a car accident. I need to get him to a hospital."

"Sure thing, man," the boy replied.

The smaller boy tugged on his brother's shirt and whispered in his ear when he bent down. A big smile crossed the older boy's face as he listened.

Greg knew he was in trouble.

The older boy straightened, and asked, "How much you got, *hombre*?"

"I'll give you twenty bucks each."

The boys consulted, both shaking their heads while they whispered. They folded their arms across their chests. "Not enough."

"How about two Honda dirt bikes?" Greg held his hands up, like gripping handlebars, and flicked his wrist in a revving motion. He used one of his favorite Spanish words. "*Motocicletas.*"

They glanced at each other and giggled, big grins revealing crooked white teeth. The older one trotted off. The younger one sidled up to Greg. "I am Juan Pablo, and that is my brother, Andre."

"Thanks for your help, Juan Pablo."

"It is no problem," the boy said with a grin.

A minute later, an engine snorted to life with a loud roar. The driver had to feather the throttle to keep the motor from dying. Engine noise blasted through a broken muffler. A rusted and worn-out single cab truck with a stake bed rounded the corner of the old barn. Andre stopped the truck beside Greg and hopped out.

He and his brother opened the gate on the truck bed and pulled out two long boards. Andre grabbed the handles on the back of Greg's wheelchair and maneuvered Greg in front of the boards while yammering at his brother in Spanish. With exaggerated hand gestures, the two boys argued back and forth while adjusting the board's width. Both boys strained together and pushed Greg into the truck bed. When he was up, they tossed the boards inside and closed the gate.

"Lock your brakes, wheelchair man," Andre called, climbing into the cab.

Greg did, and clung to the rough boards of the stake bed sides while the boys motored the truck up the hill he'd just come down. When they got close, he pounded on the cab roof and pointed at the downed tree.

Andre braked the truck and pulled to the side of the road.

"Ryan," Greg called.

There was no answer.

Greg said to Andre, who was climbing out of the cab, "He might be sleeping. Can you check?"

Andre walked into the brush and whooped. Greg figured he'd seen the dirt bikes. Then he heard him talking in a muffled voice, almost mumbling. Several anxious minutes passed as Greg peered into the brush and tried to see what was happening. Not only did the brush block his view, but the wooden slats of bed sides fell right in his line of sight, and he had to either sit up to see over the six-inch-wide plank or duck down to see under. He alternated views while he waited.

Andre came out of the brush and motioned for Juan Pablo. They went into the thicket, and a moment later, pushed out a motorcycle. They busied themselves moving it into the back of the truck.

"What about my friend?" Greg asked.

"He is sleeping," Andre said. "We take him in the cab. First we load the bikes."

Greg had trouble understanding the accent, but he got the gist. He wanted to leap out of the truck, pick Ryan up, and carefully lay him on the seat. But it wasn't to be. He was stuck in the truck's bed, waiting. He hated waiting. He should be doing something. With a white knuckled grip on the wood, he rattled the stake bed side.

Andre glanced up at the sound of wood and metal scraping together. "Hey, *hombre*, it's okay."

For Greg, it was not okay. His disability made it physically impossible to help his friend. Depending on these two slow-moving boys was driving him crazy. A scream of anger welled inside of him, and he fought to keep himself under control. He wasn't angry at the boys. He was angry at the gods, the universe, that bastard Nightcrawler who'd ordered the ambush on his convoy, and whatever had seen fit to sever his spinal column, dump him into a wheelchair, and make him useless. A fat tear rolled down his cheek. He wiped it away before anyone saw it.

The two boys loaded the bikes into the flat bed and tied them to the passenger side rail with a long piece of rope. Finally, they carried Ryan out of the brush, supported between them with his arms over their shoulders. He stumbled as he walked, chin touching his chest, trying to keep up with the quicker, shorter strides of the boys.

They got him into the cab. Juan Pablo ran around and climbed inside to keep Ryan's inert form in place while Andre shut the door. Ryan slumped against it. Juan Pablo squeezed into the middle seat, and Andre climbed in and got the engine started.

Andre backed the truck around, burying the rear half of the stake bed in the dead branches of the fallen tree. Crisp brown leaves sheared off and dropped everywhere. Smaller sticks broke off as the stake sides bent them backward. Andre muscled the wheel around and pointed them downhill. In the time it had taken Greg to wheel down to the farm, they'd driven to the hospital in Utuado.

The two boys helped Greg down the long plank ramp. An orderly appeared and asked what they needed. He scurried off with Andre bellowing and waving his arms in the air while pointing at the truck cab. The orderly returned with a wheelchair. Juan Pablo and Andre assisted in lowering Ryan into it.

Greg pressed crisp fifty-dollar bills into the outstretched hands of the waiting boys. Their eyes bulged when they saw the amount Greg had given them.

"*Gracias, señor*," Andre said.

Greg said. "I can't thank you enough."

"*Sí*," Juan Pablo said, still staring at the picture of President Grant stretched tight between his fingers.

"Better get those bikes out of here," Greg said. "Change the color so no one will recognize them."

Andre punched his brother in the arm and pointed at Greg. They spoke in Spanish, and Juan Pablo nodded. He slipped the money into his pocket and put on the shoes Andre had just kicked off. "I will go inside with you and help you with your friend. Andre will take care of the motorcycles."

Greg nodded in approval, spun around, and pushed for the automatic doors of Utuado hospital's emergency room, Juan Pablo following close on his wheels. Greg hurried after the orderly, remembering the gun on Ryan's hip. He overtook the orderly and blocked the hallway, forcing him to stop.

Holding up a finger, Greg said, "*Uno momento, por favor.*"

The orderly held tight to the wheelchair's grips. "We must get him to a room."

"Let me speak to him for a minute, alone," Greg said, waving his hands in dismissal.

Juan Pablo harassed the orderly in rapid-fire Spanish and pushed the man away.

Greg rolled up next to Ryan and pulled the gun and holster from his right hip. "Are you doing okay, buddy?"

Ryan barely nodded, croaking out a weak, "Yes."

Greg motioned for the orderly after tucking away the pistol, and Greg followed as the orderly took Ryan to a room and transferred him into the bed. A nurse came in and took Ryan's vital signs and checked his pupils and breathing. Then she disappeared.

Greg was in the middle of filling out paperwork when a doctor came in. Behind him was a female police officer. She stood silently in the corner while the doctor examined Ryan and concurred with their self-diagnosis of heat exhaustion before ordering intravenous saline solution to rehydrate the patient.

When the doctor left, the police officer said, "We need to talk."

CHAPTER FIFTEEN

Sunshine blinded Ryan. The bright light hurt his head even with his eyes closed. Every part of his body ached, and the inside of his left elbow itched. He reached over to scratch it and felt the IV tubes protruding from his skin. When he opened his eyes, his gaze followed the clear hoses up to the saline bags hanging from the IV machine.

His left arm felt like it was on fire. It had been straight for way too long. He pulled his hand back to slide it from under the covers, but it wouldn't move. Then he jerked hard and felt steel bite into his skin.

Frantic, he whipped the covers off and saw the handcuffs manacling him to the plastic bed rail.

"What the hell?" he mumbled.

Ryan flexed his arm and wiggled his wrist, trying to relieve the muscle cramp. He took a deep breath and lay back down, putting his right hand over his face to block the sunlight.

The room door opened. A short, dark-haired woman wearing green scrubs walked in. She closed the window curtain and approached the bed. In Spanish, she said, "It's nice to see you're awake."

Her name badge read "Eva." The smile on her lips could not hide the tiredness in her brown eyes.

"How long have I been out?" Ryan asked, continuing the conversation in his second language.

"Since they brought you in yesterday afternoon." She wheeled a vital signs machine to the side of the bed, attached a blood pressure cuff to his right arm, and pressed the button to inflate it.

Before she could stab the thermometer in his mouth, Ryan asked, "Who brought me in, Eva?"

"A man in a wheelchair and two young boys." She jammed the thermometer in his mouth, then clipped a sensor on his finger as the blood pressure cuff slowly deflated. While the machine did its job, she went into the bathroom and returned with a small jug. Ryan watched her squat by the bed and heard liquid splashing. It was then he realized he had a catheter shoved up his urethra.

"Can you take that out?" he asked.

Eva shook her head. "Not as long as you're handcuffed to the bed."

"Why am I handcuffed to the bed?"

The petite nurse shrugged.

"Eva, what's going on?"

She did not reply, only disappearing into the bathroom to empty his urine jug.

"Where's the guy in the wheelchair?" Ryan asked when she returned.

"I don't know. He left with some police officers."

Ryan laid his head back on the pillow and stared at the ceiling. He tried to piece together what had happened. His last clear memory was of pulling Greg into the brush alongside the road and falling onto the ground. From there, things got hazy. He had a snapshot of being helped into a truck, of being rolled into the hospital, and of Greg arguing with the attendant.

Ryan shook his head. If they'd handcuffed him to the bed, they must think he killed those guys at the Jeep in cold blood, but the bullet holes in the Jeep's body should prove otherwise.

Why did Greg have to go with the police? he wondered.

Eva sat at a wall-mounted computer to chart Ryan's vitals.

He scratched his chest and felt the leads of the heart monitor. He pulled them off.

A minute later, another nurse rushed into the room. She ignored Eva and went straight to Ryan's bed. She stopped when she saw Ryan was awake. Her eyes flicked between the heart monitor leads and Ryan's face. Then she conferred with Eva before leaving the room.

Eva rolled over to the side of the bed on a short stool. "They want you to wear the heart monitor during your stay with us."

"My heart is fine," Ryan said, aggravation evident in his voice.

"Dehydration can cause serious problems with the cardiac functions."

"With all this saline, I think I'll be okay."

Eva sighed but relented with a shrug. "I can't force you to wear them." She rolled back to the computer.

"Can you get me a glass of water?"

With a hint of playfulness, she said, "I thought you were doing just fine with the saline."

"I've got cotton mouth," he said, rolling his tongue around his teeth to remove the built-up plaque and the taste left by the infusion of saline.

Eva finished her notes and left the room. She returned a few minutes later with a large glass of ice water and a straw.

Ryan took long drinks through the straw, letting the cold liquid rinse away the funk in his mouth.

"Do you know where my clothes are?"

"They're right here," Eva said, pointing to a drawer.

"Can you set them on the table?"

She did and asked, "Anything else?"

He shook his head. "No, thanks."

He rummaged through the pockets after she left the room. Ryan found his wallet, but not his cell phone or his pocketknife. He assumed the police had taken them along with his gun and holster. They'd be able to match his pistol to the bullets in the three men he'd killed.

He had to get out of the hospital and find Greg.

After a long drink of water, he clenched the straw with his teeth and pulled it free of the cup. He reached under the bed and unhooked the urine bag from the right bed rail, swung himself into a seated position on the left side of the bed, and dropped the bag by his feet. He had no desire to experience the pain of the catheter being jerked out of his bladder if the tube snagged on something. His overused muscles and various cuts and scrapes on his arms and legs provided enough agony.

Able to use both hands together now, Ryan took the straw from his mouth. He opened his wallet and extracted his Wallet Ninja, a credit card-shaped multipurpose tool. He used the multitool's letter opener to slice off an inch of the straw then cut the piece lengthwise.

He shoved the straw between the ratcheting paw and the internal teeth of the handcuff, forcing the teeth to disengage. Ryan pulled the cuff apart and slipped his hand free. Next, he removed the tape from his elbow and pulled the IV line from his vein, leaving it to drip on the floor.

Ryan pulled his gown up and examined the indwelling catheter. He knew he needed to deflate the small balloon holding it inside his bladder. During his hospital stay after being shot in Afghanistan, he'd seen guys rip them out. They'd bled badly from the damage caused by dragging out the ball of saline. The catheter consisted of two tubes, one connected to the bed bag and the other which terminated in a small threaded plug. He used the Wallet Ninja to slice the plug off the tube, and saline rushed out onto the floor. He pulled the catheter out and heaved a sigh of relief.

Free of all the tubes and machines, Ryan got dressed. His clothes had been washed, by a nurse he assumed, and smelled like hospital disinfectant. It was better than wearing the backless gown out into the street and showing his ass to the world. Not that he hadn't done that before, but today, he'd rather not attract the attention.

Outside the hospital, Ryan tried to orient himself to where he was in town. He stopped a man in a white lab coat and asked for directions to the Y-bridge on shaky legs. The doctor told him to go west along the river. Ryan thanked the man and walked across the green lawn of an outdoor amphitheater. He crossed the river on Las Palmas Street and turned west on 111R. Ten minutes later, he was crossing the Y-bridge and headed for the pizza parlor he and Greg had eaten in yesterday. He could almost taste the cold beer.

When he entered the restaurant, he noticed Pedro staring at him.

Suddenly, Pedro wheeled around and ran into the kitchen. Ryan hurried across the dining room after him.

A man shouted, "Hey, you can't go in there!"

Whatever reason Ryan had concocted in his mind for chasing the restaurant owner evaporated and he paused, one hand on the door. "*Este no es el baño?*" *This isn't the bathroom?*

The man pointed at another door clearly labeled as a restroom in both Spanish and English. Ryan apologized, crossed the pizza parlor, and entered the bathroom. He used the urinal, washed his hands, and walked back to the small bar.

A cold bottle of Presidente appeared on the counter, and Ryan drained it in several long gulps. The alcohol made him lightheaded, so he ordered a calzone and a water.

Pedro reappeared through the kitchen door and gave Ryan a patronizing smile. "Where is your friend?"

"He couldn't make it today," Ryan said.

"A pity."

"You got a phone I could use?"

"*Sí*," Pedro said and pointed at an ancient payphone near the restrooms.

"Does that thing work?" Ryan asked, laying a ten-dollar bill on the counter.

Pedro nodded and made change to give Ryan some coins. Ryan pulled a small phone book from his wallet and dialed Rick's cell phone number.

When Risk answered, Ryan said, "Hey Rick, it's me, Ryan."

"Where you at, buddy? The hospital is going crazy."

"What do you mean?" Ryan asked.

"Dude, I'm at the police station with Greg. Where are you?"

"At a pizza place by the Y-bridge."

"Hang tight, I'm coming to pick you up."

Ryan returned to his seat to eat his calzone. It didn't matter that the hot sauce poured out like lava and burnt the roof of his mouth; he woofed it down like a starving man. Then he ordered another.

As Ryan waited for his second helping, a short, stocky man entered the restaurant, removing his mirrored aviator shades as he walked straight up to Ryan. Rick Hayes had been an Army EOD tech they'd known in Afghanistan on their last tour back in 2014. Greg had bumped into him again in Key

West, where Rick had been taking tourists on helicopter flights over the Florida Keys. Greg had invited him into the DWR fold, and he'd been part of the team since.

"Dude, what the hell?" Rick said.

"Stay frosty," Ryan said tersely, and slid a beer over to Rick.

Rick cocked his head and arched an eyebrow.

"Loose lips sink ships."

Rick began to discreetly eyeball everyone in the restaurant while sipping his beer. Ryan finished his second calzone even though his stomach was full. After fishing his wallet out, he tossed down enough money to cover the bill and a generous tip.

When Rick started to rise, Ryan stopped him. He leaned in and whispered, "I want you to bump the owner while I buy a cigar. Get his cell phone."

Rick nodded, and together they walked to the small display of cigars beside the register. Ryan pointed and asked for a Don Collins Panetela. When Pedro bent to grab the cigar, Rick leaned in with him to look at a box of Churchills.

Rick pointed. "Those any good?"

"*El major.*" *The best.*

"I'll take four and what my friend wants." Rick opened his wallet.

Pedro reached for the cigars with a pleased expression on his face. Rick gave Ryan a quick wink and paid for the tobacco. Ryan knew the man had a pair of slick hands. Over beers one night, Rick had told Ryan about growing up on the tourist-crowded streets of New Orleans. His father had been a pickpocket and had taught him the trade before being arrested for robbing a jewelry store.

Outside the restaurant, both men climbed into Rick's rental car and sped away. Two blocks away, Rick pulled a smart phone from his pocket and handed it to Ryan.

Ryan cradled it and hit the power button. "Thumbprint protected."

"Don't touch the print reader screen. I might be able to get it open."

Ryan nodded and laid the phone in the center console with the thumbprint sensor down.

It didn't take long to arrive at the police headquarters building.

"What are we doing here?" Ryan asked, glancing at his friend.

"What you would have done if you'd stayed in the hospital. Besides, the boss is waiting for you."

"Greg's in there?"

"Guaranteeing your return, squid."

Ryan climbed out of the vehicle and headed for the front door. He turned when he realized Rick wasn't coming with him.

Rick was leaning on the open door of the rental car. Ryan could see himself in the man's shades. He looked pale. Being sick had taken away some of his deep tan and dark circles swelled under his green eyes. The food had helped, but he was tired already. He wanted to take a nap.

"I'll take care of the phone," Rick said. "Go talk to Inspector Martinez."

Ryan turned and walked into the building. He found a female police officer at the front desk. When he informed her who he was and asked for Martinez, she led him back to the inspector's office.

When he pushed through the glass door, Ryan saw a woman behind the desk. Greg sat in one corner, flipping through a magazine.

The woman pointed to a chair. Ryan sat.

Inspector Martinez said, "Your friend has convinced me not to arrest you for murder."

CHAPTER SIXTEEN

Greg said, "The least I could do."

Ryan looked back at the inspector and waited for her to continue. He noticed a plaque on the wall bearing her full name, Gabriella Louisa Santos Martinez. She had thick black hair pulled back in a ponytail, and her uniform looked tailor cut to her trim figure. Ryan guessed she was around five foot three when she came around to lean on the front of the desk.

She crossed her arms and said, "The gun we took from Mr. Olsen is a match for the bullets we found at a crime scene in Ponce. He claims it is his gun, yet he has no gunshot residue on his hands, unlike you, and he had a child distract an orderly so he could take your pistol. The hospital has security cameras everywhere."

Ryan glanced at his hands as if the GSR would be visible. He vaguely remembered Greg taking the gun and holster. He asked, "What crime scene in Ponce?"

Gabriella said, "Last night we found two men shot to death outside the Ponce shipping terminal."

Ryan knit his brows and glanced at Greg again before looking back at Gabriella. "When was this?"

"Around eleven p.m.," she said.

"I'm pretty sure I was in the hospital."

Greg nodded in confirmation. "I told her that. We checked you in around two in the afternoon."

Ryan spread his hands. "Problem solved."

"No, it doesn't solve the problem, Mr. Weller," Gabriella said, shaking her head, ponytail swaying back and forth. "Would you explain how bullets from your gun killed two men in Ponce when you were in the hospital?"

"Greg, did you tell her why I was in the hospital?"

Gabriella answered, "Dehydration."

"Can I speak to my boss for a minute, alone?" Ryan asked.

Gabriella fixed both men with a stare. "No. I know you're not the killer. One, because you were in the hospital. Two, your boss was in possession of your pistol. Three, the autopsy revealed the men were shot elsewhere and the bodies dumped. The bullets were a plant." She uncrossed her arms, placed her palms on the desk, and leaned forward. "I would like to hear your explanation of events in the creek."

Ryan leaned back in his chair and crossed his feet at his ankles. He wanted a cigarette. "Yesterday, we left the pizza parlor by the Y-bridge and headed for Ponce ..."

He related the whole story of the ambush and the gunfight by the creek. He told her about dragging Greg up the hill and theorized that whoever had set up the ambush could have extracted the bullets from the dead men by the creek and placed them in the bodies at the Ponce shipping terminal.

"You're an excellent storyteller," Gabriella said, running a hand over her hair. "Your friend told me a similar tale. I went to the crash site and found your Jeep. There were no dead bodies, and no indications that a fight had taken place."

Ryan shook his head. It didn't surprise him. Whoever was after them was covering their tracks and trying to pin two murders on them to scare them away from investigating the container thefts. This might have worked if the bad guys hadn't botched the setup. Their blundering attempts did little more than to strengthen Ryan's resolve. The pushback they were receiving from the criminals indicated they were on the right trail.

"Did you show her the phones?" Ryan asked Greg.

"Yes, I gave them to her last night and they've disappeared."

"Disappeared?" Ryan said, furrowing his brows.

"Yes," Gabriella said. "I turned them over to evidence last night. Now they're gone."

"What a surprise." Ryan shook his head in disgust. "Your police force has a history of corruption. Someone here has ties to whoever ran us off the road and is now trying to frame me for murder."

"Why *are* they trying to frame you for murder?" Gabriella asked.

"We're investigating the theft of DWR's cargo containers from the shipping ports here in Puerto Rico," Ryan said. "Obviously, they don't want us to figure out who they are."

"On whose authority are you investigating these thefts?" the inspector demanded.

Greg said, "When people steal from my company, I'm going to investigate."

"You have no authority on this island," Gabriella reminded them.

"You're right," Ryan agreed, and stood. "Am I under arrest, or are we free to go?"

Inspector Gabriella Martinez waved a hand toward the door. "Get out."

Women had been telling him that a lot lately.

Greg left first, and Gabriella followed them to the door. Just as Ryan passed through, she said, "There are many unsavory characters operating in Puerto Rico. You will call me if you are in trouble." She pressed a business card into Ryan's hand.

As they were approaching Rick's car, Greg said, "Let's go back to San Juan."

Rick climbed out of the driver's seat to help disassemble and pack the wheelchair. Ryan got in the back and leaned forward between the two front seats.

"Did you get an intel from the phone?" he asked.

"Not yet," Rick said. "I need to get in front of a computer to hack it."

Ryan sat back and turned sideways on the bench seat. He closed his eyes and slept all the way to San Juan.

CHAPTER SEVENTEEN

The tropical sun caused rivulets of sweat to course down Ryan Weller's broad back. He was shirtless, clad in boardshorts and flip flops. Flakes of rust, sand, and paint marred his skin and made him itch. He breathed his own humid air through the respirator as he ran the sandblaster along *Peggy Lynn*'s flanks.

With all the modifications, she needed a paint job. The new holes in the hull contained bow and stern thrusters linked to a satellite system which would hold the salvage vessel in place over a dive site no matter the wind, waves, or currents. Even without the uplink, the thrusters would give them better maneuverability and stabilization, making everyone's jobs easier from the captain to the dive tenders. A new pair of CAT diesel engines and generators filled the engine bay and a dizzying array of modern electronics graced the pilot house.

Installing the hardware had been the easy part. It was running the wires and connecting the systems that took time. Another two weeks and the old girl would be fit for sea trials. All the crew looked forward to getting underway.

Ryan had taken on the job of scouring the hull down to bare metal for the fresh coat of antifoul. He'd been at it for the better part of a day, and he had the ninety feet of steel gleaming like new. They needed to cover the hull quickly to prevent rust from forming. Another hour and the paint crew would arrive.

The roar of the sandblaster died away suddenly, and he glanced around for the culprit. Greg Olsen twirled the end of the unplugged extension cord.

"Plug it back in." Ryan gestured. "I'm almost done."

"Come see me when you're done and take a shower. You stink."

Ryan flipped him the bird and grabbed the sandblaster as the power came on. He finished the job and stepped back to check out the bare hull. Pits and gouges marred the surface from decades of sea service. She'd need a little more work before the painters arrived. He was just glad he wasn't doing it. He coiled the hose around the sandblaster's tank and grabbed a broom to sweep up the piles of sand and paint lying under the ship. One of the dock workers walked over with a dustpan to help Ryan load the dirty sand into trash bags.

Captain Dennis Law came down the ladder from the deck and examined Ryan's handiwork. He ran a hand over the ship's side, paused, eyes half-closed, fingertips pressed against the steel. A man communicating with his true love. Ryan felt he should remove a hat or put his hand over his heart in the presence of such reverence.

After a moment, the captain's eyelids fluttered open. With a nod to Ryan, he said, "Good job, son. You better go see what Greg needs."

"Aye, aye, Skipper." Ryan oversaw the operation, but he deferred to the older man when it came to the boat. Dennis was owner and master of the vessel. None of *Peggy Lynn*'s crew needed to work after splitting twelve million dollars, but when Greg said hop, they asked how high, even if Ryan was as sarcastic as possible while doing so.

One perk of the marina was the use of the showers. Ryan turned the water as hot as he could stand and climbed in. After soaping up and rinsing off, he dragged a razor over his stubbly cheeks, chin, and neck.

Whatever Greg had in store meant more work. Earlier in the week, the former Dark Water CEO had rented a furnished apartment and installed several high-powered computers. Ryan had taken one look at the massive screens and decided they would be perfect for Spider Solitaire. He wouldn't need to squint. Then Don Williams and his fiancée had arrived on the island and occupied one of the apartment's bedrooms.

Don had originally been brought to Key West to help outfit *Peggy Lynn* before the aging salvage vessel left for Haiti. Ryan had co-opted him into becoming a member of the crew. Ashlee, from her desk at DWR headquarters, had run computer simulations to help them find the *Santo Domingo* after the hurricanes had moved the ship on the sea floor.

Their job now was to set up GPS tracking of DWR's shipping containers. For the last few days, she and Don had been running all over the island installing RFID chips and GPS trackers on containers and equipment. Ryan had hoped that by working on *Peggy Lynn*, he could avoid helping them.

Walking back to *Dark Water*, his damp towel over his bare shoulder, he saw Rick pull up in the new rental. The man had shaved his head, and his white dome looked weird compared to his tan face. He stepped out of the Jeep wearing khaki shorts, a Hawaiian shirt, leather sandals, and his ubiquitous aviator sunglasses.

"Where's your sucker at, Kojak?" Ryan asked.

"Very funny, asshole."

"You look like a cross between Telly Savalas and Tom Selleck."

Rick beamed. "That's better."

"Nah, on second thought, you're too short."

"Screw you, Weller," Rick snapped.

Grinning at his own joke, Ryan asked, "What's the boss want?"

"Don't know. He said to get over here and pick you guys up."

They stepped aboard the massive Hatteras and went into the salon. They found Greg ensconced on the settee, his laptop open on the dining table, surrounded by stacks of paperwork. Ryan brushed past the solid wood cabinets, granite countertops, and chrome fixtures of the luxurious salon and kitchen to veer down to the bunkroom, where he pulled on shoes and socks and a T-shirt to go with the shorts he already wore.

Back in the salon, Rick was getting water bottles from the fridge. Greg had transferred to his wheelchair.

"What's going on?" Ryan asked, leaning against the counter. He opened a water bottle and took a long drink.

"We're leaving for Fajardo to do equipment inventory and install trackers," Greg said.

Ryan groaned.

"Until you catch a thief," Greg said, "we need to get some work done."

"How am I going to catch him if I'm too busy working?"

They drove to the apartment operations center. Ashlee had her head buried behind two large monitors set up on the massive kitchen peninsula. White quartz counter tops gleamed over dark wood cabinets. Oversized stainless-steel appliances were inset into the walls. Don was busy inventorying RFID chips on a glass-topped table. Greg had spared no expense in finding them luxury digs to work from.

Ryan thought if Ashlee was his fiancée, he'd be too distracted to take inventory. She was cute, with thick, natural red hair in a loose ponytail, ivy green eyes, and an upturned nose. While she spent most of her time behind the keyboard, she remained trim. By comparison, her beau was rangy, with large brown eyes and a mop of brown hair under a white mesh trucker cap with the University of Texas logo on the front. They made an odd couple, her at five feet tall and him at over six foot four.

Don picked up an ongoing conversation. "Texas will win the Big Twelve this year. Tom Herman has 'em looking good."

"Bullshit," Greg said. "My Aggies will wipe the floor with your Longhorns."

"Hold on," Rick barked. "Both you idiots know Oklahoma is going to whoop your asses."

"Neither one of you will make the play-offs. Buckeyes all the way," Ashlee chimed in. "Right, Ryan?"

He shrugged. While he liked watching college football, he didn't follow it fanatically.

"Ohio State is going to lose to Michigan this year," Rick added.

"No way," Ashlee shot back. "Do you even watch football, bro? Harbaugh can't win the big game."

Greg called, "Time out on the field. You guys have the gear ready for us to take to Fajardo?"

"Right here." Don pointed at the pile of RFID chips and GPS trackers with his index and pinkie fingers extended from his fist in a "Hook 'em Horns" gesture.

"Real cute." Rick rolled his eyes and moved past the engineer to grab a box.

Ryan also picked up a couple boxes of gear, and they carried them down to the Jeep. Between the tracking equipment, the wheelchair, and the three men, the Wrangler was full. Rick climbed into the rear seat, which seemed built for his five-foot-six frame.

An hour later, they were negotiating the twisted warren of streets along Fajardo's waterfront. The dock area consisted of four long piers for ferries and freight. DWR had the contract to shore up the hurricane-damaged piers, adding concrete pillars, pouring new foundations, and rebuilding cracking and crumbling sections. They'd also added handicap ramps and features to the ferry berths.

The job foreman, Sam Tennison, met them outside the fenced-in DWR compound just down the street from the docks. He was a tall man with broad shoulders, shaggy brown hair, and a thick horseshoe mustache that reminded Ryan of Hulk Hogan. Even though Sam didn't give off the *say your prayers and eat your vitamins* vibe, he did look capable of crushing a man's skull between his bare hands.

When Greg rolled over to him, the job foreman pulled the stub of a cigar from his mouth and smirked. "What brings the boss to slum with the working man?"

"I gotta keep you stiffs in line."

"Then you better start with the riff-raff you brought with you." Sam grinned at Ryan and Rick.

"Good to see you're still cantankerous as ever, Sam." Ryan extended his hand, and Sam shook with his meaty, calloused paw. Then Ryan pointed at Rick. "This here is Rick Hayes. He's another one of those officer types."

Sam thrust his hand out. "We'll ignore the officer part. If you're running around with these two yahoos, you're all right in my book."

Rick shook hands.

"Now that Jack has met the beanstalk, let's get this job started," Ryan said.

Sam laughed, one hand on his thick chest.

Rick, on the other hand, glowered. "I told you, no more short jokes."

"Just a little one?" Ryan asked, holding up his thumb and forefinger an inch apart.

Rick extended his middle finger.

"Play nice, boys," Greg admonished, "or I'll have Sam knock your brains in."

Sam stuck his cigar between his lips and rubbed his hands together. "With pleasure."

Ryan saw the sadistic gleam in the foreman's eyes and knew the man had knocked in his share of heads to keep his men in line. Sometimes the only thing roughnecks and construction guys understood was a little fisticuffs.

"I got the gear all laid out for you," Sam said. "Let me know if you need anything else." He strode across the lot to a portable office and went up the stairs, yelling at two men who were lounging under an umbrella at a picnic table to get back to work. They jumped up and disappeared.

"Don't piss off the Mustache," Rick said.

Ryan said, "Don't piss off the guy in the wheelchair, he'll make you put RFID tags on all his shit."

CHAPTER EIGHTEEN

Three hours later, Ryan stood, placed both hands on the small of his back, and leaned into them. The constant bending and straightening had made him stiff. He walked in a tight circle, rolling his neck to loosen his muscles. While he and Rick had applied RFID chips to each piece of gear, Greg followed behind with a tablet. He'd scanned the tag and input the name and serial number of each item.

On the drive down, Greg had told them the RFID tags would last up to twenty years on passive mode, and if they were actively transmitting, three to five years. When not moving, the tags reported every two minutes, but when the equipment was in transit, the tags updated at thirty-second intervals. Not only could they tell which containers were on the move, but each tag also gave an alert if someone tampered with it. When the tags registered in DWR's system, they transmitted time, temperature, speed, longitude and latitude, and battery life, among other things.

DWR's investment in the technology would lead to more effective stop-loss measures and better tracking of equipment and material, allowing for just-in-time shipments to work sites, and this test would also allow them to track the stolen containers to the thief's hideouts.

"What's wrong with you, old man?" Rick asked.

"Nothing a cold beer wouldn't fix."

"Same here," Greg called. They'd tagged all the gear and now were each working a tablet.

"I saw a store on the way in," Ryan said. "I'll walk down there and buy some."

"Get one for me," Rick added.

Ryan strolled out onto Avenida El Pescador and headed for the convenience store he'd seen earlier. On the opposite corner of the street was a café with outdoor tables covered in white cloths. Cars, trucks, and scooters jammed the roads. Large orange barricades blocked traffic from interfering with ferry operations. Everywhere he looked, bright colored buildings crowded the street. There was barely room to walk on the sidewalk.

The store aisles were so full of goods, he had to turn sideways to traverse them. Greg wouldn't have gotten past the large rack of sunglasses at the door. Ryan grabbed a cold six-pack of Presidente from the cooler and made his way to the counter. The clerk had a radio on, blasting mariachi music, and was watching a soccer match on television. He barely took his eyes off the set while working the cash register one-handed, the other clutching a cigarette. Ryan didn't tell him it was the wrong football.

Back outside, he turned down an alley and came upon stacks of containers waiting to be loaded on a ship. Ryan started to walk to the main street when he stopped and turned back.

The bottom container was in almost pristine condition. If it was here, he reasoned, shouldn't it look like the others, carrying battle scars from years on the high seas? He sniffed his shirt. He could still smell smoke. Why hadn't he bought a pack of cigarettes?

He stepped sideways to gain a view down the length of the container. Someone had recently painted it and done a shitty job. They'd neglected to sand off the rust, leaving pits and jagged dimples where the oxidation had broken through. Near the container's center, overspray ran in long drips. Despite the heavy layer of paint, the dark shadows of the five-foot-high letters *DWR* had bled through.

"Huh," Ryan muttered. He passed his palm along the paint, stopping at a large blob at the end of a run. Picking at the blob with his fingernail, he discovered the paint inside was still wet. Then, moving around to the rear, he squatted to study the identification tag and metal door seal. Neither belonged to DWR.

Ryan hurried to where Greg and Rick were working.

"You get those beers?" Greg eyed the paper sack.

"Oh, yeah. Here." Ryan handed him the bag and quickly added, "There's something I want you to see."

Greg extracted two bottles, cracked open the lids, and downed half of one while handing the other to Rick. He held the partial bottle up to the light and wiped his mouth with the back of his hand. "Damn, that's good. What did you want?"

"Come look at something." Ryan retraced his steps to the strange container with Rick and Greg on his heels. When they arrived at the parking lot, Ryan motioned to the container stack. "See anything wrong?"

Both Rick and Greg stopped to examine the containers. They spotted the wet paint at the same time. Greg called Sam on the phone and asked him to bring a forklift.

Ryan leaned against the chain-link fence and dug out a beer. He had it three-quarters gone when Sam showed up, riding on the side of a forklift. Another bruiser sat behind the wheel. He had long greasy hair, a scar on his chin, and a cigarette dangling from the corner of his lips.

As he watched, Greg instructed Sam to cut the padlock and tag. Sam motioned for the driver to come over. The man hopped down and picked up a pair of bolt cutters. He sauntered over to the container, ashing his cigarette.

The smoke drifted to Ryan and he inhaled deeply. He wanted to wrench the cutters from the guy's grasp and beat him with them, then take the cigarette and stub it out in his eye. Why was quitting so damned hard? How long had it been since he'd had a smoke? A month? *Yeah, thirty freaking days*. The smoke smell was almost making him salivate. He rolled his shoulders and neck to relieve tension.

"One day at a time," Ryan muttered.

The big construction worker snapped the lock and handed it and the tag to Greg. They opened the doors and stared at the pallets of cement blocks.

"Missing anything?" Sam asked.

"I didn't think so," Greg replied.

Rick motioned for Ryan to hand him a beer, and the two stood sipping beers and watching Greg talk into his cell phone.

"Here comes trouble." Rick pointed at a uniformed security guard trotting across the parking lot. He held a clipboard and was screaming for the men to stop what they were doing.

Ryan pushed himself off the fence and dropped his empty bottle in the paper bag. He intercepted the security guard, and they quarreled in Spanish about who the container belonged to and why they had the right to take back their property. Finally, Ryan said, reading the man's name tag, "Ernesto, let me see your manifest."

"*Señor*, it is not possible."

Ryan's relaxed attitude snapped. He stepped into Ernesto's personal space and, in what he called his "command voice," a level louder than normal, he demanded, *"Dónde está el manifiesto de envío?"* Where's the shipping manifest?

Startled, Ernesto held up a clipboard. "I have it here."

Ryan snatched the clipboard away and flipped through the pages until he found the ones he wanted. He read aloud the name of the shipper. "Caribbean Maritime Delivery."

"What's the address?" Greg asked, having wheeled up during the commotion.

Ryan handed him the clipboard.

Greg pulled the page out of the stack and returned the clipboard to Ernesto. "This container belongs to Dark Water Research."

"Por favor, señor," Ernesto begged. "I am only the security guard. I do what I am told and do not make decisions."

"Then I'm telling you I'm taking my container back," Greg said.

Ernesto held up his hands in surrender. *"A mi, plín."*

Ryan's brow knotted. The guy had just said, "To me, plink."

Coming to Ryan's rescue, Sam said, "It's a *Boricua* thing. Means 'I don't care.'"

"What's a Boricua?" Rick asked.

Sam smiled. "You boys need to bone up on your Puerto Rican slang. It's what they call each other instead of saying *puertorriqueño*."

"Now that we have today's history lesson out of the way," Greg said. "Let's get our container back home and put a new tag on it."

"You want tags on all the concrete blocks, too?" Rick asked in gest.

"Yes," Greg said. "On every freaking one."

Rick moaned dramatically.

Sam had the forklift driver unstack the containers and take DWR's stolen merchandise to their lot.

As they walked back to the compound to finish tagging equipment, Ryan said, "Didn't Ashlee and Don tag that container when it was in San Juan?"

"They did," Greg said.

"Did they miss one?" Rick asked.

"No," Greg replied. "That's who I was on the phone with. She said they tagged it and the system says the container is still in San Juan."

Ryan frowned. "Then someone has insider knowledge of our new tracking program and has defeated it already."

When they were back at the compound, Greg rolled into the shade of the umbrella and pulled out his phone. Ryan and Rick sat down to drink their remaining beers. Ryan pushed Greg's in front of him while he spoke to Ashlee. Greg told her to get over to the port authority and find out why their tracker said the container hadn't left San Juan but was in Fajardo.

The forklift driver barreled out of the office and slammed the door behind him. He stepped into the office's shadow and lit a cigarette. Ryan took a calming breath of second-hand smoke. It smelled so good. Quitting was getting harder the older he got. When he was younger, he could pick them up and put them down with ease. Now he wasn't sure if his willpower had slipped or the manufacturers were adding more addictive shit to them. Nothing like breathing rat poison, carbon monoxide, and cyanide.

"Yo, driver, let me bum a smoke," Ryan pleaded.

The man tossed the pack and lighter on the table.

Greg snatched them up and threw them back. He pulled the phone away from his ear and said to Ryan, "Get back to work."

Ryan chugged the rest of his warm beer, slammed the bottle into the steel garbage drum so hard the glass broke, and stomped toward the Jeep to get his tablet.

CHAPTER NINETEEN

Diego Hernández leaned against the fence and watched the people swirl around him on the crowded Avenida El Pescador. Trucks and cars rolled past; their choking exhaust swept away by the ocean breeze. A ferry idled along a dock, taking on a load of vehicles and pedestrians. Further down the quay, DWR used an excavator on a barge to lower sections of corrugated steel into the water, where divers welded them to piles.

He hadn't traveled to Fajardo to watch DWR build a pier extension. He'd left his tiny mountain redoubt to check on his shipment. In two hours, *Star of Ceiba*, a deck cargo ship, would arrive. She'd take the containers to the Port of Miami, where the stolen cargo would be sold via internet auction.

They'd accumulated ten containers for the Miami run. Now there were nine since the DWR operatives had found their container.

Diego had had Phillipe Fernandez remove the tracker from the container and leave it fastened to a light pole inside the Colón terminal. Then they'd taken the container to a warehouse and given it a fresh coat of paint. Obviously, not a good one, as Ryan Weller had spotted it. It galled Diego that DWR had sent a professional after him. The other shipping companies reported their losses to the local authorities, many of whom were in Diego's pocket, and moved on with their business. Not Dark Water Research.

Taking the first DWR container had been what he'd thought was an accident, mistaking it for relief supplies. When they'd opened it at Diego's compound, they'd found surface supply diving equipment. He had quickly sold the gear except for the generator, which they'd used to provide electricity to a village.

Diego was the bastard son of a white U.S. Navy sailor and a Puerto Rican mother. He had the dark skin and long, thick black hair and goatee of a native, but the height and green eyes of his father's European ancestors. Close to six feet, he carried the bulk of a weightlifter from his days in the military and prison.

The sailor had moved his mother to Jacksonville, Florida, and then abandoned her. She'd moved to Miami and met a Boricua, who had raised Diego and fathered four other children with his mother. Diego was glad to have siblings, and had enjoyed his boyhood in Florida, but his favorite memories were of visiting his stepfather's family in the hills above Utuado.

Diego had joined the Army after high school and become an airborne Ranger. While serving overseas, he'd discovered he had a knack for finding and exploiting loopholes in the logistics train. Soon, he was diverting supplies from regular Army units.

His greed had gone beyond the supplementation of his fellow Ranger elements, and an Army criminal investigator had caught Diego selling guns and ammunition to Afghan tribal leaders. They'd arrested and court-martialed him. After serving ten years in Leavenworth, Diego had returned to

Puerto Rico. It wasn't long before he was running his own criminal enterprise.

The hurricane had been a blessing in disguise. While much of the island had been destroyed, he'd found a lucrative business in stealing shipping containers. At first, it was to deliver goods to those who needed them the most. While the governor and the U.S. president feuded over logistics, Diego and his partner took advantage of the cargo glut. They moved water, food, tarps, and medical supplies into areas hardest hit by the storms, making lives more comfortable. Stealing even a portion was like dipping a teaspoon into a firehose.

A year after the storm, the spigot had been shut off. Now they were dipping their teaspoon into puddles, and the puddles kept getting smaller.

Diego felt the pressure from all sides. The government was cracking down on gang activity, the shipping companies were utilizing technology to stop theft, and other criminal syndicates were homing in on his operation. They wished to use his established shipping routes to move cocaine and marijuana. The more he resisted them, the more they pushed back. That was why he needed to put an end to this investigation by Dark Water Research: to send a message to his competition. If he did it correctly, he could even drive DWR off the island and use his influence to help friends acquire the dock projects.

As he watched the excavator, he heard the clatter of a tow motor driving down the avenue. The driver and a man with a lustrous brown mustache riding on the side of the forklift turned into the lot and drove to the stack with the freshly painted DWR container at the bottom. He listened as the men intimidated Ernesto into giving them the shipping manifest and opened the container. The forklift driver unstacked the containers and drove DWR's back to their compound.

The puddle had shrunk again.

DWR's three operators strolled across the lot after the forklift. They passed Diego on the way back to DWR's compound. The one holding the paper sack containing beers met Diego's eyes and fire burned through Diego's body. Ryan Weller was so close. It took all his restraint to not jerk his pistol from his belt, place the muzzle to the back of the man's head, and pull the trigger. Message sent, execution style.

Rather than commit murder in the street, he looked away from the big man's gaze and walked down the sidewalk. Adrenaline and revenge pumped through his veins. He wanted to glance over his shoulder but kept his eyes straight ahead. He'd make them pay for meddling in his affairs.

CHAPTER TWENTY

When Ryan and Greg entered the apartment the next morning, Don had his feet propped on a table, and he was tossing a rubber ball into the air. Ashlee was gazing at her computer screen.

Don caught the ball and said, "What's up, boss?"

Greg ignored him and rolled straight to Ashlee. "Any luck getting the camera footage?"

She shook her head, red hair swaying back and forth, and pushed her reading glasses onto her forehead. "The port won't give it to us without a warrant."

"Did you tell them it was in their best interest to hand it over? They should want the thieves caught as much as we do."

"You can't explain anything to lawyers," Ashlee said.

Ryan went over to the coffeemaker, cleaned out the old grounds and started a fresh pot. While the coffee brewed, he pulled out his cell phone and checked for messages. He was hoping Joulie would call him and they could talk about James. He hadn't heard from her since he'd left a week ago. While he was in Haiti, they'd spoken on the phone at least once a day, if they weren't together. He missed her phone calls and her sultry voice purring in his ear, but he had known from the beginning their relationship wouldn't be a lasting one.

The screen showed no calls.

"Coffee's ready," Greg said, interrupting Ryan's reverie.

Ryan poured himself a cup, wishing he had a cigarette. He sighed, watching Greg mix a Cuba Libre. His boss rode him to quit smoking, but he had no qualms about drinking alcohol at eight thirty in the morning.

Greg's phone rang, and he pulled it from the holster on his belt and answered it. After a moment, he glanced up at Ryan and motioned for them to go into a bedroom.

When they were inside, Ryan closed the door. Greg hit the speaker button and placed the phone on the mattress.

The gravelly voice of Floyd Landis filled the room. "Why can't you boys stay out of trouble?"

"Just to bug you," Ryan replied.

"I can believe it from you," Landis said.

Greg gave Ryan a *shut-up* look, then said, "What do you have for us?"

"First, I've got names to go with the pictures of the three dead guys. They belong to a gang called the Utuado Vaqueros."

"Utuado Cowboys," Ryan translated. "Not very original."

"Original or not, these cowboys wear the black hats," Landis said. "The man with the Ranger tattoo did time in Leavenworth with the group's founder, Diego Hernández." Landis filled them in on Hernández's history, then added, "The other two guys are Puerto Ricans with minor criminal records. They were low level actors before Hernández showed up and recruited them for his gang."

"What about the phone Rick took off the restaurant owner?" Ryan asked. They'd overnighted the phone to Landis when Rick couldn't hack the password.

"We got a number we think is for Hernández. The calls coincide with the time of your ambush."

"Let's have it," Greg said.

Landis read the number.

"Is he still using it?" Ryan asked.

"It was active in Fajardo yesterday."

Ryan glanced over in time to see the shock on Greg's face.

Greg said, "We were in Fajardo yesterday."

"The trace puts him on the docks. He made several phone calls. All of them went to burners."

Ryan quickly replayed yesterday's events, wondering if he'd seen the gang leader at some point. "Can you send us a picture of Diego?"

"Yeah, I'll email it to you."

"Thanks," Greg said. "Anything else?"

"That's all I've got," Landis said.

"Any chance you can help us get our hands on the video footage from the Colón shipping terminal?" Ryan asked.

"We've circumvented the Fourth Amendment enough for one day. If you need someone to vouch for you, give them my number."

"Thanks, Landis," Greg said. "We'll talk to you later."

"Be safe, fellas."

Greg ended the call. Ryan leaned back in his chair, put his hands on his head, and stared out the window.

A moment later, Don came in and set a cup of coffee on the nightstand. "I figured you wanted it."

"Thanks." Ryan picked up the cup.

"I wish we could get a look at those cameras," Greg said as they went back into the spacious living room and kitchen that stretched the length of the apartment, from the front door to the wall of glass separating the living area from the balcony.

"Ash, did you try tapping the network?" Don asked.

Her thick hair waved back and forth. "No way."

Ryan refreshed his coffee before walking to the window. What was Diego Hernández doing with the container? Had he looked inside to see it contained concrete blocks? Was he using the blocks to rebuild houses? Ryan could get behind that cause. He'd donate money to it. Two containers of block wouldn't even build a whole house.

Landis had failed to get them access to the cameras. The next step involved local law enforcement.

Ryan pulled Inspector Gabriella Martinez's card from his wallet and dialed her number.

When she answered, he said, "Inspector, this is Ryan Weller. We spoke in your office."

"I remember. What can I do for you?"

"I was wondering if you had access to the security cameras at the Colón shipping terminal in San Juan."

"Why should I do this for you?" the inspector asked.

"Because someone stole another of DWR's shipping containers. They knew it had a tracker on it and left it on a light pole in the terminal, so we'd think the container hadn't left. Meanwhile, they were putting it on a boat in Fajardo."

"How did you know the container was in Fajardo?"

Ryan detailed their trip to visit DWR's worksite and finding the repainted container. He finished by saying, "It was dumb luck."

"The security footage should give you a lead to who took the containers."

"Yes," Ryan replied.

On the other end, she sighed. "I have a murder to solve, if you haven't forgotten."

"Look, Inspector, I'm positive the guys who are stealing containers are the same guys who killed those two punks in Ponce. In fact, we think the ringleader of the whole operation is a guy named Diego Hernández."

Gabriella was silent for a moment. "I'll see what I can do about the footage."

"Awesome," Ryan said.

"Give me the dates you need."

He did so. "Can you bring the footage over to my office and we'll watch it together?"

"Oh, you have an office now?" she said.

"We rented space in San Juan."

The inspector snorted. "Your operation is expanding."

"I told you," Ryan said defensively, "we need to stop this theft ring. They're stealing containers from other shipping companies as well."

"Why are they so interested in yours?"

"I don't know," Ryan confessed. "Every container we have staged at Colón is a decoy. If they move, they're being stolen."

"I'll get the footage, but you're not to act on what you see. That's my job."

"Yes, boss," Ryan lied.

"I'll call you when I've got the tapes."

He thanked her and hung up, then picked up his coffee from the counter. It was lukewarm when he sipped it.

"Is she getting it?" Greg asked.

"She'll even let us watch it," Ryan said, not turning around.

In the plaza below, a group of sunburnt tourists walked along the waterfront. It was easy to forget he was on an island paradise when his mind was on work. The proximity of the carefree vacationers and the hard-working locals made for an interesting juxtaposition. It was like that anywhere water met land. There were those who vacationed and those who worked for the vacationers. Then there were those like the DWR team, who worked behind the scenes to make sure both groups could enjoy their lifestyles.

"What now?" Rick asked. He'd come in while Ryan and Greg were speaking to Homeland.

"We wait for Gabriella to get the footage," Ryan said. He stepped to the counter and splashed more coffee into his mug. "I'd like to have this job wrapped up by the time sea trials start."

"Ready to get back on the water?" Don asked.

"Yes," Ryan said, returning to his spot by the window. "There's work in the Lesser Antilles."

Don came to stand beside him. "With the new systems, you shouldn't need a full-time mechanic. Do you mind if I go back to Texas?"

Ryan motioned the younger man onto the balcony. They went to the railing overlooking the San Juan skyline beyond El Boquerón Bay. After a while, Ryan said, "Ready to get married?"

Don nodded, glancing through the glass at Ashlee, who was absorbed with the computer. "Yeah, and I'm ready to be home with her. I didn't sign on for long cruises."

Ryan sipped from his mug. "We can arrange that."

"Thanks."

The young man was not only an excellent mechanic, he was a fine electrician and computer jockey. Ryan would miss having him aboard *Peggy Lynn*. He sipped his coffee thoughtfully. He was ready to move again. There were more container locations to investigate. Greg had opted to go the electronic route rather than go on what he'd deemed as a wild goose chase, but Ryan wanted to chase the leads. Their first location had been a honey hole, and they'd stirred the bees. He was more than willing to keep poking the hive.

He let his gaze travel north to the open Atlantic. Big breakers rolled in to smash on the shore. It wouldn't be long before the winds shifted to the east, signaling the end of summer.

"Have you and Ashlee gone sightseeing?" Ryan inquired.

"In the evenings," Don said. "We've been busy getting the chips and trackers set up."

Ryan glanced through the window at Greg. Normally, after they'd checked in at the apartment, the boss returned to *Dark Water* and did paperwork.

"Wait until Greg leaves and take your girl out. You guys need a day off. There're some nice beaches near here."

"Thanks."

"Enjoy it. I'll hold down the fort."

"What about the container they took?"

Ryan shrugged. "We have a tracker on it."

They stepped inside, and Ryan refilled his mug.

"I'm out of here," Greg said. "I've got work to do. Are you coming, Ryan?"

"No, I'll stay here. Ashlee is going to show me how to run the tracking equipment."

"Suit yourself. Check in with Captain Dennis and make sure he doesn't need you."

"Will do, boss," Ryan said.

Greg left the apartment with Rick. When they were in the elevator, Ryan sat beside Ashlee.

"Teach me how this works."

She spent thirty minutes giving him a tutorial and would have continued if Don hadn't dragged her away from the computers and made her pack a beach bag. When they'd left, Ryan walked onto the balcony. It was nice to have peace and quiet. Living on the salvage vessel with other people left little time to be alone. Again, he wished he had a cigarette. He leaned both forearms on the stainless-steel railing and watched the waves roll through the bay.

After *Peggy Lynn* was back in the water and they'd moved on to the Lesser Antilles, he wondered how his relationship with Joulie would end. Their argument about James had been their first real tiff. Leaving had felt like taking the coward's way out, but he had a job to do and until he finished here, he wouldn't know how things would end with her.

Turning from the balcony, he went inside, refilled his coffee mug, and sat down at the computer. After six games of Spider Solitaire, he was bored.

Then his phone rang.

CHAPTER TWENTY-ONE

"I have the video," Gabriella announced. "Where do you want to meet?"

"Where are you now?" Ryan asked.

"At the Colón terminal."

"That was fast." Ryan glanced at his wristwatch. Three hours had elapsed since speaking with her. He gave her directions to the apartment building before giving the place a once-over to see if he needed to straighten up.

Fifteen minutes later, Gabriella arrived. Ryan met her in the lobby and escorted her up the elevator. She wore black slacks with a blue blouse, her black hair hanging long and loose. Ryan liked the way it looked.

When they stepped into the waterfront apartment, the inspector glanced around, taking in the opulence contrasted by the stacks of cardboard boxes shoved against one wall.

"Moving in or out?" she asked.

"Both."

She crossed to the computer setup and tapped her oversized sunglasses against her teeth while examining the screens. Pointing at a flashing dot, she inquired, "Why is that one moving?"

He bent to look over her shoulder. The tracking dot was heading out of San Juan on the toll road.

"What the hell?" Ryan whispered. He clicked on the alarm setting. It had gone off while he was in the lobby and shut off after two minutes of audible warning.

Gabriella straightened, catching his chin with her shoulder and smacking his jaws closed. Ryan grasped his chin and sank onto a bar stool. He moaned as he rubbed his jaw. None of the teeth seemed loose as he prodded each with his tongue, but the blow had rattled them.

"I'm so sorry," Gabriella apologized, putting her hand on his cheek.

"It's okay," he mumbled.

"Do you need ice or something?"

He shook his head.

"Let me see. Open up."

She pushed his hands away and put hers on each side of his lower jaw. He opened his mouth and let her peer inside, wishing he had a breath mint.

"Looks like everything is all right."

He nodded with his mouth still agape. Her fingertips caressed the line of his jaw.

Ryan pulled away. It wasn't just concern for his jaw, it was the look in her eyes and the tenderness of her touch that made him uncomfortable. He had to remind himself he was in a relationship of sorts.

He squeezed his teeth together and flexed his jaw muscles. Through gritted teeth, he inquired, "Where's the terminal footage?"

She smiled and pulled a thumb drive from her pocket and held it up. "But first ..." She plucked out her phone and dialed the port. She told them there was another DWR container on the move and requested they send the video footage to her via email.

Taking the USB from her, he slipped it into the port on the side of the computer. A minute later, they were watching the grainy footage of the front gate shot from a video camera mounted above the guard shack. A tiny window in that footage displayed the license plate of the vehicles as they approached the gate arm.

Thirty minutes in, they spotted a semi-tractor towing a DWR container through the gate.

Gabriella jotted down the tractor's license plate number while they watched the flashing dot of the moving container. She called the port again for an update on the video. They were sending her the footage but had viewed it themselves and gave her the license plate number.

"That's the same one," Ryan mouthed, pointing to the number she'd written just a minute ago.

"I'll put out a BOLO for the truck and driver." The Be On the Lookout notice would have every cop on the road searching for the rig, and they'd stop it if they spotted it.

"You can't put out a BOLO yet," Ryan said when Gabriella ended the call.

"Why not?"

"We need to know where they're taking the container. It could lead us right to Diego's hideout."

"I doubt it," she retorted. "They know we bugged the containers."

"We put multiple bugs on it. Look." He used the mouse to zoom the computer screen in on the seaport. "See that tracker number? That's the one we wanted them to find. They took it off and left it, just like last time."

Comprehension dawned on the inspector's face. "So, they don't know the container is still being tracked."

"Correct."

"Okay. I'll hold off on the BOLO for the moment."

"You could at least run the license through your data base and find out who owns the truck."

Gabriella reached for her phone. At the same time, it chimed. "I got the email." She used the computer's internet connection to download the surveillance video.

"We can get 1080p color video and high-resolution images beamed from halfway across the galaxy, but all the San Juan Port Authority can manage is black-and-white nineteen-eighties tech," Ryan lamented.

Gabriella chuckled. "At least they have footage."

"I guess that's the bright side."

In the video, a day cab semi-tractor stopped at the pole gate. The guard stepped out of the booth to examine the driver's paperwork. He scanned it with a hand-held device and handed it back. Then the guard stepped backward into the booth and the gate lifted. The license plate was clearly visible in the tiny window.

"Can we take a picture of the driver?" Ryan asked.

"Not with this program."

"I'll leave a note for my computer tech to crop stills of the driver and the license plate and try to figure out what rig he's driving."

"The tractor is easy. It's a Kenworth T800 day cab." Gabriella pointed at the truck's chrome badge, which looked washed-out white in the footage. In answer to the dumbfounded look on Ryan's face, she said, "What? My dad drove a truck for a while when I was little. I loved riding with him."

Ryan rose and walked into the kitchen. "Do you want some water, or coffee, or soda?"

"Water is fine."

He took a Mountain Dew and a water bottle from the fridge and set the water on the counter.

As he did, Gabriella looked up at him. "Did you know the

U.S. uses fifteen hundred plastic bottles every second? How many of them end up in the ocean?" She plunged on without waiting for an answer. "I'd think you, as a man who makes his living on the ocean, would be more eco-conscious."

The fierceness of her indictment stunned Ryan. After a moment, he said, "Uh ... would you like tap water instead?"

"Just make sure you recycle these." She opened her bottle and took a drink, then typed on the computer again. Ryan came around the counter and sat beside her. He watched as she accessed the police data base and ran the license plate.

"The driver is Phillipe Fernandez from San Juan. Want his address?"

"Sure." Ryan wrote it on a note pad lying beside the computer.

"When we put out the BOLO, we'll have someone watch his house."

"What now, Inspector?"

Gabriella checked her watch. "We should have a destination in the next two hours." She glanced out the tinted glass window. "Let's go for a walk. I didn't have lunch, and something tells me you don't have anything here the eat."

Ryan went to the fridge and held the door opened for her to see there were only condiments and a pack of hot dogs. "The kids mostly eat out."

"What kids?"

"Don and Ashlee are living here while we got the tracking system up and running."

"How old are they?" she asked, still puzzled.

"In their twenties."

"But you're only ten years older than they are."

Ryan shrugged. "They're kids."

She waved a hand, dismissing the conversation. "Let's go. I'm starving."

Ryan rubbed his face. Jokingly, he said, "I don't think I can eat. My mouth still hurts."

Gabriella stuck her lower lip out. "Poor baby." She moved around the counter and stood toe to toe with him, placing her fingertips on his jaw. She slipped them tenderly along the bone. After a moment, she declared, "Nothing's broken."

Ryan stared down into her dark brown eyes. She bit the corner of her lip as she stared back. He was aware of the seven inches of height difference, the softness of her fingers, the white of her teeth over the pink of her lip, and an aroma of vanilla and almonds.

"Think you can chew something now?" she asked, her eyes glowing with concern.

"Maybe a few more minutes of massage will help." He closed his eyes and tried to reason why he was allowing her to continue touching him. The old cheating joke that used to make the rounds in the military popped into his mind: *It ain't cheating if you're in a different zip code*. It had variations from *a different country* to *a different house*, but the joke was the same.

Her hand slid to the back of his neck and exerted pressure. Before he was conscious of it, he was bending down. His lips found hers, and his hands moved to her shoulders. He wanted to pull her in and push her away at the same time. When her arms snaked around his neck and pulled him closer, he lost the willpower to fight.

When the door handle clicked, and the front door swung open, they jumped back in surprise.

CHAPTER TWENTY-TWO

Rick Hayes stood in the open doorway, taking in the scene. He had a half-smile on his face. "Well, well, well ... while the cat's away, the mice will play."

A jolt of adrenaline surged through Ryan at being caught. He glanced at Gabriella and saw her face was flush. She ran her fingers through her hair then smoothed her blouse.

Ryan cleared his throat. "What's up, Rick?"

"You, apparently." He grinned and glanced at Gabriella. "Where's Don and Ashlee?"

"I gave them the day off."

Rick rolled his eyes. "Greg wants you to come to the marina."

"Why?"

"I don't know, bro. The boss says, 'Go find Ryan and drag his ass back here,' and I do it." Rick pulled a Mountain Dew from the fridge. "I'm sure he'll be thrilled to know you're stepping in for him and giving his people the day off."

"Don is *my* people. He works on *my* salvage boat."

"You can justify it anyway you want, but I'll go tell him." Rick took several long swallows of soda. "No." He rethought his original statement. "You go tell him you're screwing around when we have work to do."

"Actually, I'm doing my job," Ryan shot back. "I'm an independent contractor working on a case. And if you must know, we have a container moving right now. Plus, we reviewed the video footage and found our truck driver."

Rick held up his palms. "You don't need to justify it to me, dude."

Ryan pulled out his phone and dialed Greg.

By way of greeting, Greg answered, "What are you doing?"

"We had a container leave the port just over an hour ago, and Gabriella is here." He told Greg everything that had happened in the past hours.

"You left a few things out," Rick stated, loud enough for Greg to hear.

"Shut up, Kojak," Ryan snapped.

"What's he talking about?" Greg asked.

"Nothing," Ryan replied. "I gave Don and Ashlee the day off because they've been busting their butts for a week."

"Next time, talk to me beforehand, yeah?"

"What did you need?" Ryan asked.

"Never mind," Greg replied. "Send Rick back here and let me know what happens with the container."

"Will do." Ryan ended the call and looked at Rick. "You heard the man—get your ass back to the boat and let me do my job."

"There's a lady present, or I'd tell you where to stick it."

"Don't let the door hit you in the ass on the way out." Ryan grinned at Rick until Rick turned and strode to the door. As the door closed, Rick stuck his hand in the gap, middle finger extended, then jerked his hand back.

"What's with you two?" Gabriella asked.

"He doesn't like me because I'm tall and I give him shit because he's short."

Not comprehending the feud, she shook her head. "Let's go eat."

"My jaw still hurts."

"Don't be a baby."

"Go to the restaurant in the courtyard. We have a tab there, so get whatever you want. Bring me back a hamburger with everything."

Gabriella left, and Ryan was grateful she hadn't argued with him. Going to eat would have felt like a date now, and they'd inevitably talk about their pasts, the case, and the kiss. Well, he didn't need to talk about any of it. He wanted to forget about it. He wondered if Joulie's vodou spirits were whispering in her ears. They weren't married, and he hadn't talked to her since he'd left Haiti. She wasn't leaving her fiefdom, and when *Peggy Lynn* was back in the water, well ... they'd cross that bridge when they came to it. But until then, he felt obliged to stay faithful to his Haitian vodou priestess. *Yeah, be faithful or she'll put a hex on you.*

The refresh button kept telling him the container had stopped at the Rafael Cordero Santiago Port of the Americas in Ponce. He zoomed in on the wharf and saw the container sitting near the water's edge. When he checked the tracker deviation, it read plus or minus fifteen feet. If the container were fifteen feet to the right, it would be in the bay or on a ship.

Just then, the alert sounded on the computer, and he zoomed out to watch another container exiting the Colón terminal.

"Is that another container moving?" Gabriella asked as she entered the apartment again. She held a white paper bag in one hand and used the other to close the door.

"Yes, and the other one has stopped at the port in Ponce."

She set the bag beside the computer monitor. "Interesting. He's using multiple ports. First Fajardo and now Ponce."

"Can you call Colón and ask them for a copy of the driver's manifest?"

The port agreed to send over copies of the bills of laden used to remove the DWR containers. While they waited, Ryan called Greg and gave him an update.

"I hear containers aren't the only thing you're bird-dogging," Greg teased.

Ryan ignored him.

Greg continued, "At this point, I'm inclined to think they're toying with us. They either knew there were trackers, or they don't care."

"You think someone leaked?" Ryan asked.

"We can narrow it down a little," Greg said. "On this island, there were five DWR employees involved with tagging those containers, and I told Shawn Lindowel at L&F."

"How many port workers saw us tagging gear?"

"Maybe Diego has people watching the ports," Greg agreed.

"Or us," Ryan suggested.

Gabriella laid her phone on the counter. "They claim their internet is down right now, so they can't email them."

Ryan nodded, then said to Greg, "Hey, Gabriella and I are going to Colón to check out the manifests."

"Who's watching the trackers?"

Ryan said, "We have an app for that."

CHAPTER TWENTY-THREE

The Luis A. Ayala Colón San Juan Terminal was massive. Cargo containers, oil and natural gas storage tanks, docks, cranes, and roads covered acres of blacktop. Gabriella parked her silver Honda Accord in front of a two-story building covered in blue metal siding with large picture windows in the front. Off to the left side was a giant portico extended almost fifty feet, and to the right was the large shell of a building Ryan assumed they used for vehicle inspections. A chain-link fence ran around the perimeter of the structure's parking lot and on the other side it looked like a giant had used the colorful cargo containers as building blocks to erect the walls of a fort.

Ryan stepped out of the car and glanced over at the steam plant, an enormous jumble of pipes beside red-and-white cooling towers. Clouds of steam leaked from pipes lower to the ground. A large sign read *Puerto Rican Power Authority Authorized Personnel Only*.

Gabriella led the way into the office. Chipped linoleum tiles supported government surplus metal desks weighted down with computers and papers. A long row of filing cabinets stood against the far wall. At least the air conditioning worked.

A man stood and walked to the counter. "Can I help you?" he asked in Spanish.

Gabriella flashed her badge and replied, also in Spanish, "Inspector Gabriella Martinez. I'm here for the shipping manifests."

He smiled. "Yes, we spoke on the phone." With a glance at Ryan, he lowered his voice. "Is he a cop, too?"

Before Ryan could answer, she said, "He's a representative of Dark Water Research."

"Wait here, please." The man pointed at two plastic and steel chairs that reminded Ryan of a high school cafeteria.

When the clerk pushed open a heavy steel door, Ryan glimpsed a room full of computers and electronic boards showing which ships were coming and going, cargo to be unloaded, and available dock space and cranes. The San Juan Port Authority was one of the busiest in the Caribbean, so the modern electronics didn't surprise him.

The two investigators waited half an hour for the clerk to return. When he did, he was bearing two sheets of paper. He set them side by side on the faded linoleum countertop. Ryan and Gabriella stepped to the wood-paneled counter and studied the paper.

In the boxes labeled *Shipping Company* was the printed name *Caribbean Maritime Delivery*. Under the name was a company address, and below it, a delivery address. Ryan used his phone's map application to find the company's Puerto Rican headquarters, zooming in on an office building. Then he looked at the delivery address in Miami.

Gabriella thanked the clerk for his time, and they left the office. She waited until they were in her car before asking, "Do you recognize the address?"

"It's L&F Logistics. Now I know they're screwing with us."

She pulled up the Secretary of State's website on her phone and searched for Caribbean Maritime Delivery. "It says the sole member and manager is Shawn Lindowel."

CHAPTER TWENTY-FOUR

As Gabriella and Ryan climbed from the car at the apartment, Ryan peered at his watch. The sun had arched through its zenith and fallen halfway to the western horizon.

"It's time for margaritas," he said, looking at Gabriella.

"No, here we drink piña coladas," she corrected as she slammed the car door. "We did invent the drink, you know."

Ryan smiled as the lyrics to Garth Brooks's "Two Piña Coladas" played in his head. He remembered a version of the song where, instead of burying problems in the sand, Brooks had buried the woman in the sand. They strolled past the shops in the courtyard and stood by the water that glistened in the low-hanging sun.

They stopped and stared at the water. Gabriella pulled her hair into a ponytail and tied it back with a rubber band to keep the wind from blowing it into her face. She looked up at him expectantly. "Are we going to get those drinks?"

The big American shrugged, missing her cues and instead focusing on the case. He had several ideas of how to approach things, the first being to pick up the truck driver and interrogate him into revealing the location of Diego's hideout. The other option was to wait until they stole a third container and follow it. Ryan stared at the buildings on the far shore. He was ready to put an end to this theft ring and return to working underwater. Everything was less complicated there. It was man against the elements. Screw up and you died. On land, the elements felt muted.

Gabriella sighed, her eyes searching his face before turning away. "I'm going to my office."

"You're driving to Utuado?"

She nodded.

They both leaned on the rail, not looking at each other. Neither wanted to discuss the kiss, but it was foremost in their minds. Ryan glanced at the woman out of the corner of his eye, appraising the police officer. She was pretty, and he felt an attraction to her or rather the softness of her lips. Maybe it was the fact she carried a gun and knew how to use it?

She straightened. He turned to face her, still leaning on the railing. Gabriella put a hand on his, her brown eyes searching his. She gave off an expectant vibe, and he knew what she wanted. Instead, he bussed her cheek.

Her eyes narrowed ever so slightly, and her smile was plastic. "Call me."

Standing by the rail, he stared after her. He should have explained his reservations and the relationship he was in. She might have understood his reluctance. He remained rooted to the spot by the rail, unable to make himself go after her. When she turned the corner, he took the elevator upstairs.

His mechanical engineer and computer geek had returned. Ashlee sat in front of the computer, wearing shorts and a yellow bikini top. Her skin had the reddish glow of sunburn that would hurt in the morning.

She turned and gave Ryan a smile. "Thanks for the time off."

"No worries," he declared. "But you missed the excitement. Our thieves stole a container and drove it to Ponce, and we got the security video from Colón, which I need you to freeze and take a picture of the driver."

She began working on it at once. Ryan fetched a Mountain Dew and sat down beside her. Don came out of the bedroom dressed in lounge pants and a T-shirt. He, too, had burnt red skin. They ordered food from the downstairs restaurant and had it delivered to the apartment.

Once they were done with dinner, Ryan called it a day and headed for *Dark Water*, but his night was far from over.

CHAPTER TWENTY-FIVE

An alarm screamed. Ryan ran toward a door and banged into it with his shoulder. The push bar slammed open, but the door didn't move. He hit it again and again.

Behind him, a sheet of flame burned, racing toward him along the walls, floor, and ceiling. Beyond the walls, he could hear the whistle of incoming mortars and rockets. Shrieks of scared and dying men blended with the return gunfire and the sounds of tanks flinging their heavy projectiles across the sky. The warning siren continued to blare, signaling for the EOD team to rally for bomb disposal. Somewhere out there, a team needed him, but the damned door wouldn't open.

He cried out in frustration. His body shook and when he glanced at his hands. They were red with blood.

Ryan screamed. He trembled as he fell to his knees, the fire rushing over his body, eating his flesh and his clothes. Still, his skeletal hands remained stained blood red.

A vise-like grip on Ryan's arm shook him. His eyes snapped open and his back arched, lungs drawing a giant breath, fists swinging. Rick jumped back, barely avoiding Ryan's thrashing arms.

When Ryan finally came to his senses, Rick said, "That must have been some nightmare."

Holding his hands up, Ryan stared at them. Satisfied they were no longer covered in blood, he rolled his legs off the bed and sat up. He put his head in his palms, breathing in through his nose and out through his mouth. He could still feel the heat, the rage, the solidness of the locked door, and the screams of dying men. The dream had been so real and in vivid colors.

"Your phone alarm was going off," Rick informed him.

Ryan reached for the device. He opened it to the home screen. A warning flashed for the tracker app. The thieves had taken a third container from Colón.

He rubbed his face again. It was eleven p.m. He'd only been asleep for an hour.

"You going to be okay?"

"Yeah," Ryan answered. "Just a bad dream. You know, the one where you're in Afghan."

Rick nodded. Whether he understood or he had similar dreams, Ryan didn't know. Rick had been an Army officer stationed at Kandahar Air Base. His primary job was analysis, not bomb disposal on the front lines.

Ryan stood and found his sea legs wobblier than normal. Steadying himself with a hand on the wall, he left the bunk room and went forward to the V-berth to find Greg.

"What do you need?" Greg called from the salon.

Ryan climbed the stairs and found Greg with a drink in his hand and a half-empty rum bottle on the island. Ryan found a glass and splashed a finger of rum into it before slamming it back. The alcohol did nothing to calm his post-dream jitters. He rolled his tongue around in his mouth to rid himself of the burn. "Another container just left Colón."

"Dammit," Greg said, smacking his glass onto the granite. "Three in one day. I smell a rat."

"What do you want to do?" Ryan asked, bending to rest his forearms on the island, still feeling dazed by his dream.

"Where's it at?"

Ryan consulted the map. "Southbound on the toll road."

"How far out?"

"Couple of miles."

"Get your gear and let's follow that bastard."

Ryan staggered to his bunk room and removed his KRISS Vector Gen II submachine gun from under the bunk. The gun's five-and-a-half-inch barrel had a six-inch silencer threaded to it. He folded the stock and slipped the rifle into a soft case attached to a backpack. Then he filled a pack with extra magazines and a medical kit. He dressed in cargo pants, a dark shirt, and boots, then accessorized with a folding tactical knife and a Glock handgun.

Back in the salon, Greg and Rick were checking their own pistols.

Rick beamed at Ryan. "Can't let you independent contractors go stomping around in the night all alone. You might get lost."

Ryan ignored the dig and carried his gear to the Jeep, including a set of dive gear and a tank from the cockpit locker on *Dark Water*. Once he'd dumped the gear in the rear of the Jeep, the three men climbed in, and Ryan gunned the Wrangler out of the parking lot, heading for Luis A. Ferré Expressway to follow the truck.

"Open the tablet and find out where they're going," he instructed.

Rick handed the tablet to Greg, open to the tracking screen.

Greg checked the locator then scanned the road ahead. "Looks like we're going to Ponce."

CHAPTER TWENTY-SIX

Rick Hayes reached back and touched Ryan's leg. Ryan came awake instantly and sat up. He'd gotten his back flat on the lumpy seat, then twisted the rest of his six-foot-frame to fit the tight confines of the Jeep's back seat. He'd gone to sleep with his arms crossed and intertwined in the seatbelt. Falling asleep anywhere was a skill he'd mastered in boot camp and had carried with him after his time in service: Grab shuteye whenever you can.

His back ached, his bent legs were stiff, and his head felt groggy, but two hours of sleep was better than none. Even though a surge of adrenaline had blasted through his veins at Rick's touch, all he wanted to do was lie back down. Ryan forced himself to stay upright and rubbed his eyes. They were parked in front of a side gate to the Rafael Cordero Santiago Port of the Americas.

"Looks like standard chain-link and razor wire here," Rick said.

Ryan had believed a modern port facility such as this would have roving security guards and cameras. He couldn't see any, but that didn't mean they weren't there.

A closed guard shack stood in a pool of light, and two heavy-duty steel swing gates blocked access to the container yard. On the left were three large warehouses, and behind a six-foot-high mound of dirt were multiple oil storage tanks. To their right at the far end of several acres of vacant paved lot, two massive gantry cranes moved over a container ship. Another ship lurked against the berthing. Sparse sodium vapor lights on high poles cast everything into shadow.

"Which one of those is ours?" Ryan asked.

"The one being unloaded," Greg said. "More good news. The other container is sitting on a semi right over there." He pointed toward the stern of the closest ship.

Ryan leaned down between the two front seats to see out the windshield. "How did they get in?"

"Must be another way," Rick said, sliding the Jeep's transmission into reverse. He backed out of their parking spot, pushed the shifter into drive, and swung around to follow the fence line away from the main gate.

Greg guided them through the tangle of streets with help from the tablet's map. They found an open gate off Highway 123, just after a bend in the road and before a clump of trees surrounding a drainage ditch. Chain-link fencing lined both sides of the road. Ryan wished he had brought a set of night vision goggles.

Greg craned his neck around to look at Ryan. "What's the plan?"

"Find the containers and kick some ass."

"Stick to the drills," Rick said, referring to the standard checklists for bomb disposal.

Ryan pulled on his backpack. "I don't remember any drills about stolen cargo containers."

"Recognize, disarm, neutralize," Rick said. He shut off the Jeep's lights as he coasted to a stop near the gate.

"Got it."

Ryan slipped from the Jeep and crouched by the fence as Rick sped away.

He watched the Jeep fade into the darkness, then turned his attention to the cargo facility. If they were dealing with Diego Hernández's group, he knew they would be armed and ready for his assault. Three containers appearing at the same place felt like a trap.

Ryan rubbed his sweaty palms on his cargo pants and tugged the backpack's straps tighter on his shoulders. He'd forgone the chest rig, feeling it would make him stand out too much. The KRISS Vector was in a pouch on the exterior of the backpack, and he carried a Glock on his right hip. The Glock's magazines were compatible with the KRISS—both took nine-millimeter hollow points.

Weeds and saplings grew up through the cracked pavement and gravel. Weather-stained concrete barricades directed traffic to the left, away from the rusted and padlocked entrance gates toward a mobile trailer set on concrete blocks. Light spilled from three windows, illuminating two cars parked in front. More eight-foot-high chain-link fence topped with barbed wire ringed the trailer and parking lot. Someone had run into the fence and buckled three of the posts.

Ahead, the white seven-story superstructure of the freighter gleamed in the lights of the crane. Highlighted in white on the blue hull was the name *Southern Star*. Based on the size of the ship, Ryan knew it was a feeder. The feeders were used to collect cargo from smaller ports and move them to a consolidation point, or to transport cargo between smaller ports the super max carriers couldn't access. Still, it was a massive vessel.

At the base of the ship's stern, men were transferring the contents of the DWR decoy container into a van body semi-trailer. Based on the cargo previously stolen, Greg had loaded the decoys with items he knew would be attractive to the thieves: concrete block, large blue tarps, two-by-fours, and plywood. If they lost the cargo, it was Greg's way of donating to the cause. The robber's track record indicated they would put the supplies to use in their continuing project to rebuild the storm-ravaged island.

Ryan stopped running after he passed the office trailer. He had assumed the semi had come through the gate and driven to the ship. He'd been wrong. The fence he was following did not have a serviceable gate in it. It merely separated the trailer office from the main port. Fortunately, no razor wire topped the chain-link.

A bushy tree had grown almost dead center between two light poles and the branches had intertwined with the chain-link, embedding the metal in its thick trunk. Ryan used the darkness of the tree's shadows to conceal his scaling of the fence.

Landing on the ground, he froze in a crouch. His eyes were the only thing that moved as his gaze roved from right to left, taking in everything to ensure he hadn't been seen. The men continued to unload the cargo container using a yellow forklift.

His gaze shifted to the ship and for a few moments, the synchronized ballet of cargo unloading mesmerized him. The crane cab, mounted on a trolley under the jib, ran out over the *Southern Star* and let the cargo spreader down into the ship's hold. It withdrew a container, slid it backward along the jib between the tower legs, and lowered it onto a trailer chassis. The truck driver ensured the container had locked onto the chassis, and he drove away to be replaced by another in a seemingly endless parade of trucks.

Between the crane's lights and the halogen lamps on the back of the freighter, illuminating her name, there were fewer shadows near the ship. Ryan moved closer, pulling a tracker free from his backpack. When the men were all facing the DWR container, he sprinted to the van trailer and slid beneath it. He activated the tracker and used the device's powerful magnet to hold it in place.

Ryan rolled out from under the trailer and sprinted toward two lone cargo containers on the ground by the crane closest to him. He needed to gain a better vantage point to survey the ship and its security. He stumbled over the railroad track embedded in the pavement.

As he approached two containers sitting on the tarmac by the crane, movement in his peripheral caught his attention. Ryan turned his head to see a roving guard with an M16 rifle walking between the stern of the ship and the amidships gangplank. Ryan paused at the container and peered around it. Another guard stood watch at the gangplank, and a third stalked between the gangplank and the bow. All three men kept their heads swiveling around, their hands locked on their weapons.

He'd been right. Diego had laid a trap.

Behind him, the semi-trucks idled in a long line, waiting for a container. The humid air was thick with carbon monoxide. He glanced around to see if he'd attracted any attention.

Ryan let his gaze rove over the ship, searching for a way around the guards. He considered approaching the ship from the starboard side but was uncertain if guards patrolled the water. He had also left his scuba gear in the Jeep, which meant he would need to retrograde out of the port, meet with Greg and Rick, then make a long swim up the channel in the dark. There wasn't time for any of that.

Ryan watched the cranes work and considered climbing on a spreader and riding it to the ship. He discarded that idea as well. Too many people would see him and raise an alarm. The most logical way was up the rear stern line. He was about to make his move when he heard a woman whisper his name.

CHAPTER TWENTY-SEVEN

Ryan cranked his head around, reaching for the Glock at the same time. The gun came out of its holster, hand swiveling a fraction behind his head. When his hand stopped moving, he was staring down the sights at Inspector Gabriella Martinez.

Gabriella held her hands up in surrender and whispered, "What are you doing here?"

"What the hell do you think I'm doing here? I'm tracking DWR's containers. There's two on the ship and they just unloaded the third into another truck." He jerked his head in the direction of the container.

"I followed that one here," Gabriella said.

Ryan considered this for a moment.

"Can you put the gun down?"

Without taking his eyes off the inspector, Ryan holstered the Glock. "I need to get on the ship."

Gabriella shook her head, the light shining off her black hair. She wore dark blue cargo pants, a similarly colored long sleeve T-shirt, and black boots. She had a gun on her hip and a badge beside it. "Come on."

Ryan followed her back toward the empty DWR container. The tractor that had brought it had hooked to the van body and left.

"When you called about the video footage, I had them watch for DWR's containers. This one left shortly after we tapped into the feeds. I decided to follow it."

"I planted a tracker on the van body," Ryan said.

Gabriella nodded. "I watched you. Who do you have following it?"

"Greg and Rick."

They stopped by the empty container, and Gabriella crossed her arms. "I did some digging after I talked to you at my office."

"Should we be discussing this right now? There's armed guards protecting a ship with at least two stolen containers on it."

"Yes." Gabriella nodded. "I put your name into the system, and I got a phone call from Homeland Security asking me what I was doing."

Ryan snorted. "I need to get on the ship, not discuss my past with you."

"Well, for your information, *bichote*, I agreed to help you." When Ryan looked puzzled, Gabriella translated, "*Big shot*. It's *Boricua* slang."

"I'm just a guy trying to make a living."

"But you work for the U.S. government."

"Not anymore. I'm a salvage consultant. I get paid based on what I recover, and I need a payday, so let me get on that ship and retrieve my cargo containers."

Gabriella crossed her arms. "What's your plan?"

"We use your badge to walk past the guards."

"Those guards are private security. They won't let me on without a warrant."

"Tell them we're investigating the theft of a container,"

Ryan said. "They have to let you on."

"I'm not authorized to do that."

"You're not authorized? You're a law enforcement officer."

"I can't." She turned away.

"Then why did you come here?"

She snapped her head back to glare at him. "I need to know who's behind the thefts. If I gather enough evidence, I can make a case to my superiors."

Ryan shook his head. "I can't wait that long."

"You're still wanted on suspicion of murder. I can arrest you."

"No," Ryan said, shaking his head. "I'm going on the ship."

He turned and darted away, leaving Gabriella behind the trailer.

Southern Star's mooring ropes stretched like a spider's web from her bow and stern to massive bollards set along the waterfront. Ryan crouched behind the aft bollard, waited for the guard to turn and begin his patrol back to the center of the ship. With the guard out of sight, Ryan sat down on the pier, slung his legs over the edge, and grasped the stern rope. He slid off the pier, wrapped his feet around the rope, and shinned his way up to the opening just above the ship's name.

Once he climbed aboard, Ryan knelt in the darkness. His hands hurt from gripping the thick rope, and his chest and arm muscles burned from the exercise. He pulled his cell phone from his pocket and turned on the tracker app Ashlee had installed earlier. The app was syncing with the satellites when Ryan heard a noise behind him.

He spun and saw Gabriella's head poking through the hole in the hull.

"Help me," she hissed. "I'm going to fall."

Ryan dropped the phone onto a coil of rope and grabbed Gabriella's wrists. He hauled her partway in and grabbed her belt to finish hoisting her aboard. She landed in a heap at his feet. Slowly, she sat up and rubbed her shoulders and wrists. Ryan picked up his phone. The satellites had locked onto the containers' tracking signals. They were close to amidships, either side by side or on top of one another.

He lowered his phone and looked at Gabriella. "You okay?"

"Fine," she said. She got to her feet, tugged down on her pants, and wiggled, trying to relieve the wedgie Ryan had given her by grabbing her belt. She glanced at his phone. "There's no way to get close to them."

Ryan ignored her and moved forward under the covered walkway along the starboard side. The tracking indicator flashed to tell him he was near the container. He slowed and peered into the cargo hold. Tracks on both sides of the hold allowed the crane spreader to precisely stack the containers, so all he could see were the tops. He sent a text message to Ashlee informing her of the need to have the containers picked up at their destination.

"All that just to verify they are on this ship?" Gabriella asked. "You could have done that from the luxury of your apartment when the ship left port."

"We wouldn't get a chance to tangle with the infamous Diego Hernández while sitting in the apartment," Ryan said. He brushed past her, heading toward the stern. "Let's get a beer. I saw a bar by the port's main entrance."

"Are you asking me out?"

"No, I'm getting a beer. You can do what you want." Ryan continued walking toward the stern. Halfway back to the superstructure, he paused so abruptly that Gabriella ran into him.

She whispered, "Why did you stop?"

Ryan held a handout to silence her and brought a finger to his lips to reinforce the gesture. They pressed their backs to the cargo containers and stood stock still, listening to the faint sounds of water gushing out of the bilge, the hum of diesel engines, and the clatter of steel on steel as the spreaders moved cargo boxes.

Gabriella whispered, "What is it?"

Ryan drew his handgun, wishing he had taken the time to pull the KRISS Vector from his backpack. He swiveled his head back and forth to view the length of the passageway. What light that did filter through the passageway's covering did little to push back the dark shadows that Ryan and Gabriella had used to infiltrate the ship. Those same shadows hid the men Ryan suspected were now stalking them. He had seen fleeting movements in the darkness, the crafty positioning of men about to spring an ambush. The companionway was a shooting gallery and its unyielding steel would ricochet any bullets. No hiding place would be safe.

Instinct ingrained from his years of service said to flee to the water, but Gabriella had barely made the climb up the mooring line. She would certainly tire during a long swim. Even if they took to the water, they were in a C-shaped harbor and their adversaries could easily follow them to their egress point. They had one way off the ship: the amidships gangway. To reach it, they would have to run toward the ambush.

He wanted to delay the gunfight if possible.

Every hundred feet along the companionway were ladders leading up to the lashing bridges that crossed the ship, allowing crewmen to apply the lashing gear to the cargo containers to prevent their lateral movement while at sea.

Ryan pointed to the one closest to them. "Go, up the ladder."

He followed right behind her, his hands on the same rung as her feet. Her small frame forced her to stretch her legs for each rung. He willed her to move faster. They climbed through an opening onto the lower deck of a two-tier lashing bridge. Once on the catwalk, Ryan knelt on the metal grating and unslung his pack. He plucked the KRISS Vector from the side pouch, extended the stock, and slapped a thirty-round magazine into the mag well. He handed the gun to the wide-eyed inspector.

"Do you know how many laws you've broken by having this gun?" she asked.

He shouldered the pack. While stuffing a handful of magazines into his cargo pockets, he said, "Arrest me after it saves your life."

Taking the gun back from Gabriella, he glanced toward the ladder. They were still fish in a barrel, caught on the narrow steel walkway. He ran along the bridge toward the dock, dodging the thick, threaded metal rods and turnbuckles comprising the lashing gear. The containers rose three tiers above them.

Halfway across, Ryan realized the crane was unloading the bay to their right. The spreader dropped into the bay, sliding along the tracks. He slowed, unsure what to do next. They were losing their cover. Once past the open bay, they would be exposed. But would the gunmen shoot during the middle of the unloading process?

A loud burst of automatic fire answered his question. Bullets sparked off the steel. Amid the distinctive sounds of ricochets, Ryan spun and pushed Gabriella behind the edge of the cargo containers.

As Ryan pushed her backward, he saw a man ascending the ladder they had used to gain the lashing deck. He brought the KRISS to his shoulder and fired a two-shot burst, striking the man in the shoulders and head and he fell back through the opening.

Ryan sprinted toward the ladder. A second man appeared from below. Ryan fired from the hip, and the man ducked below the deck. Before he could show his head again, Ryan stepped over the opening and fired through it. Both men lay dead in a heap on the deck below.

He turned and climbed the ladder to the upper level of the bridge, Gabriella following in his footsteps.

Part way across the bridge, he stopped and climbed the cable railing. He leaned his back against a container and braced his feet on the cable. Interlacing his fingers to form a cup, he said, "We're going up."

She looked at him incredulously. Bullets chirped off steel near her feet. She scrambled up the railing and used Ryan's hands and shoulders to boost herself halfway up the container. He turned and pulled himself up, using the long rods of the locking bars and the curves in the metal. He rolled onto the top of the container just after Gabriella. A storm of bullets buzzed their heads from gunmen who were converging on their former position.

"Let's go," Ryan said, rolling onto his belly and levering himself to his feet. He fired the KRISS over the edge of the containers into the men on the lashing bridge below, sweeping back and forth as he emptied the magazine. Grunts and cries of wounded men filled the air.

Ryan and Gabriella ran on top of the containers, angling toward the stern. Two rows of containers butted against each other between each lashing bridge. They leaped over the bridges as they came to each. Ryan changed magazines, leaving the empty where it landed.

Bullets sparked off steel near their heels as they approached the bridge. Based on the angle of the shots, Ryan guessed a gunman had climbed into a crane cab. The man was walking his shots up, letting the gun muzzle rise as the magazine emptied.

Ryan pushed Gabriella sideways, causing her to stumble

and fall. He saw her rolling toward the edge of the containers, out of the line of gunfire.

He jumped the gap between the container tier and the superstructure catwalk. He landed feet-first and rolled to lessen the impact to his body, but he still slammed into the unyielding bulkhead. Fire spread through his feet and legs from the impact. His lower back spasmed.

Bullets pinged off the wall above him as he rolled toward the railing, preventing him from being seen from the crane cab, but the shooter still tried to pin him down, a reconnaissance by fire. Ryan looked around for the KRISS. It was lying on the catwalk a few feet in front of him. He scrambled forward on hands and knees and scooped it up, then rolled under the railing and dropped to the next deck.

Pain flared up through his feet and legs from the impact, and he almost dropped his gun again. He staggered backward, colliding with the bulkhead. While taking in several deep breaths, he glanced around for Gabriella and spotted her climbing down the containers. She jumped backward, spun in midair, and grabbed the lip of the catwalk above them. With the ease of a gymnast, she allowed her body to swing forward, and she dropped lightly beside Ryan.

Gabriella's eyes were wide, her face flush. Her chest heaved from exertion. She drew her Smith and Wesson M&P pistol.

"Are you okay?" Ryan asked.

She swore in Spanish. Her hands shook, probably from fright and adrenaline. "How do we get off this ship?"

Ryan wanted to reassure her everything would be fine, but with three gunmen on the dock and one in the crane cab, their chances of escape were slim. Checking the KRISS, he said, "The gangplank."

"Let's go."

"Watch where you point that thing," Ryan said. Her gun

muzzle aimed at his legs, reminding him of how untested she was. Cops carried guns, but that didn't mean they knew how to use them or had spent hours on the range like professional soldiers. Gabriella turned away.

Ryan brushed past her, then ran to the port side catwalk on the edge of the freighter and stopped in the shadows. He lined the sights of the KRISS on the amidships to stern guard. The guard drew abreast of Ryan. He let the sight drift forward just a hair, leading the guard's movement then he stroked the trigger. Two hollow points streaked out the barrel. The first missed the man's nose by a fraction of an inch. The second slammed into his temple a second later.

Ryan sprinted toward the gangway. The guard there turned toward his mate, who had crumpled to the ground. Ryan slowed and brought the KRISS back to his shoulder, pulling the trigger again. Two-shot bursts stuttered out of the gun. The first set went wide, and the guard brought his own gun to bear.

Ryan came to a stop before emptying the rest of his magazine. Bullets riddled the man's chest. He staggered backward with the punch of each hollow point until he fell over.

Gabriella fired her pistol. Ryan glanced over her shoulder. An armed man was running toward them, up the catwalk. The guard ducked behind a pillar in the companionway, pinned by Gabriella's shots.

Ryan reached into his thigh pocket and grabbed a magazine. It jammed in the fabric as he tried to pull it free. As he used two hands to extract the magazine, he regretted not bringing the load bearing vest. He slammed the mag home and charged the gun with a fresh round.

Gabriella was out. She dropped the magazine and reached for another on her belt. Ryan saw her execute the maneuver with perfection as he brought the KRISS up and pumped several rounds at their assailant to keep him behind cover.

He turned to the narrow gangway when she was back in firing position. The gangway extended out fifty feet from the ship. Small wheels on the land side of the plank allowed it to move as the ship rose and sank in the water according to her cargo weight and the tides.

The bow security guard fired wildly as he ran toward them.

Gabriella's gun spat again. Their assaulter screamed in pain.

Ryan squatted down and aimed his KRISS at the running guard, centering the holographic site on the man's torso. His bullets tore through the guard's chest and ripped apart his neck. The man stumbled forward and toppled over, his gun skidding away.

Behind him, Gabriella was shooting again. He heard her gun lock open. She dropped the magazine, and it hit the deck at her feet. Still in a crouch, he spun and put two bullets into the wounded man when he stepped out from behind the pillar to take advantage of Gabriella's reload.

"Let's go," Ryan yelled. His ears ran from the bark of her pistol.

They charged down the ramp toward a semi pulling under the massive gantry crane. The truck looked like a toy model in comparison to the crane.

Suddenly, something blocked the overhead lights. Ryan glanced up to see a falling container, its shadow centered on the gangway.

"*Correr, correr,*" Gabriella shouted. *Run, run.*

Ryan didn't need the encouragement. He lifted his knees and sprinted harder. He felt her shoving him in the back. Their legs tangled and they fell, rolling forward and down the gangway, trapped by the handrails. The skin on the back of Ryan's left hand peeled away.

The container slammed into the gangway, ripping it away

from the ship. Then, like a giant seesaw, the gangway heaved violently upward. It threw Ryan and Gabriella into the air.

Ryan flew over the railing and slammed onto the asphalt. Gabriella landed on his back, causing him to grunt in pain.

Both lay stunned on the pavement, the wind knocked from their lungs. He made wheezing sounds while his lungs struggled to inflate. They needed to move. Ryan's hand clutched in vain for the pistol grip of the KRISS Vector.

Gabriella rolled off him and flopped to the ground, clutching her chest as she struggled to breathe. Ryan glanced around, spotting the sub gun under the gangplank. Then he looked up.

The container was rising into air and moving toward them again.

CHAPTER TWENTY-EIGHT

Diego Hernández peered through the metal mesh of the maintenance walkway on the crane jib. From the height and the lack of light, he had a hard time determining whether the cargo container had taken out the two people who had snuck onto the *Southern Star*. Once again, Ryan Weller had escaped his well-laid trap. His men were to converge on the DWR container and cut Ryan down in a withering crossfire. From the gantry crane, Diego had a bird's-eye view of the action and a perfect sniper's nest.

He'd expected the ex-Navy man to approach from the water using either a small Zodiac boat or diving gear and ascend the rope dangling in the water off the freighter's bow. But, no, *el canto de cabrón*—the piece of shit—had come up the stern ropes and snuck through the superstructure. It hadn't been until Ryan was exfiltrating the ship that Diego's men had discovered the intruder.

As the container rose into the air and the crane cab glided silently beneath him, Diego thought he might have one last chance at stopping Ryan. The salvage consultant and the woman lay tangled on the ground beside the wrecked gangway.

This was the moment Diego eliminated the man interrupting his business model. This was his island, and the people needed the supplies he delivered to rebuild their shattered homes and lives. The U.S. government and the military didn't care about helping anymore. They were off to the next natural disaster, skirmish, or political hot potato, leaving the fate of its citizens in Puerto Rico to fade into the background. That was the way it always was. Puerto Ricans were U.S. citizens, but they didn't get the benefits of being a state.

Diego didn't care if Puerto Rico became a state. He was tired of his island being treated like a bastard child.

The big corporations cared about the money they could make from government contracts, not for the island or its people. Contractors such as Dark Water Research had plenty of cash to spare.

Diego's police contacts in La Uniformada had diverted attention away from his activities, but he'd known someone would investigate the theft of their cargo. He had not expected it to be DWR and it pissed him off. When they sent professionals after him, it was time to strike back.

"Drop it now," Diego shouted in Spanish.

The operator threw the lever forward. They could hear the shrieking of the crane's running gear as the cable drum freewheeled. The container plummeted toward earth at a rate it was not meant to travel.

When the container landed, one edge smacked the gangway again. The flimsy metal container buckled, and the door lock rods snapped. One door burst open and cardboard boxes spilled onto the dock. The crane cables continued to drape over the container in big coils before the operator could apply the drum brake. When he tried to pick up the container again, Diego saw the spreader had popped loose.

He shouldered his gun and stared through the sight, ready to execute any survivors.

CHAPTER TWENTY-NINE

Ryan felt relief as the extra weight of the inspector rolled off him. He tried to breathe. His lungs were devoid of air. His ribs ached. Why did everything have to happen to his ribs? He was tired of reinjuring them.

His lungs inflated, his body coming back online after the sudden shock, and he took several deep breaths. They needed to move. His eyes fixed on the KRISS.

Gabriella let out a scream, and he twisted his head. The container was falling again. He closed his eyes; certain it would crush them both.

The gangplank saved them, keeping one end of the container off the ground. The narrow angle of the container's slant pinned Ryan to the ground. His backpack ground into his ribs, making it even harder to breathe.

His eyes met Gabriella's. They were wild with panic and fear. He touched her hand. She interlocked her fingers with his. After a moment, he let go and wiggled forward, though the pack made it hard to move. He pushed with his feet to free himself.

He crawled on hands and knees toward his rifle lying

under the twisted wreckage of the gangway. The lights reflected off Gabriella's pistol, just past it. She squirmed forward, head and shoulders clearing the container.

Bullets fell like rain, and she scrambled back undercover.

"The shooter is on the crane," Ryan said.

Gabriella gave him a *no shit* look. "How are you going to get us out of this one?"

Ryan shrugged out of his backpack and rolled onto his back. He pulled a thirty-round magazine for the KRISS from his cargo pocket and exchanged it for the fifteen rounder in his Glock.

"What are you doing?" she asked.

"I'm going to slide out and provide cover fire. You get the guns and hightail it to the semi."

"I can't drive one of those," Gabriella blurted.

"Kidnap the driver."

"Are you serious!"

Ryan rolled to face her. "Look, Inspector, we're not walking out of here alive unless we do something drastic. I guarantee you there are more tangos coming to blow off our heads. I can pin one guy down, but you need to help."

Gabriella swallowed hard. A tremor seemed to run through her body. After a moment, she shook her head.

Ryan grabbed her by the shoulder, forcing her to look at him. He'd seen this same reaction from soldiers in combat. Even with all their training, the situation could be overwhelming. "We need to get out of here."

A snarl passed her clenched teeth. Crouching on all fours, she looked almost feral.

Over the idling of a diesel engine, he could hear her hyperventilating. The ringing in Ryan's ears had receded, but he was confident he'd added a new level of annoyance to his tinnitus. Ryan screwed the suppressor to the barrel of his pistol. Not only did it reduce the noise level of the gun, but it also improved accuracy by reducing recoil.

He brought his feet up to his butt and planted them on the pavement. In one fluid move, he rolled his head and arms out from under the box. Eighty feet above them, the sniper stood on a catwalk with his weapon to his shoulder. Ryan fired without aiming, just pointed the gun and sent lead into the sky. He continued to maneuver from under the container, shouting for Gabriella to follow him.

The sniper returned fire. Bullets sparked off the asphalt. Ryan could feel the roiled air, followed by the smack of the bullets into the ground. He fired straight up until his pistol locked open.

Rolling toward the gangway, Ryan tried to make himself a moving target. He managed to reload the Glock and found he was back beneath the container with the sobbing Puerto Rican inspector. He was closer to the KRISS Victor. By fully extending his arm, he was able to grasp the stock and drag it back to him. He shouldered the backpack.

"We're going out on three. Run to the semi."

Gabriella shrank back, trying to wedge her body further under the container.

Ryan tugged at her wrist and forced her to look at him. "You're not going to die here."

Her wide eyes stared back.

"Listen to me," Ryan begged. "We need to go."

She shook her head.

Time was running out. Shooters had to be approaching their location. He wasn't going to die under some stinking container, and he wasn't going to leave Gabriella behind. Taking a firm grip on her wrists, he planted his feet and dragged her to the gangplank where there was room to maneuver onto hands and knees. She rolled on her back and tried to squirm away.

Ryan put his hand on the other side of her body, pinning her in place. Her eyes were wild and uncomprehending. Tears streamed down her cheeks. She kept shaking her head back and forth.

Normally, he'd just give his troopers a swift kick in the ass when they blanked out in combat, but with Gabriella he needed something different to jar her out her panic, so he kissed her full on the lips. In his haste, their teeth clicked together. Then she was reciprocating, pressing her mouth into his.

He broke away and dragged her clear of the container. Two steps into the footrace, Ryan pointed the KRISS over his shoulder and fired up at the crane as he ran. Incoming bullets slapped at the ground all around them.

The bolt locked open as he rounded the back of the trailer. The driver's door was open, with no one in the seat. Ryan shoved Gabriella into the cab and climbed in behind her. Bullets perforated the cab roof and shattered the windows.

When Ryan had been sixteen, he'd learned to drive a Datsun station wagon. It had a four-cylinder engine and a short throw, five-speed manual gear box. He used those rusty skills to force the semi's transmission into first gear. He wound up the engine and disengaged the clutch. The big vehicle hopped as it started to roll.

"Come on, ya big turd, I can get out and walk faster than this," Ryan said through gritted teeth. He jerked the shifter back into second and stood on the gas. The semi picked up speed, slowly taking them out of the direct line of fire.

He glanced over at Gabriella. She was quiet and staring out the window. Her head was at an odd angle, and when he reached across the cab to touch her, she slouched forward. He could see her blood-soaked hands from where she had pressed them against her thigh. More blood streamed from a shoulder wound.

"Shit," Ryan shouted. "Don't quit on me now, Gabby."

He tugged her off the dash, but her limp body refused to stay upright. Letting go of her, he spun the truck's steering wheel hard to the left. The big truck's tires screeched in protest at the violent maneuver. Ryan angled the truck toward the chain-link fence at the entrance to avoid the long, serpentine road out of the facility.

Ryan pressed the accelerator and shifted into third gear. The parking lot was two feet higher than the road. It was too late to turn back.

The Kenworth's long, sloping nose stayed level as the front wheels left the pavement. A few feet further and the front end slammed into the grass, burying the bumper deep in the small ditch and throwing up a cascade of dirt. The truck's suspension bounced violently, tossing Ryan and Gabriella around like rag dolls. Chain link fence tore free of its anchors and posts, screaming as it grated against the metal cab and trailer. Ryan sawed at the wheel, trying to keep the truck from wrecking.

Gabriella fell and lay in between the driver and passenger seats, legs still trapped in the passenger footwell. Her clothes and hands were crimson with blood. Ryan fought the semi back onto the road, screaming curses and sawing the steering wheel. He was angry at himself for allowing her to accompany him, and angry that he didn't know in which direction to find a hospital.

How could he have been so careless? He had kept Greg and Rick from coming with him, but he hadn't been able to stop a stubborn woman. Now she was bleeding to death in a shot-up tractor-trailer.

Ryan checked the rearview mirrors, amazed both were intact. He saw no headlights on the road behind him. The men who had ambushed them wouldn't stop now. They could find them easily enough.

Ryan reloaded the pistol and jammed the barrel under his right thigh. Next, he extracted his phone and dialed Greg.

"Where are you?" Greg asked.

"I just left the port. I'm heading north on Route 12." Ryan glanced over in time to see a sign directing him toward the Luis A. Ferré toll road they'd driven from San Juan. "I need a hospital, now."

"Are you all right?"

"I'm fine. Gabriella's been shot. Give me the directions."

"How did she get shot?" Greg asked.

Ryan's voice rose to a shout. "Get me to a hospital."

"Okay." A moment later, Greg said, "If you're on 12, get off at Avenida Las Américas. Make a left and you'll see Hospital Metropolitano on your right. We're coming to you."

Ryan squinted into the wind blasting through the shattered windshield. He passed the exit for Highway 2 and saw the sign for Highway 163, the Avenue of the Americas. He slowed to take the exit ramp and barreled through the stop light at the bottom in a hard-left turn. The rear of the trailer swayed and jerked, smacking the bridge support pillar. The whole truck shuddered, and in the mirror, Ryan saw a shower of sparks behind the trailer, trailing like the tail of a comet. The tires had blown and shredded, leaving the rims to grind on the asphalt.

He pulled the wrecked rig into the grass of the road verge in front of the hospital and jumped down from the cab. As he dashed around to the passenger side door, a Jeep Wrangler stopped in front of the Kenworth. Rick jumped out and ran back to where Ryan stood in the Kenworth's open passenger door.

"Help me get her out of the truck," Ryan said. Together,

they maneuvered Gabriella from the cab, and Ryan took her in his arms. "Get my guns and pack."

"Roger that," Rick said, but Ryan was already running toward the emergency room.

At the entrance, he dumped the wounded inspector into a wheelchair and pushed her through the automatic double doors into the waiting room.

"I need help," he yelled at the nurse behind the counter.

Her expression of disdain shifted to dismay when she saw Gabriella dripping blood onto the linoleum. The nurse screamed for a doctor and motioned for Ryan to follow her through another set of doors.

They raced along a hallway to a trauma bay. The nurse helped Ryan lay Gabriella on a bed. Suddenly, people in white coats and medical scrubs flooded the tiny room. They pushed Ryan out of the way.

Absorbed in the task of saving the woman's life, they missed Ryan slipping from the room.

He spotted a bathroom and hurried inside to scrub his hands. Gabriella's slick red blood coated them. It reminded him of other times when he'd held wounded comrades while they bleed out.

With clean hands, he stepped out of the bathroom, picked up a white lab coat from a stretcher, and donned it over his bloody clothes. Then he walked out of the emergency room.

Greg and Rick were waiting in the Jeep just outside the hospital's entrance. Ryan climbed into the back. "Did you follow the semi with our stolen goods?" he asked, surprised they were still in Ponce, yet thankful for their help.

"Yeah, we did," Greg said. "When it headed north on 123, I figured it was going to Utuado, and I had Rick circle back to the docks."

Ryan nodded while staring out the window. To the east,

the sky was turning yellow over the mountains. His adrenaline flow had shut off, and he felt an immense weariness flood his body. He wasn't sure how he had survived the ambush. He could have taken a bullet just as easily as Gabriella. Maybe the one she had taken was meant for him?

If God smiled on drunks and fools, Ryan thought everyone in the Jeep was making Him grin.

"Where are we going?" Rick asked, turning out of the hospital parking lot.

Ryan rubbed his face with both hands. "Crap. I can't leave her."

"Dude, you were just in a gunfight," Rick said. "The cops will be all over you."

"Yeah, I know. Pull over."

"Check that," Greg said. "Gabriella will be in the hospital overnight, at least. Let's find a hotel and get some rest so we don't make any irrational decisions."

CHAPTER THIRTY

Six hours later, the bells of the Cathedral of Our Lady of Guadalupe woke Ryan. He rubbed his eyes and focused on his watch. It was noon. He'd slept for six hours.

His stomach grumbled. He needed coffee and something to eat. And a cigarette. He sat up, rubbed his face, and massaged his temples with his fingertips.

He glanced at the other bed. Rick lay spread eagle on his stomach under the comforter. Greg still slept beside Ryan in the queen-sized bed.

They had settled on the Ponce Plaza Hotel and Casino. Located in the historic zone, it was only seven minutes from the hospital. More importantly, it had available rooms and would allow them to check in right away.

Ryan stepped into the shower and let the hot water beat against his sore muscles. After toweling off, he pulled on cargo shorts and a gray T-shirt with the words *Dark Water Research* circling a brass dive helmet on the left breast pocket. He slipped into his Salomon shoes and filled his pockets with his tactical knife, wallet, cell phone, and lighter. One never knew when fire would come in handy. His Walther PPQ went into an inside-the-waistband holster, and he dropped a spare magazine into each of his cargo pockets for balance.

Behind him, Greg stirred but didn't wake. Ryan slipped out the door and kept a hand on it to keep it from banging closed. In the lobby, he ordered a breakfast burrito and a large cup of coffee from a woman behind a bistro counter, then walked through the tiny outside pool area, wishing he could sit down and relax at one of the umbrella-shaded tables and watch the clear blue water shimmer in the noonday heat.

He continued through the casino and found a taxi. By the time the cabbie dropped Ryan at the hospital, he'd eaten his burrito and drank most of the coffee. He tossed the rest into a trash can at the hospital entrance. At the front desk, he asked for directions to Gabriella's room.

"We have no one here by that name, sir," the attendant said politely.

Ryan stared her in the eyes, but he saw her hand drift below the counter.

Two men in police uniforms came striding toward the desk. Ryan surmised that the woman had pressed a silent alarm.

The older of the pair addressed Ryan. "*Señor*, what is your business here?"

"I'm looking for Inspector Gabriella Martinez. I brought her here last night."

The two uniforms glanced at each other before placing their hands on their pistols. Both men stepped back, blading their bodies.

Ryan held up his hands. "I want to speak to your supervisor."

The two men stood firm.

His focus was drawn to another man hurrying toward them. He had slicked-back black hair and stood taller than the two uniforms he brushed past. He extended his hand.

"Mr. Weller, thank you for coming. I'm Inspector Manuel Vargas."

Ryan hid his surprise that the man knew his name.

The Puerto Rican inspector turned and clapped a hand on Ryan's shoulder. "Come, let's go somewhere private to talk."

"How's Gabriella?"

Vargas glanced around the lobby. "She's recovering from surgery."

"Can I see her?"

"We have her under protection," Vargas said.

This was a good thing. La Uniformada was circling the wagons around their own.

Ryan let himself be escorted through the hospital to an empty room. Sunlight streamed through the window and onto the neatly made mattress.

Vargas closed the door and sat in a chair with his back to the window. He pulled out a smart phone, fiddled with the screen for a moment, then laid it on the bed. "Start from the beginning." He pointed at the phone. "I'm recording this conversation."

The sun made the temperature in the room hotter than normal. Ryan wondered how Vargas could stand wearing a suit. He had to be baking. "Which beginning? Last night or the first time I met Gabriella?"

Vargas glanced up. "The first time you met?"

Ryan chuckled. "I met Gabriella at her office last week. It was right after I'd been in a car wreck." He detailed the accident, the gunfight at the car, their work together in San Juan, Diego Hernández's involvement, and the shootout on the *Southern Star*.

When he was done, Vargas looked up. "Is that all?"

"Pretty much." Ryan shrugged. "I'm going to use the head and then I need coffee."

Vargas was staring out the window when Ryan returned

from using the room's bathroom. He straightened his jacket and motioned for Ryan to precede him out of the room. Outside, one of the uniforms from the lobby pushed off the wall.

He followed them to the cafeteria. Ryan offered to buy coffee for both men, but the uniform refused and maintained a vigil near the entry door. Ryan and Vargas took their paper cups from the counter and filled them from a large urn. While Vargas stopped for cream and sugar, Ryan took a sip of his. He wished he had some rum to cover the foul taste.

They sat at an outside table in the shade of a sun-faded canopy. Ryan nursed his coffee and waited for the inspector to speak.

"Why didn't you come to us when you first learned of the thefts?" Vargas finally asked.

"We did," Ryan replied. "Our shipping agent, Shawn Lindowel, gave a report to your people in San Juan. I also told Gabriella."

"Why did you go to the ship?"

"Because three of our containers were stolen yesterday. Now, my guess is that Diego was setting a trap since his plan to pin the deaths of the men in Ponce on me didn't work."

"You believe Hernández wanted you out of the way?" Vargas asked.

"Yes. I think he sees me as a threat to his enterprise."

Vargas nodded and sipped coffee.

"Hernández has people inside your organization, doesn't he?" Ryan said.

Vargas nodded again.

To fill the silence, Ryan asked again, "Can I see Gabriella?"

"No," Vargas said. "They performed emergency surgery right after you dropped her off. The doctor says she'll pull through. She needs her rest."

"Good."

His mind had added the image of her blood-stained body lying between the seats of the semi to the catalogue of images he'd never be able to forget. How many people had he cradled in his arms while they bled? How many times had his hands been stained with their blood?

A door slammed somewhere nearby, and Ryan jumped. Coffee sloshed out of his cup and down his bare leg. "Dammit," he snarled through gritted teeth. He threw the cup in anger before shaking the liquid from his hand.

The firefight last night and hearing the door slam had set off his alarm bells. This whole trip was aggravating. Ryan wanted to return to the ocean. It was amazing how calm he felt both above and below it, but he had to exist on land as well, and that meant learning to cope with the surprises and paranoia in his brain.

"Are you all right?" Vargas asked.

Ryan turned to the inspector. His voice rose with his aggravation. "No, I'm not all right. I'm tired. I just spilled my coffee. I got shot at last night and a good woman almost died. These thugs will not stop until I'm dead. If they keep coming after me, I will put everyone of Diego Hernández's men in a shallow grave."

Vargas leaped to his feet. "You will do nothing of the sort. You're a civilian and you have no authority."

The two men locked eyes.

Ryan growled, "When men are hunting and shooting at me, that gives me all the authority I need to protect my life."

"You didn't protect Gabriella's," Vargas shot back. "She almost died."

They continued to stare at each other, lips twitching in sneers, brows furrowed in anger.

"We can either do this together or I can finish it myself," Ryan said.

Vargas broke eye contact and shook his head. "I can't let a vigilante run loose on my island."

"Are you talking about me or Diego?"

"You," Vargas sneered.

"*I'm* the problem?" Ryan pointed at his chest. "I'm not the one running a theft ring. On *your* island. I think I'm the only guy here trying to stop it. Your police force is so corrupt, they're willing to turn a blind eye to what's happening because you're either being paid to or you think Diego Hernández is Robin Hood. He's not. He's a criminal. He's a killer. He's a threat to law and order on *your* island."

"Are you done?" Vargas asked.

"No," Ryan said, the anger still in his voice. "I won't be done until Diego Hernández and his band of merry men are in jail or dead."

Vargas reached behind his back and calmly said, "You're under arrest."

"Bullshit," Ryan snapped.

Vargas continued with the Miranda warning, pulling a set of handcuffs from his belt. Ryan backed away.

"Don't make this harder than it has to be," the inspector warned.

"I came here to see Gabriella and I'm cooperating with your investigation. There's no need to arrest me." Ryan saw the uniform, who'd trailed them to the room and to the cafeteria, step outside. He held his baton at the low ready.

Vargas continued, "You're a danger to this investigation and to the people of this island."

"Dude, I'm trying to help you," Ryan said, emphasizing every word.

"Put your hands behind your back."

"No." Ryan maneuvered to keep the table between him and Vargas, who held the handcuffs out in front of him. Ryan had established an escape route as soon as they'd walked outside. Now he needed to implement it. The only police presence he'd seen were the two uniforms and Inspector Vargas. On the ride from the hotel, he'd seen no other cops or patrol cars.

"Put your hands behind your back and turn around," Vargas ordered.

Ryan spun on his heels and sprinted north into the residential neighborhood. Vargas attempted to chase after him, but he stopped at the edge of the parking lot with his hands on his knees. The uniform paused with Vargas.

When Ryan saw they were no longer following him, he turned a corner and slowed his pace to a jog. He could eat through the miles. His training had taught him to stuff the pain inside and keep moving at all costs.

His cell phone rang, and he slowed to a walk to answer the call.

"Where are you?" Greg asked.

"I went to the hospital, but some inspector named Vargas tried to arrest me."

"I heard."

"What do you mean, you heard?" Ryan asked.

"The police have named you a person of interest in the shooting of Inspector Gabriella Martinez," Greg said.

"Damn, that was fast. But you didn't answer my question. Who told you?"

"Shawn Lindowel. He said his contact in La Uniformada called him."

Why would the cops tell him about my movements? And why would he tell Greg?

"Where are you now?" Greg asked.

"I'm at a Puma gas station a block north and west of the hospital."

"We're on our way to pick you up."

Ryan stopped dead in his tracks. The puzzle pieces began to snap into place. "Shawn is the key to this whole operation."

"What are you talking about?" Greg demanded.

"I'll tell you when you get here." Ryan hung up the phone and went into the convenience store. He glanced around at the other customers, categorizing them into possible threats and noncombatants. After grabbing a bottle of Mountain Dew, he looked longingly at the racks of cigarettes behind the counter. Ryan steeled his willpower and paid for only the soda. Subconsciously, he checked the entrances and exits in the mirror over the counter.

Walking back outside, he felt like he could breathe again. He took a long swig of the soda and stood in the shade of a tree on the back corner of the lot. Ryan made two phone calls while he waited.

When a black, four-door Jeep Wrangler pulled up to the pumps, he slowly walked toward it. It wasn't until Greg rolled down the window and snapped, "Get your ass in gear, Weller!" that Ryan knew it was the Jeep he was waiting for.

CHAPTER THIRTY-ONE

When Rick had them headed for the hotel, Greg turned to face Ryan. "Why is Shawn Lindowel the key to this operation?"

Ryan knew this would be a tough sell. Shawn was a likeable guy. He seemed capable of doing his job, and Greg apparently had a long history with the guy. Ryan stared out the window, watching a motorcyclist weaving in and out of traffic, wondering if it was a tail. When the bike turned away from them, Ryan looked at his employer.

"What do we know about Shawn?" he asked.

Greg faced forward and braced his hands on the center console and the door to lift his butt off the seat in a pressure relief. "Shawn's been our contractor for several years."

"How long?"

"I don't know." Greg shrugged, and his torso moved up and down. He relaxed back onto the seat. "I'd have to ask Muriel. Dad set things up with Shawn years ago."

Ryan nodded. Muriel Johnson was the secretary at DWR. Greg's grandfather had hired her when she was eighteen. She knew the ins and outs of the business almost better than the Olsens.

Ryan asked. "When did DWR start having problems with container theft?"

"Around the same time as the hurricane," Greg said.

"You think Shawn is the mastermind?" Rick asked, looking in the rearview mirror at Ryan.

"It makes sense." Ryan ticked off points on his fingers as he talked. "He knows what's in the containers. He's on the paperwork for Caribbean Maritime Delivery. He knew where we would be to orchestrate the first ambush, and he knew about the trackers. My money is on this guy as the mastermind."

Greg shook his head. "I can't believe Shawn would be involved in this. Why would he call to tell us about our containers being stolen?"

"Because he needs to look like the good guy. I bet he didn't expect us to go snooping around. If he did, I think he would have left our shipments alone."

"So now what?" Rick asked. "How do we prove Shawn's the one in charge?"

"We need to put the puzzle together." Ryan leaned forward between the two seats. "Shawn knew we were going to Utuado. How else did Diego get it set up so quickly? Then they set us up in Ponce."

"The guy from the restaurant called him," Rick said. "We have his phone records."

"Yeah, he did," Ryan conceded, "but Diego didn't have enough time to put together the manpower and weaponry to set up an ambush between when Peeping Pedro called and the time we were hit."

"I'll play devil's advocate here," Greg said. "Shawn knew where we were going, but if Diego has a base near Utuado, it would be easy for him to dispatch men."

"Shawn's involved somehow," Ryan replied. "He knew where we were going and why. We're a threat to his enterprise. If he had us eliminated, it would look like a random act of violence."

The three men debated the validity of Shawn Lindowel's involvement with Diego Hernández's band of merry men until they reached the hotel. They split up, Greg going to the casino, Rick to the pool, and Ryan to the weight room.

The tiny fitness room contained several workout machines, free weights, medicine balls, and tread mills. Ryan used the free weights to burn off some energy. He hadn't worked out in a gym in at least two months. He knew his muscles would be sore if he overdid it, and he couldn't afford to be any sorer than he already was.

After an hour spent alternating between lifting weights and staring out the window overlooking the rooftops of downtown Ponce, his cell phone rang.

"What's up, Ashlee?"

"I tracked the container to a place near Utuado. It's in a national forest or something."

"Cool."

"I did some digging into Shawn Lindowel like you asked. I ended up hacking his company server. He should have a better security software. His passwords are pretty weak. Anyways, I got into his company records. L&F was in the red after the 2008 recession. Things picked up in 2010, but they were slow. When Maria hit, he was suddenly handling all kinds of cargo."

"From legitimate contracts?" Ryan asked.

"I'm not a shipping expert, but everything I see looks right."

"What about bank records?"

"I can't access them. I'd have to hack the bank, and I'm not doing that."

"Thanks, Ashlee." Ryan hung up. She hadn't found the smoking gun he'd hoped she would.

Ryan gave up the pretense of working out. His mind kept trying to fit the pieces of the puzzle together, and he was worried about Gabriella. The whole point of going to the hospital had been to check on her condition. Other than the fact that she'd had surgery, which he'd known she would, he'd learned nothing.

He was glad for the solitude of the empty fitness room. The only sound was the hum of the air conditioning unit trying to combat the sun's rays streaming through the windows and leaving brilliant squares of light on the black floor matting.

His phone rang again, and he answered it even though he didn't recognize the caller.

"It's good to hear your voice."

"Joulie," Ryan cried, joy and surprise in his voice. A smile played across his lips. "How are you?"

"I am well, as is James."

"Awesome."

"You were right," she said. "He is a wonderful boy."

"I know. Did you get him into a school?"

"Yes, but that's not why I called."

Ryan rested his elbow on the windowsill and leaned on it, the phone pressing tighter against his ear. "What's up?"

"Have you heard any news from Haiti recently?"

Her voice gave him shivers. "No, why?"

"The people are protesting in the streets again. This time over the mismanagement of two billion dollars from an oil program sponsored by Venezuela. They attacked a road crew and murdered the family of one of my top security guards in their house. Ryan, someone poisoned them, and we do not understand why."

"It sounds like someone is trying to undermine your accomplishments."

"I believe that as well."

"Are you okay? Will you be safe?"

"Yes, I think so," Joulie said. "I don't want you to come back. It's too dangerous. The U.S. State Department is calling for all nonessential Americans to leave the island."

"I was looking forward to seeing you again." He wanted to hold her in his arms, caress her smooth skin, and kiss her soft lips. A niggling guilt over the kisses with Gabriella crept in.

"*Ou se kè mwen.*"

You are my heart. Ryan had heard her say it many times. It meant she loved him, or at least he thought that was what she meant. Staring out the window, he could feel her breath whispering those words across the skin on his neck. It made him shiver.

He'd wondered how she had felt after their last argument. She'd told him she didn't want children and wouldn't leave her island with so much work to do. Whatever she meant by *you are my heart* now, he was glad to hear her purr them into his ear. They lightened the burden on his shoulders. He thought of how joyous their reunion would be.

"I can't wait to see you again."

"It is not possible, *cheri mwen*." *My love.*

"Why?" The burden came crashing back down. This time to settle in his heart.

"You would be in danger here."

"That's never stopped us before."

Joulie was silent for a long moment. Then she cleared her throat before saying, "I can't allow you to come back. There are those who wish to use our relationship as a wedge. They claim you are distracting me from my job. I cannot allow our relationship to undermine my authority."

"Did you poison those people?" Ryan asked.

Her answer wasn't convincing. It wasn't beneath her to eliminate those who spoke ill of her. She liked to say she maintained power through her status as a mambo, but Ryan knew the truth. Joulie was a ruthless Haitian warlord who preserved her power through violence when needed. Ryan was certain the eradication of the security guard and his family was retribution for something he had done wrong.

"Joulie, what's going on?"

"Nothing, Ryan. I miss you."

She missed him, yet she had told him not to come back.

"Can you do me a favor?" Ryan asked, not wanting to rationalize their conversation into something it wasn't.

"*Wi.*"

"Can you check to see if shipping containers are being stolen from your ports or stolen containers are being brought in?"

"Why?"

Ryan gave her a rundown of the last weeks, ending with his theory about Shawn Lindowel spearheading the container theft operation. He left out the ambushes and gun fights.

"I'll see what I can find out."

"Thank you, Joulie."

She hung up without saying goodbye. Ryan took the phone from his ear and slid it into his pocket, then placed his crossed arms on the windowsill and let his chin rest on them. Two-day stubble stabbed his skin. He stared out over the rooftops, listening to the church bells toll.

Ryan couldn't help wondering if the bells tolled for the death of his relationship or the death of another good woman.

Introspection was another plague of aging. Had he reached the point in life where his choices were met with more doubt than satisfaction?

The door opened and he heard Rick say, "He's in here."

Ryan shook off his funk and turned to the interlopers, leaning back against the window, arms crossed. He glanced at the wall clock. How had he lost three hours?

Inspector Vargas stepped into the room. He shifted side to side, having trouble meeting Ryan's gaze. "Gabriella is awake. She's asking for you."

"Are you going to arrest me?" Ryan asked.

"No." Vargas shook his head. "She read me the riot act for not letting you up to see her. She explained the whole thing." His gaze shifted to Ryan's face. "Thank you for rescuing her."

Ryan shrugged. "It was the only thing to do."

"She would like to see you," the inspector reiterated. "I can take you in my car."

"I need a shower first." Ryan rubbed the chin stubble.

"Take your time," Vargas replied.

Ryan wondered if it had been the tongue lashing from Gabriella or a call from the Department of Homeland Security that had cowed Vargas. Ryan had called Floyd Landis while at the gas station and asked him to check the inspector out, and to vouch for Ryan if he was on the level. "Did you get any strange phone calls this afternoon, Inspector?"

Vargas cocked his head. "I would like you to explain how a salvage consultant receives the blessings of Homeland Security."

"It's a long story. I'm sure you'd find some of it amusing, but I don't want to bore you."

Vargas stared blankly at him.

Ryan brushed past the Inspector. "I'll meet you at the hospital."

CHAPTER THIRTY-TWO

Gabriella's eyes were closed when Ryan and Vargas entered the room. A short man with close-cropped hair motioned for them to step back outside. As he rose from a chair beside her bed, he straightened his rumpled shirt. Ryan noticed the folded jacket over the back of the chair.

The stranger eased the door closed and extended his hand to Ryan. "I'm Eric, Gabby's husband. Thanks for saving her life."

Ryan's eyebrows rose.

"We've been divorced for a year," Eric explained. "I'm still her emergency contact." When neither Ryan nor Vargas replied, he continued, "She's been sleeping since she talked to you, Manny."

"Is she doing all right?" Ryan asked.

"Yes, the doctor says she'll be just fine. She needs rest and time to heal."

Ryan glanced up and down the hall. "Where's her protection detail, Vargas?" He didn't think he could get away with calling him Manny.

"We don't think she's in danger," Vargas said.

Squaring to Vargas, Ryan whisper shouted, "You don't think she's in danger? Those guys have been trying to kill me, and if they find out she's alive, they'll come after her, too."

"Who?" Eric asked, stepping between the men.

Ryan turned to him. "What did Inspector Vargas tell you?"

"He said someone shot her during a robbery."

"That's partially true," Ryan said. "It was an ambush, and the robbers got away."

"How do they know it was Gabby?"

Ryan rolled his neck, trying to loosen the tension. "There's a mole inside La Uniformada, isn't that right, Inspector?"

Vargas held his hands up, palms out. "It's not me. Call your Homeland guy. He can vouch for me."

A nurse pushed through the group and turned her back to the room door. She placed a hand on the handle before addressing the men. "If you continue to argue, you'll need to leave. You're disturbing the patients."

Ryan knew she was right. They couldn't stand in the hallway and argue about who did what. The important thing was that Gabriella was okay. Everything else they could work out later. Ryan glanced down at the name badge hanging on a lanyard around the nurse's neck. It read Yarah. The faded picture did not do her justice.

"I'm sorry," Ryan apologized. "We care about Gabriella and want the best for her. Can we see her now?"

"I'll check." The short nurse pushed through the door. A minute later, she returned to the door. "Is one of you Ryan?"

Ryan raised his hand.

"She would like to speak with you." Yarah held the door open.

The big salvage consultant moved past her, and she shut the door as he walked to the bedside. Gabriella's eyes were open but clouded from the pain medication. Her skin was a shade paler and slick with a sheen of sweat.

Yarah busied herself, checking the IV tubing and bags. She opened something on the machine, and it began to beep loudly. Ryan hated the noise the IV machine made, especially when it woke him from sleep.

"Hey, Gabriella," Ryan said softly, leaning over the bed.

She gave him a weak smile.

"I'd ask how you're doing, but you look like shit."

"Always the charmer." She coughed, and Yarah glared at Ryan.

He pushed a lock of hair from her face. "What can I do for you?"

Gabriella moved her hand up and grabbed his wrist. "Get those assholes."

"We'll get them. Can I trust Vargas?"

Gabriella nodded. She let go of his hand and pointed at the water pitcher on the tray table.

Ryan poured water into a cup and held it so she could sip through the straw. "Eric seems nice."

She released the straw from her lips and rolled her eyes.

Ryan glanced up at Yarah. "We're about to discuss classified police procedures. Do you need to be here?"

"I don't want you to stress our patient."

Ryan lifted his shirt and showed her the surgical scar on his abdomen. "I know all about hospitals and gunshot wounds. Trust me, I won't stress her out."

Yarah sighed with indignation and left the room. Vargas came in and stood by the window.

Ryan sat down on the edge of Gabriella's bed. "The semi I put the tracker on at the port went to the Río Abajo State Forest."

Vargas furrowed his brow. "When did you plan to share that knowledge?"

"I asked my Homeland contact to get satellite footage of the forest. Google Maps shows nothing but trees."

Ryan had had to convince Landis that this was a valuable use of satellite time after Landis had denied there were satellites flying over the area. To Ryan, this was a preposterous statement. With the unrest in Venezuela, Nicaragua, Cuba, and Haiti, along with the U.S.'s continual need to spy on its neighbors, Ryan knew there were satellites orbiting the earth with the ability to shoot a few photos of a Puerto Rican gang's hideout. The government could put a feather in its cap if they brought peace to the island and justice to the shipping companies. It would show the people of Puerto Rico that the U.S. government had their best interests at heart.

"When will you get the photos?" Vargas asked.

"He told me he'd call when he had them," Ryan said. "I expect it to be soon."

"I want to go with you," Gabriella said.

"No way," the two men said in unison.

"I can't just lie here in bed and do nothing."

"That's exactly what you'll do," Ryan said.

"You're being sexist," Gabriella retorted. "Stop trying to protect me."

"I'm not being sexist," Ryan said. "You just got shot and had surgery. It will take time to recover. Trust me."

Gabriella looked away. Tears glistened on her cheeks.

Ryan placed a hand on hers and said quietly, "You're going to be fine."

She neither met his gaze nor moved her hand from under his.

"He's right, Gabby," Vargas said. "You need to rest. We can handle this."

Yarah came into the room, took one look at Gabriella, and told the men to leave.

Ryan glanced up at the nurse, then over at Vargas. "Can you give us a minute?"

"We got this, Gabby," Vargas said. "I'll be back in a few days."

Ryan and Gabriella stared at each other until Vargas and the nurse had left the room.

"Thanks," she finally said. "You saved my life."

"You're welcome." He leaned down and kissed her forehead. "Get better."

Ryan walked out before she could respond. He passed Eric without acknowledging him, and said to Vargas, "I'll call you when I hear from Homeland."

CHAPTER THIRTY-THREE

Ryan, Greg, and Rick sat around a small table beside the hotel pool, shaded by an umbrella. Cold beers sweated in the heat and several empties stood in the center of the table. Ryan had used the hotel's computer and printer to print out the satellite photos sent by Floyd Landis. The eight-and-a-half by eleven images were a little blurry due to the low resolution of the printer. It had run out of colored ink partway through the pictures.

"Looks like a small compound," Rick said. "Hard to tell with the tree canopy blocking the view."

"Think we might need to do a little recon mission?" Ryan asked.

Rick grinned and nodded. "Sounds like fun."

"We need to include Vargas on this," Greg said.

"I agree," Ryan replied after a moment of silence. "This is an island-wide theft ring. The police needed to be involved, especially if Homeland's feeding them information."

Ryan's phone rang, and he picked up. "*Buenos días*, Inspector Vargas."

"I assume you received the satellite images?"

"We did."

"Where are you?" Vargas inquired.

"Still at the Ponce Hotel and Casino," Ryan answered.

"Don't go anywhere."

"Come to the pool area."

Fifteen minutes later, Vargas strode across the pool deck, wearing his usual suit and tie. In one hand he held a ream of glossy photos, and in the other, a cup of coffee. Ryan wondered if the man was sweating to death or his body had acclimated to wearing a suit.

Vargas sat down at the empty fourth seat and dropped the oversized photographs on the table. Ryan could detect no sweat on the inspector's face.

"I think we need to do some recon," Rick said, spreading out the glossies.

"No." Vargas's reply was firm. "I don't even want to inform Utuado Regional Command that we're investigating crimes in their district.

Ryan stopped sifting through the photos and looked up. "What's the plan?"

"We hit them hard and fast."

"I agree, but we need more than the three of us to pull this off. You'll have to trust someone in the police force."

Vargas nodded. "I've called in a few favors. We have an M1083 to transport our troopers. We'll infiltrate through the woods and up this road here." He pointed to a small, dirt track snaking under the trees in one photo.

"When will this happen?" Greg asked.

"Two days. Until then, I've got lookouts posted around the area to let us know if Diego gets wind of our operation. If he moves, we'll have people tracking him."

Ryan said, "I'm trying to work an angle to catch the broker. I called a friend, and she said she would negotiate with our man for some stolen containers."

"A friend?" Greg asked dubiously.

"Is this person law enforcement?" Vargas asked.

"No, she's more of a warlord."

Vargas cocked his head and furrowed his brow. He stared at Ryan, waiting for him to explain, but Ryan did not.

"How long will that take?" Vargas asked after a moment of silence.

"I'm not sure," Ryan replied.

The inspector took a sip of coffee. "We don't have time to waste setting traps. If it involves your man, we'll find out later."

Ryan glanced at Greg, who nodded. That one movement indicated Ryan should drop the trap and move forward with the plan Vargas had suggested.

"Do we need two more days?" Ryan asked.

"Yes," Vargas said. "We'll need to assemble a force and brief them on the situation."

"Waiting only gives Diego a chance to escape," Rick said. "You need to move up your timeline. If this guy is anything like the bomb makers we hunted in Afghanistan, he'll just go to ground and wait for us to forget about him. If he leaves the island, we might never catch him. And he can still run his operations."

Vargas nodded in agreement, the said to Rick, "I understand your concern, and my superiors have agreed to allow you and Ryan to accompany the assault force."

CHAPTER THIRTY-FOUR

The tan, snub-nosed M1083 lumbered up the dirt road under a canopy of old-growth trees. Twelve members of Puerto Rico Police's *Fuerza de Choque*—Shock Force—sat with Ryan Weller and Rick Hayes in the cargo bed. Vargas was by the tailgate, ready to lead the assault.

The Shock Force wore dark-blue battle dress uniforms, black chest rigs over bulletproof vests, elbow pads, shin guards, and helmets with shields. Each carried an M4 rifle and Beretta M9 pistol. By comparison, Ryan and Rick looked underdressed. They had on black BDUs, chest rigs with ceramic chicken plates instead of the full body armor, and black combat boots.

The plan was to drive to the compound while another team infiltrated through the woods from the north. In theory, the pincher movement would trap Diego Hernández and his men, forcing them to either surrender or stand and fight. Ryan hoped Diego surrendered.

According to the satellite photos, the narrow access road dead-ended in a tiny hollow nestled at the base of a sheer, fifty-foot-high, limestone cliff. Camouflage netting, entwined with the trees, stretched over cargo boxes and equipment to hide the operation from the air.

The M1083 driver slowed to make the turn off the blacktop, then accelerated through the single metal pole serving as a gate. It snapped lose from the fence post like a dry twig.

Trees scraped the sides of the six-wheeled transporter as it bounced through deep, water-filled ruts. Ryan kept his head on a swivel. So far, there had been little sign of resistance. There wasn't even a guard posted at the end of the road. If he'd been running the show, he'd have a guard near the gate, a sensor to inform him when the gate opened, and booby traps ready for any raiding force. Maybe the advance force had taken out the guards? Was Diego relaxed enough in his sanctuary to think he was immune to attack?

Ryan's thumb brushed the selector switch on the KRISS. It was still in the safe position, as it had been the last dozen times he'd checked since leaving Utuado. Each touch trained the muscle memory to flick the switch from safe to single shot. The constant reaffirmation was calming for him. It had always been, even in combat during his Navy career.

No matter how hard they trained, the first shot of battle changed their plans. The enemy was unpredictable. Even the men riding on the truck were an unknown. He'd never met them outside this combat zone.

Mopping the sweat from his brow, he tensed and cringed at each sound. The closer they got to the camp, the lower he tried to sink into his seat. The cab contained armor, the tires were equipped with a central inflation run-flat system, and the troopers had fixed a winch to the beefy front bumper. None of it mattered when the men dismounted, and the bullets flew. Ryan wished the police had mounted a machine gun on the truck roof for backup.

With each passing minute, his heart rate increased. He wiped his palms on his pant legs to keep them dry and breathed deeply through his nose to steady his nerves. *I'm too old for this.*

An explosion shattered the stillness. Ryan and everyone in the truck ducked. A second detonation rent the air. Men screamed, shouted orders, and demanded information. Swiveling in his seat to look over the cab, Ryan could see smoke drifting through the trees. Then the truck sped up, bouncing and tossing the assault force with each bump in the road.

They broke out of the forest, and the driver slammed on the brakes. Ryan's shoulder crashed into the bed side. Policemen stood and rushed toward the tailgate. Rick rose with them, but Ryan grabbed him by the back of the flack vest and jerked him down. Bullets cracked all around as Diego's force resisted the assault.

The officer in front of Rick slumped forward, his helmet dented from the impact of a bullet. Blood gushed from a second wound on his neck. More men pitched backward as bullets dissected the Shock Force.

Inside the truck bed, men writhed and screamed. Half of the raiding force had bullet wounds. A medic scrambled from man to man, checking wounds and treating the most serious injuries. The other half had dismounted and spread out in the woods around the compound.

Ryan came to his knees and peered through the truck's windows and bed slats. The truck driver had abandoned the M1083 at the mouth of the clearing, which was barely large enough for a semi to turn around. From the top of the cliff, a machine gun hammered them with bullets.

Abutting the cliff base were three cargo containers. Two sat with their ends facing the road, with the third crossways on top. A wooden stairway led to the upper container, which had windows installed along its length. To Ryan's left were two rusty van body trailers parked side by side. Their dry-rotted tires had sunk into the dirt. Several cargo containers on trailer chassis had been backed into the woods on the right.

An explosion rocked the stone wall, cascading dirt and rocks onto the cargo container office. Ryan glanced up in time to see the damaged machine gun fall and bounce off the top of the containers. The infiltration group had done its job, but not soon enough to prevent massive injuries.

Sporadic gunfire continued to pop and blast as the Shock Force fought with Diego Hernández's gang of criminals. Ryan and Rick clamored from the truck and moved through the trees on the outskirts of the compound.

They paused to assess the situation. The camouflage obscured their view of the cliff. There was no way to estimate the number of tangos still hiding there. They spotted Vargas behind a tree, trying to rally the troopers to make an assault. The six uninjured men of the Shock Force were spread throughout the trees between the M1083 and the old semi-trailers some fifty feet away.

Suddenly, gunfire erupted through the office windows. The vicious hail of lead sent the Shock Force diving behind whatever cover they could find. Red and green tracers blazed across the clearing as the two groups exchanged fire. Vargas huddled behind the tree, trying to make his whole body as narrow as possible. Bullets chewed on the bark. The two Dark Water Research employees slunk farther back into the woods. Ryan believed they could get close enough to either breach the containers or provide flanking cover fire for the rest of the Shock Force. He wondered why the infiltration team's flanking action had stopped after taking out the machine gun.

Someone screamed, "*Cuidado!*" *Watch out!*

A grenade exploded outside the office, and the wooden steps fell away. Ryan squatted in the dirt behind a tree. The stench of musty leaves and cordite filled his nostrils. The Shock Force had refused to give him a wireless headset because he and Rick were civilians, tagging along on the mission. He was unable to coordinate with the others now that the mission had gone to hell.

Suddenly, the gun fire stopped, and silence fell on the compound.

Ryan swung his gun up and nearly shot Vargas as he ran toward them and dove to the ground beside the two kneeling men. He rolled and came up to a knee.

As if on cue, Diego's men opened fire. Lead rained from the cliff, the containers, and throughout the woods. A man leaped from the container to the ground. He landed hard, rolled, and came up in a limping run toward the base of the cliff.

Vargas yelled, "That's Diego."

Without thinking, Ryan bolted after the man.

He trailed Diego down a path through the woods and saw the man disappear into a cave. Ryan cut to the left to approach the cave without being seen. Surely Diego would fire at anyone charging after him.

When Ryan reached the mouth of the cave, he peered into the entrance. The man was kick-starting a dirt bike. He recognized Diego Hernández from his photograph, even from a dozen feet away and wearing a helmet. It was the eyes, hard and dark set wide over a thick nose. The dirt bike's engine came alive, and Diego revved the motor, locking eyes with Ryan.

Diego grinned, then pinned the throttle open. Ryan planted his feet and brought the KRISS to his shoulder. He pulled the trigger without aiming. Diego ducked; the bike squirming beneath him.

Before he could fire again, Diego and his motorcycle were almost on top of him. Ryan dove out of the way just as the bike swept past, showering him with a spray of dirt and leaves.

He knew he had no hope of catching the guy on foot, so he ran into the cave in search of another dirt bike. He found one leaning against a wall with a helmet hanging from the bike's handlebars. Ryan jammed on the helmet, but it was tight, squeezing his ears and scalp. He discarded the KRISS and kicked the starter lever. The Suzuki RM came to life with a roar, the blat of the four-stroke exhaust echoing off the rock walls.

He jammed the bike into gear with a loud thunk and dumped the clutch. Diego had ridden straight through the center of the compound and Ryan had no choice but to give chase through a hail of lead.

CHAPTER THIRTY-FIVE

The bike danced and bucked as he accelerated. Tracers whined through the air. The battle was ending with the leader escaping. The heavy gunfire had been a mask for Diego's defection.

Beyond the clearing, a rutted, single track wove through the trees and heavy undergrowth. Ryan felt the dirt bike's knobby tire claw and bounce over slick tree roots and exposed rocks.

Diego was gaining ground. He knew the route better than Ryan, who tried his best to keep his fleeing suspect in sight. As the brush tore at his clothes and face, he was thankful he'd taken the extra second to strap on the helmet.

He thought about the end game. Where was Diego going?

They quickly left the sounds of battle behind, climbing up a steep hillside and dropping into another valley. The tight trail snaked through the trees; the roar of the four-stroke engines drowned out all other sounds.

Diego glanced over his shoulder to gauge the distance to his pursuer. At each turn, they passed limestone cliffs and rounded sinkholes. Through an opening in the thick leaves of the subtropical forest, Ryan glimpsed the muddy banks of a river.

Ryan heard Diego downshift, and the pitch of the bike's engine changed. He, too, slowed. Diego had disappeared. Ryan glanced around before spotting the churned soil where Diego had left the trail. He turned his bike and pointed it down the perilously steep hill. The trail was almost vertical, and Ryan found his butt hanging over the rear fender. He dared not touch the front brake. He kept his eyes glued to Diego's tire tracks.

At the bottom of the steep hill, the trail widened and flattened onto the sandy bench of the river. Ahead, Ryan could see him standing on his bike, knees slightly bent, elbows up. Diego's tires tore deep grooves in the wet sand and a rooster tail cascaded from the rear wheel. Ryan ripped the throttle wide open. Under him, the suspension squatted, and the rear tire dug deep into the sand. Then it grabbed traction, and he rocketed after his quarry.

This was what it was like to be alive. Blood pounded through Ryan's veins, carrying the heavy doses of adrenaline to every part of his body. A grin split his lips. He was fully in the moment. Right now, there was nothing in the world but the two men on dirt bikes, racing through the river canyon.

He gained on his target. Diego glanced back, and Ryan saw the devilish grin on his face. Diego angled toward the river. Ryan followed, almost abreast of Diego's Suzuki.

They hit the water together. Spray filled the air, soaking both men. Ryan gunned his engine, sliding his butt back on the seat to keep the front wheel light. If he let it sink, the bike would wreck, and he'd fly over the bars.

Ryan was the first onto the rocky beach, turning into Diego and forcing him to run through the shallows. Water ran off his clothes and squished in his boots. To their right, a towering limestone cliff, pockmarked with caves, guided their path. The cliff bent toward the river, becoming a near vertical hill of dirt at the water's edge.

Diego leaned his bike toward Ryan, pushing Ryan to within inches of the cliff.

The rock wall flew by in a blur. Ryan held the bars in a death grip, the slightest twitch would cause him to scrape the rock.

Diego let go of his throttle and reached over Ryan's clutch hand, punching the kill switch on Ryan's bike. The motor died and his bike suddenly decelerated.

Ryan pulled in the clutch lever, downshifted to second, and popped the clutch. The engine caught. He cranked the throttle open, dodging the spray of rocks and sand shot up by Diego's rear tire. He tucked his chin to his chest, staring at the ground in front of him. Debris pelted off the helmet's visor. A pebble smacked his left knuckles, stunning them.

He hazarded a glance up and watched as Diego veered off the bench, up a steep path carved into the side of the hill where the cliff met the dirt wall. The roots of thick, mature trees made the earthen bank slippery. Even Diego had problems keeping the power to the ground. Ryan gained on him as the trail twisted and rose straight up for the final push to the summit. He had the power on to make the climb.

At the top, he went airborne. Before he left the ground, Ryan knew he would wreck. To his left, Diego disappeared up the dusty road.

Time seemed to stand still for an instant at the apex of the flight. Then the front tire dipped.

When the bike slammed into the ground, it wrenched the bars from his hands. Ryan flew over the frontend. His right knee struck the throttle body, sending a blast of pain through his leg. Instinctively, he stuck his hands out to catch himself. Skin tore from his palms as he slid through the dirt before coming to a halt in the ditch at the side of the road.

After a moment, he scrambled to his feet. Every part of him ached and blood dripped from his ruined skin. His left hand was still numb from being struck by the rock. He worked his fingers in and out to restore blood flow and feeling. He shook them to throw off the pain, muttering curse words at Diego, the dirt bike, and his incompetent riding skills.

Then he picked up the bike, remounted it, and kicked it back to life. He revved the throttle and spun the tire as he pulled away, racing after Diego.

The crash had given the Puerto Rican the advantage. Ryan would have to work hard to catch up. He leaned forward over the bars to streamline his body. The road straightened then curved to follow the steep karst cliffs through which the river flowed. Ryan had no idea where he was or where they were going.

A flash of yellow showed where Diego turned off the road. Ryan downshifted and braked to make the turn. Again, they were on tight single track through dense forests. They climbed over a mountain and down into another valley. The trees were sparser and the riding easier. Ryan increased his speed to catch Diego. This time, he would get close enough to put a bullet in the man and end this chase. He had to keep a light hand on the bars, or the ripped skin of his palms became searing pain. His knee throbbed, and his knuckles were numb. To top off his worries, he didn't know how much fuel the bike had left.

On a far mountain peak, Ryan could see the three towers of the Arecibo Observatory. Diego angled toward them, charging up one of the steep mountains to where the thousand-foot diameter spherical reflector nestled in a giant sink hole.

The dense underbrush made for difficult navigation, but it was obvious Diego had been this way before. When they crested the summit, he cut around a massive concrete anchor for the reflector support cables and onto a small access road just wide enough for one vehicle. Low stone barrier walls ran along the sides of the road. Overgrown vegetation clutched at them as they passed.

Coming abreast of Diego's left side, Ryan kicked him in the leg. Diego flinched and swerved away, ducking under a low branch. As Ryan came abreast of him again, Diego veered toward him. Ryan hit the front brakes, and the tire skidded on the pavement, letting Diego slide past.

Ryan released the brake and twisted the throttle. The bike shot forward and his front tire rammed Diego's rear.

Diego's tire skidded on the pavement. The whole bike turned sideways, tires spinning on the slick pavement. Without warning, the rear tire caught traction, whipping the bike back straight and catapulting Diego into the air.

Both Diego and the riderless motorcycle flipped and rolled.

The spinning motorcycle knocked the front tire out from under Ryan's bike. He fell off, sliding across the pavement. He tucked his arms into his sides and rolled. He had a weird view of the scene as he spun, watching the motorcycles crash and flip, then rolling to a view of open road and sky.

When he came to rest, he lay on his back. Pain radiated from every nerve. His knees were skinned and bloody where the asphalt had torn away the pants. Purple bruises formed on his elbows, and his palms had lost more skin. The helmet visor hung by one screw. Ryan closed his eyes, muscles sagging. The stars behind his eyelids flashed with the pounding in his brain.

Hearing movement, his eyes snapped open, remembering why he was here. One of the Suzukis lay on the road, its seat missing, the handlebars snapped in two. Diego was picking up the other one. It looked rideable. One side of Diego's helmet had a gash in it, exposing the white composite material below the painted shell. His knees were a mass of bloodied blue jeans, and his right arm was missing its skin from wrist to elbow. Still, the injuries weren't preventing him from trying to escape.

Ryan rolled to all fours. His skull pounded, but Diego already had the bike upright and was kicking the starter. The engine roared to life.

A white truck sped toward them and came to a screeching halt, blocking the road. Diego feathered the clutch, using the bike's spinning rear wheel to pivot the bike around his planted leg, and charged away from the truck.

Still on all fours, Ryan jerked his Glock from its holster and tried to bring it around. As he rocketed past Ryan, Diego stuck out his leg and kicked Ryan solidly in the ribs.

The stars that had circled his head earlier returned. He fell face first onto the pavement, wrapping his rib cage with his arms. He moaned in pain and rolled onto his back. His fingers trembled while he worked the chin strap loose. The pressure on his skull lessened as he pushed off the helmet and drew in a deep breath.

"Oh, man," he moaned, wrapping his ribs again. "That freaking hurt."

A tall man with a salt-and-pepper beard and dark brown hair knelt beside him. "You okay, son?"

"No," Ryan groaned.

"Well, if it's any consolation, you don't look like the belle of the ball, either." Salt and Pepper glanced around the accident scene, then back at Ryan. "I'll be right back."

Ryan nodded and watched the man walk to the truck. He stood in the open doorway and called someone on a two-way radio. Ryan sat up, holding his ribs with his right hand and used his left to help scoot himself backward to lean against the stone wall.

When would his ribs get a break? He'd first injured them jumping from the roof of a house in Mexico almost a year ago and had been bumping them ever since. At least today the chicken plates in his chest rig had kept the sharp points of pistol magazines and knife handles from stabbing him and had provided some protection during the accident. But they did little for the kick in the side.

He pulled a knee up to examine the gravel imbedded in the skin. Blood oozed out from the open wounds. Arching his back to loosen it, he sat up straighter and got more comfortable against the rock wall.

When Salt and Pepper returned, he had a first aid kit. He knelt beside Ryan. "I called in the accident." He used a pair of trauma sheers to cut off Ryan's pants above his knees. Then he sprayed antiseptic on the hamburgered skin. With great care, he pulled the small chunks of rock from Ryan's flesh with tweezers. Before bandaging, he washed away the blood with water.

"You're pretty good at that," Ryan said.

"I was an FMF corpsman back during Desert Storm."

"I was Navy EOD," Ryan said.

Salt and Pepper glanced up and met Ryan's eyes. The two men shared an instant bond of service, even if one had been a Navy medic for the Marine Corps. Ryan wouldn't hold it against him. The Bullet Catchers needed to be patched up, too.

"Ryan Weller."

"Dane Jones."

Ryan coughed. "Nice to meet you, Dane."

Dane continued to work on a large cut on Ryan's left leg. "What are you guys doing up here?"

"I'm working with the police. Diego, the guy who rode away, is the leader of a theft ring. He escaped a raid on his compound, and I gave chase."

Dane nodded. He taped the knee wound closed and sat back on his haunches. "I asked the office to call an ambulance. It won't get here anytime soon."

"I need to call my partners." Ryan slipped a cell phone from his pocket.

"There's no signal up here. That's why I used the radio."

Ryan put the phone away.

"Let me see your hands," Dane said.

Ryan held his hands out, palms up, for the man to examine.

"Those will be painful for quite some time." He dumped antiseptic on them, and Ryan howled. "Sorry." He pulled a roll of gauze from the first aid kit.

When he finished wrapping his hands, Ryan stood up. His head ached, and he wobbled for a moment, bending down to place his hands on his knees—a decision he regretted instantly, as pain coursed through both. Dane guided him back to the stone wall, and Ryan dropped heavily to his butt. Dane handed the water bottle to Ryan and he took several long drinks.

Far in the distance, he heard the faint sound of the four-stroke dirt bike engine as Diego applied full power. He'd escaped, and Ryan wasn't looking forward to telling Vargas or Greg.

CHAPTER THIRTY-SIX

Ryan and Dane Jones watched from inside the cab of the white Ford pickup as a Kawasaki BK117 helicopter settled onto the landing pad near the Arecibo Observatory administration building. When the chopper's rotors slowed, the co-pilot waved Ryan forward.

Ryan gingerly shook Dane's hand and exited the truck. He ran to the helicopter and climbed in beside Rick and Vargas.

They lifted off, and Ryan had a bird's-eye view of the terrain he and Diego had negotiated on their dirt bikes. He pressed his head to the window and looked down at the yellow bike still sprawled on the pavement. The pilot dipped the nose of the bird and turned west.

Ten minutes later, they landed at the Utuado hospital. They escorted Ryan to the emergency room to have his wounds treated. When he walked in, the male nurse who had wheeled him in several weeks ago looked displeased.

Ryan grinned at him.

The man narrowed his eyes and held up his hands in surrender. "*Ay, papi.*"

Vargas laughed. "Your reputation precedes you."

"I may or may not have escaped from custody here. Nothing has been proven."

"We can prove it," Vargas said. "It's on video."

The nurses treated Ryan's wounds, applying more antiseptic ointment to his hands and cleaning the rest of the gravel from his knees. They bandaged his road rash and left him to wait for discharge instructions.

Greg and Rick came in after the doctor had seen Ryan.

"You doing okay?" Greg asked.

"I'll be all right." Ryan sat on the edge of the bed. He held his ribs as he did so.

"Hurt the ribs again?"

"Yeah. Doc says their bruised and I should take it easy."

Rick said, "I'm ready to go back to my hammock and piña coladas. Maybe even fly some tourists around."

"I'm with you," Ryan agreed. "I need a break from all this action."

"You had six months off to play in the Florida Keys," Greg said.

"Yeah, and I need another six months off to get my ribs healed up. I'd like to breathe without sharp, stabbing pain."

Rick grimaced. "I'm with you there, buddy."

Ryan eased himself back down in the bed. His breath caught in his throat when he tried to fill his lungs. "Holy shit, that hurts."

Greg wheeled over to the window. "We still don't know if Shawn is part of the operation."

Rick added, "If he is, he'll need to find another transporter."

"Guess there's only one way to find out," Ryan said.

"What way is that?" Vargas asked as he entered the room. He carried two cups of coffee and set one down on the tray beside Ryan's bed.

Ryan leaned forward, wincing as he did so. He raised the cup in a silent toast to the inspector.

Everyone waited for Ryan to answer. He took a sip of the coffee and glanced around at the expectant faces. "We go ask him again."

"We tried that, remember?" Greg said. "He got indignant and threw us out of his office."

Ryan shrugged. "All the more reason to poke the bear again."

Vargas made a hand gesture to quiet the others. "Forensics is digging through the paperwork we found at the compound. Some of it was burnt deliberately. Let them piece together the puzzle on their end and see what we get."

Everyone nodded.

"In the meantime," Vargas added, "get that ship of yours refitted so you can get off my island."

Ryan grinned. "I was just beginning to like it here."

CHAPTER THIRTY-SEVEN

Joulie Lafitte pushed the stack of paperwork to one side of her desk and let out a sigh. Running businesses and funding infrastructure projects was more taxing than being a warlord.

While she missed having Ryan's help, she admitted the situation with him had gotten more complicated than she'd expected. Their personal lives and monetary funds had comingled, and then there was the con job he'd pulled to get her to look after James.

He was a sweet kid and charmed everyone he met, but Joulie hadn't wanted to be a mother. She barely had enough patience to deal with incompetent employees, let alone raise a child. She realized the same attitude, coupled with abject poverty, led many Haitians to turn their children over to more affluent relatives or other members of society in a process known as restavek, a form of slavery. Joulie was loath to tackle the issue without providing her people with economic means of support, first, so children wouldn't need to be enslaved.

Ryan had put her in a bind with James. She had prayed to the loa and asked for advice, but they were strangely silent.

Joulie had also hired a nanny to help her care for James. Esther was older than Joulie. She had raised several children of her own and used a firm hand with James. It wasn't until Joulie had confided in her late one evening about the silence of the loa that Esther had told her she was asking for the wrong thing. Joulie should not be asking for a sign, but strength to keep the child. The loa had given her the sign by bringing James to her.

Joulie had asked the new question and received an answer. If she respected her lover, she would do as he asked.

But they had also given her a message about Ryan. The loa had brought him to her and now they were sending him away. She must trust they knew best.

Mambo Joulie reached for the phone and dialed the number Ryan had given her. A woman answered in Spanish. In English, Joulie asked to speak to Shawn Lindowel.

A moment later, Lindowel answered.

Joulie said, "I understand you have containers for sale?"

"Yes," Shawn replied. "We sell used containers for several shipping companies."

"You misunderstood my question. I want to buy containers with … certain legal discrepancies."

"I don't know what you mean."

"You do, Mr. Lindowel," she purred. "I want to be part of your pipeline to dispose of your stolen containers."

The phone line went dead.

"He hung up on me," Joulie muttered to herself.

She redialed the number and asked to speak to Shawn again.

The man's anger carried through the phone line. "Lady, I don't know what game you're playing, but my shipping company operates above board. We do not sell illegally acquired goods or containers."

"Sir let me explain," Joulie said, trying to let honey drip from her voice. "It's my understanding that Diego Hernández is helping you move stolen containers out of Puerto Rico. I would like to purchase those containers and have them shipped to Haiti."

"Look, lady," Shawn said. Joulie could tell he was straining to keep his voice under control. "I don't know ...." Shawn stopped, drew in a deep breath, then asked, "What is it you're looking for?"

"Construction materials, food staples, clothing, car parts. Whatever you can send. I'm trying to improve my country, and your resources would be of great help."

"How did you get my number?"

Joulie smiled. "A mutual friend gave it to me."

"Diego?"

"He is one of our mutual friends." Joulie stood and walked to the window. The manicured hotel grounds reminded her of her home when she was a child, before the earthquake had destroyed her village and killed her parents. Near the high stone wall, surrounding the property, James and a valet were playing catch.

Silence filled the phone line as she waited for a response.

"What's your name?" Shawn finally asked.

"Joulie Lafitte."

"And you're in Haiti?"

"Yes, Mr. Lindowel."

"How will you pay for shipment?"

"Cash via courier, perhaps gold bars if you're inclined."

"Gold?"

"*Wi.*"

"Let me get back to you."

"I'll give you my personal number." Joulie recited her

digits. There was something about his behavior she couldn't put a finger on. He'd started out indignant then changed his tack. It was as if he were gathering information from her.

Joulie continued to watch James toss the ball after she'd hung up the phone. In the weeks since Ryan had left, she'd spent every evening with James. The loa Ezili Dantò was forging the mother-child bond within her.

Damn Ryan for being right.

CHAPTER THIRTY-EIGHT

Shawn Lindowel turned his chair, rested his right hand on the desk, and drummed his fingers on the desk blotter while staring out the window. He stood and picked up his putter. He always thought better with a golf club in his hand.

Bending over the club, he positioned his feet and set his body over the ball. With a short stroke, he nudged the ball across the thick, gray carpet toward the putter returner. He missed the returner, the ball's path diverted by the carpet fibers. Shawn used the club to move another ball in front of him and sent it down range. This one hit the hole, and the returner shot it back to him.

A smile crept across his face. He loved the short game. After he retired from the shipping industry, he could make the rounds on the amateur golf circuit. He already played in local tournaments and had won several. He happened to be one of seven scratch players on the island.

His smile faded with the memory of the phone call from the Haitian woman. She believed he was dealing in stolen cargo. He'd stolen nothing since he'd taken a candy bar from a convenience store in sixth grade on a dare from his friends.

His Catholic guilt had made him return to the store, confess his crime, and pay for the candy.

Not only was he accountable to his partner but to the businesses they dealt with. They put their faith and trust in him to deliver their goods on schedule. What made this crazy woman think he was involved in anything illegal? And who was this Diego who'd given her his number?

Shawn leaned his club against the bookcase and poured a shot of rum. He started to recap the bottle, then poured himself another shot. His Catholic guilt didn't extend to drinking. Maybe his drinking resulted from Catholic guilt? He held up the liquor in a mock toast to his father, a devout Catholic who had driven him to succeed and to drink. While sipping the liquor, he sat down at the desk and opened a web browser. He typed in *Diego Hernández*.

He sipped the rum again. It burned down his throat, and bile roiled in his stomach when he saw the mugshot of Diego Hernández under a headline about a raid on his compound in Utuado. He knew Diego. The man had been in his office multiple times to visit Marcela Fuentes. The viper had nested in Shawn's den.

CHAPTER THIRTY-NINE

Marcela Fuentes hung up the phone and straightened papers on her desk. When she was nervous or angry, she cleaned or did something productive to soothe her soul. She thought of it as nesting. As she filed paperwork and examined every manifest, she tried to think of other things besides Diego and their failed attempts to have a baby.

She and Diego had first met when she was eleven, and she remembered it like it was yesterday. She had been in the yard outside her house on the outskirts of town and had looked up to see a gangly boy about her age coming down the hill, leading three other children. He wore a mischievous grin as he approached and pointed her out to his siblings. Diego danced in, snatched her rag doll from the chair it was sitting in, and tossed it as far into the bushes as he could. Marcela had burst into tears, and Diego's gang had erupted in laughter.

She recalled the words she had hurled at him, using the fact that his skin was lighter than his siblings as leverage: "*Está brutal hijo de lechero de pendejo.*" *You brutal, slow-witted son of a milkman.*

He'd been furious, and she remembered the look of anger clouding his face. She'd touched a raw nerve she didn't know he had. Diego kicked over her small, plastic table and stomped the doll's wooden chair until it lay broken in dozens of pieces. She fled into the house to hide from his tantrum.

Four years later, he apologized, and at the tender age of fourteen, they'd shared their first kiss. She was positive that even though he lived in Miami, she would one day marry him, and when he returned from his stint in military prison, she had. It didn't bother her to marry a criminal. She adored the man, and his logistical genius was providing them money for a family.

What had started as a way to help the people of the storm ravaged island had turned into a lucrative business, selling stolen shipping containers for profit through a Miami auction site they'd found on the dark web. The money went to fertility clinics and expensive drugs for both her and Diego, yet her womb remained barren and, now, their criminal enterprise was in jeopardy.

Diego's shaky attempts at two ambushes had gone spectacularly wrong, forcing him into hiding. His knees and palms were missing hunks of flesh, and he'd sustained a concussion from falling off a motorcycle and hitting his helmet against a stone wall. She never liked those noisy dirt bikes. If he hadn't been wearing a helmet, he would be dead, and then where would she be? Alone again, living with her parents, with no prospects of a child or a life?

No, she needed to resolve this. The best way was to escape. A plan began to formulate in her mind. The deck cargo ship, *Island Trader*, sister of *Star of Ceiba*, was due to arrive in Fajardo in four days to take their shipment to Miami. For a little more money, the already handsomely paid captains would give her and Diego a ride to Florida, where they could blend in seamlessly with the large Puerto Rican and Latino populations.

Selling the containers at auction meant extra money, but there was an easier, faster way. She opened an incognito browser on her computer and searched for Joulie Lafitte. Marcela had no use for gold bars, but she'd take cash. The monitor froze for a moment, and a swell of disgust flowed through her for the island's slow Internet service.

When the results loaded, she clicked on the images tab and scrolled through the photos of the Haitian warlord. At the bottom of the page, she saw a photo that made her pause. Joulie's face was lit by candlelight flickering from small jars on a snowy white tablecloth. A handsome white man leaned in, arm around the back of her chair, lips near her ear. With the other hand, he refilled a wine glass from a bottle wrapped in a towel. His tanned face gazed intently at Joulie, not the wine splashing into the cup. Even in the low-resolution image, she could see the sparkle in their eyes.

From the angle of the photo, Marcela thought someone had taken it in secret, as the restaurant looked empty and the couple intimately cozy. Joulie Lafitte had a *blanquito*—an uppity white person—as a lover.

Marcela knew the little *chota*—snitch. Ryan Weller.

CHAPTER FORTY

Inspector Manuel Vargas knocked on the door of the small, neatly kept residence in the San Juan suburb of Bayamón while Ryan Weller sat in the front of the cop's car. Standing behind Vargas were two uniformed officers. A second pair of cops were just disappearing around the back of the house.

Ryan glanced up and down the street. Every house had bars over the windows and doors. The single two-story house he could see had spikes pointing outward on the railing of the second-story balcony. The shutters and bars made the homes look particularly uninviting. He wondered if the crime was really that bad or if these people were preparing for the zombie apocalypse.

Several houses had well-trimmed yards, while others were nothing more than bare dirt or ragged weeds with scraggly bushes and shaggy trees. A few palms peeked over the neighboring roofs. Clouds raced across the sky, overcasting the neighborhood, turning the houses into shabby, dark shells.

Phillipe Fernandez's front yard was one massive slab of concrete. A driveway extended from the street to the rear of the property, allowing Phillipe to park his tractor and trailer. This morning only the Kenworth T800B tractor sat beside an ancient Ford pickup, painted a mixture of battered green and rust primer gray. The house's tan stucco contrasted with the white vertical bars, giving it the appearance of a prison cell. The iron door was more ornamental, with curved scroll work.

Vargas beat harder on the metal, making it rattle. It had been breezy when Ryan awoken that morning, but now a harsh wind swept over the island, lashing at the trees and men's clothing. Even though it was near eighty, Ryan only rolled the window halfway down to ward off the chill.

The inspector hammered the door again.

The shape of a woman moved onto the porch, staying behind the bars. Vargas held up a warrant to search the premises and his badge. Ryan couldn't hear what they were saying over the wind, but he got the gist of the conversation. They were searching for her husband, Phillipe, and demanding she either let them into the house or tell them where he was staying. Ryan had been instructed to remain in the car while La Uniformada searched the property, but when they had the truck driver, he could sit in on the interrogation.

The heavy bars swung outward, and Ryan saw an old woman, strands of gray hair blowing across her wrinkled face. She wore a colorful apron over a white skirt and a yellow blouse. Vargas went through the door, the wind slamming it shut behind him, and the uniformed officers spread out to flank the iron gate.

Ryan glanced at his watch and wondered how long it would take to go through the place.

Fernandez would, hopefully, give them a lead to find Diego Hernández. After the criminal's escape from the observatory, Vargas had put out a BOLO and released Diego's picture to the media. There had been a large write-up in the morning paper and several news stories filmed and broadcasted from the compound near Utuado.

Greg had congratulated Ryan for putting a stop to the thefts, but Diego was still on the loose, and there were plenty of other bad actors who needed to be rounded up, especially Shawn Lindowel. Ryan couldn't, in good conscious, stop the investigation. He needed to see it through until the end.

A uniform held the ornamental door open to keep it from blowing closed as Vargas stepped through, pushing a man in front of him. The prisoner was in his fifties, with neatly trimmed dark hair, a weather-lined face, and downcast eyes. Wind whipped at his flannel work shirt and blue jeans. With his hands cuffed behind his back, he shuffled toward Vargas's car and climbed inside when the inspector opened the rear door. Vargas bent and retrieved one of the man's flip-flops and tossed it onto the seat beside the prisoner.

They rode across town to the police station, where Vargas booked Phillipe Fernandez with accessory to theft.

Vargas put him in an interrogation room. The driver detailed every aspect of his misadventures. Knowing he'd eventually be caught, he had planned to turn state's evidence and had kept a journal of dates, times, container numbers, and ports of call.

Ryan watched through the two-way mirror as Vargas hounded Phillipe about various aspects of the operation. The driver described how he had received fictitious manifests, picked up the load, and delivered it to the destination. Diego paid him via direct deposit into a local bank account in his wife's name. When asked why he had taken to a life of crime, the man had shrugged and said, "*Mucho chavos.*" *Lots of money*.

Then Vargas got around to asking the question Ryan wanted him to ask from the beginning: "Where's Diego?"

Phillipe shrugged. "You raided his hideout in Utuado; that is the only place I saw him."

"Give us the names of other truck drivers Diego used," Vargas demanded.

"They are in the notebook," Phillipe said. "I only knew a few from Guaynabo."

Ryan guessed they wouldn't get any more information from the old man and wandered out of the room to find a cup of coffee. They needed a new plan to find Diego.

CHAPTER FORTY-ONE

Peggy Lynn hung by a web of straps between the massive blue legs of the TraveLift. Ryan always held his breath when the TraveLift was moving his boat. There were so many things that could go wrong. He watched the lift driver use a remote control to maneuver the lift toward the purpose-built piers and the safety of the water where *Peggy Lynn* lived.

Glancing to his right, Captain Dennis Law, dressed in his usual khakis, red T-shirt, and white tennis shoes, stalked the driver, watching his movements like a hawk. Behind him, Travis Wisnewski and Stacey Coleman, fresh from their trip to the States, walked hand in hand. Out front, the octogenarian first mate, Emery Ducane, kept an eye on the two men helping to guide the driver.

The heavy tires rolled onto the piers; black rubber glistening wet from the early morning rain. Everyone breathed a collective sigh of relief when *Peggy Lynn* nestled into the cool, blue water. Workers scrambled to unweave the straps and pull them free before they backed the lift off the pier.

Travis and Ryan used the bow and stern lines to pull *Peggy Lynn* to the dock. Dennis jumped aboard and stepped onto the bridge. A moment later, the twin diesels snorted to life. Ryan smiled. He loved that sound. Whether on a work boat or a dive boat, the starting of the engines signaled the beginning of the adventure. *Peggy Lynn* had a new lease on life, and new journeys awaited her and her crew. Greg had found them salvage work further down the island chain, but they needed to test the new systems, break in the engines, and do a shakedown cruise before going anywhere.

As he worked, Ryan mulled over the theft investigation. Vargas and his crew were serving warrants for Shawn's home and office as *Peggy Lynn*'s crew refloated her. Ryan had elected to help splash the salvage vessel.

Travis wrapped the stern line around a cleat. He had foregone his shirt to even out his farmer's tan. His muscular arms were deep brown, and the rest of his body printer paper white. He was a Yooper, from Houghton, on the finger of Michigan's Upper Peninsula, which stuck into Lake Superior. He'd taken Stacey to meet his folks before driving south to Alcoa, Tennessee, where Stacey had grown up. Somewhere in the Smokey Mountains, he'd put a ring on it. Stacey beamed with happiness, and the diamond on her finger reflected the sparkle in her eyes. Ryan patted himself on the back for bringing the couple together.

Stacey had re-dyed her hair to a deep purple. A fresh tattoo of a kraken stretched from the elbow of her right arm to her shoulder, the tentacles spreading out across her collar bone and shoulder blades.

Ryan coiled a line while Emery and Don Williams huddled beside the open engine bay doors, monitoring their performance on a mobile app. The diesels snarled quietly. Everything about the ship seemed new. Even the crane boom and supports, which sprouted out of the deck to form an A-frame tower above the wheelhouse, had been reinforced and the drum winch motors overhauled. Shiny, braided steel cable replaced its rusted and frayed predecessor.

Something nagged at Ryan, making his guts ripple and his pulse race. There was too much unfinished business in his life to just climb on *Peggy Lynn* and sail away. Between the cargo thieves and Joulie, he needed closure. At least he could assist Vargas or chase his own leads, but there was nothing he could do about Joulie until she told him what she was thinking.

With no other leads, he was at the mercy of Vargas's team of forensic officers. They'd found more evidence in Diego's compound linking Diego and Caribbean Maritime Shipping to Shawn, even recovering manifests signed by Shawn from the burned piles of paperwork.

"Hey, Ryan, get your head out of the clouds," Dennis yelled.

Ryan looked up to see the captain leaning on the railing, staring at him. "What?"

"I've hollered at you five times now, and you just stood there holding the line."

"Sorry, I was thinking about something else."

"I know you was, but we got work to do here. Don't fret none about what you can't change."

Ryan tossed the rope on the quay. "What did you need?"

"I wanted you to cast off, so we can move to the other slip."

"Roger that," Ryan said, picking up the coiled rope and unwinding it from the cleat.

When he stood, everyone was looking at him. He shifted his gaze to Dennis. At his signal, Ryan tossed the line aboard, went to give the bow a push with his foot at the same time Dennis gunned the bow thruster, and almost fell off the pier.

Ryan regained his balance, smiled sheepishly at everyone laughing at him, and shoved his hands into his pockets, watching the vessel get underway for the first time in two months. Travis leaped aboard as Dennis backed *Peggy Lynn* away from the dedicated lift dock, taking her to the transient pier where'd they be until they left Puerto Rico when sea trials were complete.

Peggy Lynn drifted backward out of the slip. Dennis bumped the throttle to goose the right propeller to swing the bow, then engaged both drives when the old boat straightened. For decades, he'd been the master of the throttles and drives. Once he got the hang of the thrusters, he'd always use them.

Ryan's ringing cell phone startled him from his thoughts.

"Do you want to hear some juicy gossip?" Gabriella asked from the other end of the line when he answered.

"Do I want to know where this juicy gossip came from?"

"No, so don't ask. Turns out Diego Hernández and Marcela Fuentes, the secretary for L&F Logistics, are married."

"Are you kidding me?" Ryan said.

"I'm not. What are you doing right now?"

"Not much."

"Walk to the parking lot."

He spun, phone still pressed to his ear, and walked past the ungainly boats sitting "on the hard" a sailor's term for a boat sitting on dry land with their intricate cribbing and blocks. Stepping out of the boatyard, he spied Gabriella's silver Honda Accord idling near the marina office. She waved to him from the passenger seat.

Ryan ended the call, walked to the car, and squatted by the window. "Aren't you supposed to be in the hospital?"

"They discharged me yesterday."

He glanced at Inspector Vargas in the driver's seat. "What are you doing here? You condone this?"

Rolling his eyes, Vargas said, "Get in the car, Weller."

Ryan got in the back seat.

Vargas asked, "You got a gun on you?"

"Yeah."

Twenty minutes of driving brought them to Calle Roberto Clemente Calderon, the eastern border of San Juan. Beyond a chain-link fence, the land had a marshy quality, Ryan's map app showed a creek and several large ponds. Stands of royal poinciana trees with orange blossoms, palms, and smaller patches of woods bordered the road.

To the west were houses, some brightly painted and well-maintained, while others were half-finished with incomplete upper stories, partial rows of concrete block halted in mid progress. Nearly every home had hurricane damage. Garbage littered the street, and parked vehicles on both sides of the narrow road forced Vargas to weave in and out.

He eventually slowed and pointed at a two-story home. "That's where Marcela Fuentes lives."

Ryan leaned over to gaze at the residence through the rear passenger window. The bottom bore a depressing shade of gray, almost indistinguishable from the upper story's bare block. A blue border painted above the three arches of the front porch matched the frayed blue FEMA tarp on the roof. The jalousie windows were open, and the only bars were in the fence at the edge of the sidewalk, set atop a twelve-inch-high poured concrete footer. Various gardening tools crowded the back of an attached carport, but it was devoid of any vehicles. Untamed vegetation grew between the carport and the neighbor's fence, covering a set of stairs to the upper level of Marcela's home.

Ryan said, "That's a big house for one lady, especially here in Puerto Rico."

Vargas nodded. "She's got family living with her, a brother, and his wife and kids, and her mother."

"Diego is in there?" Ryan craned his neck to see out the back window as they rolled past.

"Possibly," Gabriella replied.

Vargas pulled the car into a parking spot and put the transmission in park. He turned to face Ryan. "We received a tip that Diego's been spotted here. I didn't have time to get a warrant, so we can't go in there, but you, *amigo* ..."

"*Gufiao*," Ryan replied. *Cool*. It wasn't lost on Ryan that the inspector had taken a new tone with him. He was using Ryan to flush out their quarry, and Ryan was okay with being the bird dog.

"This dude is *mas trucos que la carrea de Batman.*"

Ryan was picking up the Puerto Rican slang, but this one was new to him. He looked at Vargas questioningly.

Gabriella translated for him. "Diego is tricky, lots of tricks up his sleeve."

"Oh," Ryan replied, picturing the caped crusader with his utility belt and high-tech gadgetry. Diego was no Dark Knight. In a gravelly voice, he added, "No, I'm Batman."

The two puzzled inspectors glanced at each other and back at Ryan. He shrugged.

Gabriella then grinned at Vargas. "*Sí, el esta loco.*"

"Hey, I'm not crazy," Ryan retorted.

"Go check it out, bichote."

Ryan used his map app to acquire a satellite view of the neighborhood. Marcela's property had high walls on three sides and iron bars across the front. There was no choice but to scale walls. On the street to the west, all but one house had fence along the sidewalk.

"Drive around the block. I'll get out, and you circle around, and park close to Marcela's place."

As they came to the property Ryan had identified as his entry, he saw it was a low-slung single story with an overgrown lot beside a larger home with extensive damage to its roof. Mature trees shaded the backyards and fences.

"Slow down to walking speed," Ryan instructed.

He poised himself, hand on the door lever, ready to step out. His muscles tightened; a tingling pervaded his flesh. Abreast of the weed infested yard, he stepped from the slowly rolling Accord, swung the door closed behind him, and jogged alongside the house. His skin was the wrong color to be hanging around, taking in the sights. If Diego had guards or lookouts, they'd tell him a blanquito was prowling the fences and, hopefully, Diego would bolt into the inspector's waiting arms.

Ryan scrambled up the concrete block wall and paused at the top, hidden in the foliage of a calabash tree. Diego's hideout was one yard away. Carefully, he crawled along the narrow fence to clear the low-hanging tree limbs then stood, balancing with his arms outstretched and walked to the corner. He turned it, using a tree limb for balance, and moved through a thicket of Puerto Rican hat palms. When he came to Marcela's property, he dropped to the ground, fighting through the large leaves of a banana tree. He started swiping furiously at a spider web plastered across his eyes and mouth. Spiders didn't bother him, but getting a web stuck to his face caused near hysteria.

No matter how hard he shook his hand, the sticky web clung to his fingers, and he had to wipe it off on the rough bark of a palm. His heartbeat, already high from the exercise and stealth tactics, had sped up exponentially, and he took several long, calming breaths to get it under control. While he did so, he studied the layout. Three steps led up to a rear entry door. Stone paths radiated out from the steps, and flowers grew between the paths. Nothing moved except the trees swaying in the wind. A dog barked far off, and somewhere; a baby cried.

Moving cautiously toward the house in a crouch, Ryan listened for any indication that someone had spotted him. He stopped moving when he glimpsed yellow plastic. The Suzuki dirt bike leaned against the carport wall.

Then, a rattling at the front of the house drew his attention. It sounded like a garage door running up its track, but he knew there wasn't a garage door. It had to be the gate opening. He wished he could communicate with Gabriella and Vargas. What was happening out front?

He raced to the house and pressed his shoulders to the rough stucco on the hinge side of the door. Standing on tip toes, he could see through the open window. The slant of the panes gave him an unobstructed view of a small but tidy kitchen.

Diego dashed down a hall, pulling a helmet over his head. He plunged through the door, slamming it open so hard it smacked the wall beside Ryan and made him jump. Diego leaped from the threshold, not bothering with steps on his way to the dirt bike.

Ryan ran after the smaller man, crashing into him as he tried to mount the motorcycle. He wrapped his arms around Diego's muscular torso and drove the escapee into the dirt. Ryan's chin hit the helmet, and his teeth rattled. He kept his grip as Diego struggled under him. The man freed an arm and wrapped it around Ryan's neck in a headlock. Pinned against Diego's side, face in the dirt, Ryan thrashed to free himself. The grasp was too powerful.

Diego rolled, tightening his hold and clamping his other arm against Ryan's head to complete the choke hold. Ryan could barely breathe, the constricting lock pinching his arteries and slowing the blood flow to his brain. He'd pass out if he didn't escape. Diego circled Ryan's waist with his legs, locking his ankles together and clinching his muscles.

Ryan stopped struggling and took several shallow, ragged breaths, trying to force oxygen into his lungs. Blackness ringed his vision. This was not how he wanted to die.

He rolled, forcing his opponent onto his back, Ryan spread eagle on top of him. His elbow strikes missed everything but hard earth. Darkness formed hollow tunnels of vision, the world's vibrant colors fading away. Each heartbeat pounded in his head as his heart slowed. *Thump. Thuummmp. Thuuummmpppp.* He was going out.

In a desperate move, Ryan struggled to all fours and swiftly stood. Diego cinched his holds tighter, his legs crushing the bruised ribs. Pain radiated through Ryan's chest. Even if the Boricua wasn't choking him, he'd struggle to breathe against the bruised muscles. He ran backward at full speed and slammed Diego into the wall of the carport.

With a loud cry of pain, Diego let go, and Ryan's knees gave out. He fell face first into the dirt, chest heaving as his diaphragm struggled to draw in air, hand clutching his raw throat.

Ryan thrashed himself onto his knees, knowing Diego was coming for him again, and Diego wasted no effort this time, slamming his foot into Ryan's rib cage. He howled with pain and curled into the fetal position.

Diego ran for the Suzuki. Through the fog of pain and oxygen deprivation, Ryan heard the bike's engine start with a throaty roar. He closed his eyes as grass and sand pelted his face and body. Then Diego was gone.

CHAPTER FORTY-TWO

Ryan heard shouting through the open windows, followed by running footsteps on hard tile floors. Clutching his torso with both arms, he rolled to see the house's back door. Two men jumped into the yard, taking up positions on either side of Ryan. Both screamed in Spanish as an old woman wobbled bow-legged down the steps. She used a corn broom for a cane as she approached the prostrate American.

This wasn't good. He was on the ground with three unknown persons surrounding him. He discounted the woman, probably Marcela's mother, and focused on the men. They had spread out to flank the matriarch. To get to his gun, he needed to roll to his left, which put his back to the threat. They had to know why he was in their backyard, and he had no doubts they'd kick him while he was down.

The old woman smacked him with the broom head. The stiff bristles left welts and cut his forearm. He twisted and snatched the Walther from its holster, pointing it at the woman.

"*Alto, alto,*" *Stop, stop,* he tried to shout, but his words came out in wheezes. He squeezed his elbows against his sides, struggling to quell the ache and keep the pistol trained on the broom-wielding threat. She glowered at him, holding the broom at port arms, ready to pelt him again. The men put their hands into the air and backed up.

Ryan pushed backward with his feet to put more ground between him and Diego's posse, but gave up because the movement hurt too much. He swung the pistol, aiming at the base of a large palm, and pulled the trigger.

The gun roared, and Marcela's mother ran into the house, leaving her broom.

A moment later, Vargas rounded the carport with his handgun drawn. "Are you okay, bichote?"

"No." Ryan holstered his pistol and rolled to his hands and knees. He paused and crouched on the balls of his feet, fighting through the pain before rising to his feet.

Ryan and Vargas climbed into the Honda. Ryan saw concern on Gabriella's face. He sprawled on the rear seat and let out a deep moan.

"Suck it up, Batman," Vargas said with a grin.

Ryan flipped him the middle finger.

Vargas drove to the marina, and Ryan led them to *Dark Water*. Gabriella hobbled along the dock on crutches, keeping the weight off her injured limb. It amazed Ryan that she had the fortitude to use crutches with the damage to her shoulder.

He found an ice pack in the freezer, wrapped it in a towel, and laid it on her wound when she was sitting on the salon couch. Vargas dropped down beside her with a sigh. Ryan gave him a beer and opened one for himself.

"Hey, what about me?" Greg demanded.

Ryan grabbed him a beer and set it on the table.

"What happened to you guys?" Greg asked after a sip.

"I got my ribs kicked in, again." Ryan eased into the settee alongside the boat's owner.

"And he let Diego get away. Again," Vargas said before taking a drink.

"What were *you* doing?" Greg asked Vargas.

"He was sitting in the car," Ryan interjected, "letting me do all the work."

"You volunteered," Vargas shot back.

Gabriella rolled her eyes. "It doesn't matter."

She was right. Either way, Diego was gone.

Greg asked, "What happened to Diego?"

"He disappeared into the swamp on his motorbike," Vargas said. "There was no way we could follow him."

"What about your forensic people?" Greg asked.

Vargas glanced at his watch, then checked his phone. "They're still rooting through Lindowel's computers."

"Let's think about this for a minute," Greg said. "Everything points to Shawn, but his secretary and Diego Hernández are married. What if she's feeding the information to Diego? She has the forms, access to the shipments, and knew we were putting trackers on the containers."

Gabriella cut in, "She knew you were investigating the thefts and had opportunity and motive to set you up for the ambushes and the murder of those men in Ponce."

"She tried to murder a cop," Vargas added.

"But is she the mastermind of this whole operation?" Ryan asked.

With indignation, Gabriella said, "A woman can't be a mastermind?"

"I'm questioning *if* she is the mastermind."

"We need to go to talk to her," Gabriella said.

"Right now?" Ryan moaned, then finished his beer.

"Yes." Vargas stood. "They're holding Shawn and Marcella at the office. I texted them not to let her out of their sight."

Ryan groaned and went to his bunkroom. The doctor he'd seen at the hospital after Diego's first kick to his ribs had given him a prescription for pain medication. He shook three from the bottle and dry swallowed them, then shoved the pills into his pocket.

When he returned to the salon, Vargas and Gabriella were stepping onto the finger pier, leaving the boat.

Ryan heaved himself into the cockpit's fighting chair. "Let Marcela go."

The inspectors turned to him.

"Have her followed," he explained. "She'll lead us to Diego, and we can capture them both."

Vargas nodded and reached for his phone. Gabriella rested on the transom, stretching her injured leg out. Ryan saw the strain etched on her face under a sheen of sweat. He had experienced the same discomfort of a gunshot wound. With his aching ribs, they both needed to take time off to recover.

When Vargas ended his call, he told them he had arranged for multiple cars to tail Marcela. They could switch off, lessening the likelihood they would be spotted.

"Good," Ryan declared. "Get some rest, Gabriella."

He watched her hobble up the dock, not taking any help from Vargas.

Greg rolled out to the cockpit and gave Ryan a beer, then asked, "You sure you're okay? Do you need a doctor?"

"I'm all right," he lied. He tugged his shirt up, and they gazed at the purple and yellow bruises spreading across this chest and rib cage. "Got any cigars handy?"

Greg went into the cabin and returned with a pair of hand-rolled Don Collins. They cut the cigars and lit them. The first hit of smoke to his lungs was a tonic, the nicotine washing through his body clear to his toes.

"Don wants to go back to Texas with Ashlee."

Greg nodded. "He told me."

"Do we need a mechanical engineer?"

"With all the new engines and electronics, you need someone who can fix them if they break."

"True," Ryan agreed. "We're training Stacey on the Kirby Morgan hard hats, but we could use another diver. If you pull me off the boat to do something else, that leaves Travis, and he needs a standby."

"I'll see if I can find a diver-engineer," Greg replied.

The men clinked bottles in a toast. While they were no closer to capturing Diego, Ryan was ready to go back to sea, but it would be much sooner than he expected and not on the salvage vessel as he planned.

CHAPTER FORTY-THREE

Marcela Fuentes drove aimlessly through the city. After being released by the police, she had gotten into her Ford Explorer. She had pulled out the prepaid cell phone while eyeing the silver-and-black .380 semi-automatic. The police warrant for the search of L&F Logistics hadn't extended to her vehicle, and she was thankful she had left the phone and gun in the glovebox.

She'd been afraid they wouldn't let her go, that someone would finally see how she had manipulated Shawn's business for her own gain, but the cops were too fixated on him. He'd spent the afternoon alternating between screaming at the forensics team and drinking rum. Shawn had also blamed her for his problems. She wasn't sure if he knew the truth or was just lashing out. Whatever the case, she was happy to leave.

A text message from Diego said Ryan Weller had tried to apprehend him at their home. Diego had kicked Ryan in the ribs, again, which made her smile.

If they knew where she lived and her connection to Diego, then she couldn't go home. She turned down one street and then another, trying to decide what to do. *Island*

Trader would arrive in Fajardo tomorrow evening, providing their escape from the country. Until then, she needed a place to stay and needed to collect the things she'd packed to take with her.

Really, she didn't need any of it. They had saved enough money in Cayman Island bank accounts to never have to work again. Other than spending money to maintain their criminal enterprise, she and Diego had lived frugally. They'd paid off the house, so her family would be taken care of if they were caught. And they tried to have a baby. She was glad they didn't have a child. It would complicate things now that it was time to run.

Pulling to a stop in the parking lot of a grocery store, she texted her sister-in-law, Esmerelda, asking her to bring her bags. She waited for Esmerelda to answer the text and watched the surrounding traffic. A car, with a man and a woman inside, pulled into a spot near her. The woman got out and ambled toward the store. There was something suspicious about the way she moved and the furtive glances she cast at Marcela.

Diego had explained how tails worked. Out of the corner of her eye, she saw the man in the car speak into a radio. They were watching her!

How could she be so stupid?

The woman was halfway to the store and the man had his head down when Marcela dropped the phone into her purse and gunned her car out of the lot. Watching her rearview mirror, she waited for the vehicle she suspected was following her to move, but it stayed put. A sigh of relief escaped her lips.

Her phone chimed, and as she glanced down to check the message, one of the two unmarked police cars in position to pursue her slid in behind the Explorer.

Esmerelda had Marcela's bags in the trunk of her car and

agreed to meet when Marcela found a place. Marcela tapped the steering wheel in time to the music blaring from the radio. She liked it loud, and her mood was turning, enough so that she danced in the seat, wiggling her bottom and waving her arms. Things would work out.

Marcela drove to Atlantic Beach and rented a hotel room in a seaside hotel. Then she called Esmerelda to tell her where to meet. An hour later, they'd transferred the boxes and bags to the Explorer. She hugged her sister-in-law, both shedding tears of goodbye. Then she strolled out to the beach, sure her luck had turned, and the night was about to get even better for her.

CHAPTER FORTY-FOUR

Ryan was feeling good. The pills and the beer had taken the edge off the pain, turning it into a dull ache. To the west, the sun had set behind the cityscape, and he had a perfect view from the fighting chair. Greg had called out for a food delivery and brought another round of beers. How the hell did Greg put away so much alcohol every night?

His phone rang, and Ryan glanced at the caller ID before answering. "What's up, Gabriella?"

"How are you?" she asked.

"I'm okay. What about you?" His head reeled, and he took several shallow breaths, but not seeming to satisfy his body's hunger for oxygen. Gritting his teeth, he forced himself to take a slow, deep breath, expanding his diaphragm against the bruised ribs and muscles.

"I'm fine," Gabriella said. "Would you like to go to dinner?"

He was about to say no but changed his mind. "Sure."

"Good, I'll pick you up in ten minutes."

"Roger that." He went back inside and glanced at Greg as he got ready. "You're on your own. I gotta date."

"What? With whom?" Greg inquired.

"Gabriella."

"Your vodou mama won't like you cheating on her."

Ryan shrugged. He didn't feel like telling Greg about the end of his relationship.

Gabriella called him from the parking lot, and he walked to her Honda. She moved over to the passenger seat. Ryan slid behind the wheel before she directed him to a restaurant on Atlantic Beach.

The couple found seats at a table. Gabriella arranged her crutches on one of the free chairs. The buzz Ryan had felt on the boat was gone and he ordered a margarita on the rocks with salt. He wanted to reinvigorate the hazy feeling of being half-drunk. Not only did it take the edge off his pain, but it sedated his emotions as well. If things went well tonight, Gabriella might just be the rebound shot he needed.

CHAPTER FORTY-FIVE

Marcella wandered along the beach, the sun turning the blue water into a giant reflection of oranges and yellows. Further out, white breakers capped black waves as they foamed over the reef lines. She wished Diego were with her, holding her hand and helping to quell the queasiness in her stomach. Someone had tailed her to the grocery store, but had they been able to follow her here? She should be in the hotel room, not strolling the beach like a common *turista*.

She decided to go back to her room. Tomorrow, she'd drive to Fajardo, meet Diego, and leave her home for good. It made her sad that she could never return to her childhood home or kiss her mother goodnight, but this was the life she had chosen. Diego had warned her of this possibility before she had become involved.

As she made her way toward the hotel, Marcela glanced over at the restaurant. Hunger pains gnawed at her stomach. Room service would have to do. Suddenly, she paused, all thoughts of food vanishing from her mind.

Her adversary sat with the female cop Diego had shot in Ponce. They were enjoying adult beverages and ordering dinner. They looked rather cozy. Doubts about Ryan's relationship with Joulie Lafitte crept into her mind.

Would Joulie pay a ransom for him if he was dating another woman?

There was only one way to find out. She pulled out her cell phone and dialed Diego's number.

He answered on the second ring, and she told him where she was and what she wanted him to do.

Marcela consulted her phone's clock. The couple's food had arrived just as she'd hung up. Diego needed to get into position quickly. Marcela positioned herself where she could watch the couple.

As she waited for Diego to arrive, she keyed the power button on the side of her phone for at least the one hundredth time in the past thirty minutes. Where was Diego? Just as she pushed the button again, a text message came through. Diego was in place. She stood and walked toward Ryan Weller and the female police officer. What did he see in that puta anyway? Marcela threw some exaggerated sway into her hips just as she had when she'd led Ryan and his boss to Shawn's office. Time to bait the trap.

CHAPTER FORTY-SIX

When they'd finished their meal, Ryan moved from across the table to sit beside his date. They watched the people parade past their table and poked fun at the crazy tourists.

Then someone caught Ryan's eye and he nudged Gabriella. She clutched his hand, acknowledging she had also seen their person of interest. The woman seemed to be watching them, taking quick glances over her shoulder, pretending to tend to her windblown hair.

"Where's her tail?" Ryan inquired.

"I don't know." Gabriella sent a text to Vargas, who replied they had reduced the number of watchers since she had checked into a hotel.

Marcela walked along the sand, shoes in hand, gazing directly at them.

Gabriella leaned in and whispered, "Let's follow her."

Ryan nodded and emptied his margarita. The flush of alcohol had burned off, replaced by adrenaline.

"You pay for dinner and I'll follow her," the inspector said, shouldering her purse and jamming a crutch under each arm.

"I see what's going on," Ryan joked. "You're skipping on paying. I thought this was Dutch treat."

She paused, leaning on her crutches. "What is this ... Dutch treat?"

"Both parties split the check."

"You are mistaken. You're paying, and I am following Marcela." She spun on her good leg and hobbled down the steps to the sand.

Ryan flagged down a waiter, explaining he was in a hurry because his date had left him, and he needed to catch her. The man scurried off with Ryan's credit card. When he returned, Ryan signed the bill and tossed a generous cash tip on the table. Then he jogged after the two women, holding his ribs as he moved.

Marcela stayed just ahead of Gabriella who labored through the soft sand on her crutches. The woman in the lead kept glancing over her shoulder to ensure she was still being followed.

Ryan hung back, observing the scene. Beyond the shore, the relentless Atlantic smashed onto the reef line. The boom of surf ever present background noise to the city traffic. A quarter moon had risen, low and fat against the horizon. Lovers strolled hand in hand while others sat silently, watching the waves break on the sand.

Near the eastern end of the beach, Marcela turned into an alley. Ryan watched Gabriella follow behind a minute later. Darkness swallowed her, and Ryan ran to the edge of the building and stuck his head around the corner.

Gabriella was hobbling along the alley, but Marcela had disappeared. He jogged up to his date, checking the darkened doors and windows of expensive swimwear and clothing shops as he went.

"Where'd she go?" he whispered.

"Up there." Gabriella nodded to the entrance of a parking

garage. Her face was white, her steps slowing from the lengthy walk on a strained leg and the force of the crutches on her shoulder.

They walked together to the entrance. Ryan figured Marcela was gone, even with the cat-and-mouse game she had played on the beach.

A single bulb lit the garage entrance near the elevator. Off to the left, a row of parked cars sat in darkness between the massive concrete pillars that held up the second and third floors of the structure. Something was not right. His alarm bells jangled. As he'd told James, his Spidey sense was tingling.

He grabbed Gabriella by the arm. She stopped, and he gestured for her to wait, but she shook him off and continued. Ryan slipped his pistol from the holster and followed. Everything about this seemed wrong.

Gabriella led the way, hurrying down the dark hallway. He passed a small depression in the concrete on his right. Normally, he would have swept it with his gun, clearing the hiding spot of any tangos, but he was trying to keep up with the inspector. He hissed at Gabriella, "Slow down."

Then he heard a scraping noise on the wall behind him. Before he could spin, the hard metal of a gun barrel pressed into his right kidney. Ryan raised his hands. His assailant ripped the pistol from his fist. He started to shout a warning to Gabriella.

It died on his lips when he saw Diego Hernández put a gun muzzle to her temple. She froze midstride.

"Walk straight ahead," Marcela ordered.

Ryan moved forward. A third person emerged from the shadows, holding a semi-auto shotgun with a cut down barrel and a birdshead grip, reminding Ryan of an old pirate pistol. Shotgun leveled his weapon at Gabriella. Diego opened the rear hatch of a Ford Explorer and pulled out a roll of silver duct tape.

Ryan had trained for the scenario of disarming a person behind him, but the large bore of the scattergun just inches from Gabriella's torso kept him from reacting. The man could pull the trigger faster than Ryan could seize Marcela's pistol. Then there was Diego, able to shoot either of them. Neither he nor the inspector needed an extra hole in their bodies. He knew the agony of a gunshot wound all too well, having sustained two in Afghanistan on his last deployment. The misery in his ribs was a pinprick compared to the intensity of being shot.

Diego pulled Ryan's hands in front of him and wrapped tape around his wrists. Then he took a few turns around Ryan's waist, locking his arms against his belly. With Ryan confined, Diego searched his pockets, taking his tactical knife, wallet, and the extra pistol magazines and holster, along with Ryan's pain pills. Diego held up the bottle and rattled the contents. He pocketed the knife, pills, and wallet, then tossed the rest onto the Explorer's front passenger seat.

Shotgun and Diego picked up Ryan and set him on the rear bumper. Then Diego started wrapping Ryan's ankles. He sadistically ripped the tape off, pulling the hair from Ryan's bare leg.

Diego smirked. "How's your ribs, blanquito?"

Ryan just glared at him.

Gabriella received wraps around her ankles and wrists before being thrust into the cargo bay beside Ryan. Diego threw a tarp over them and closed the hatch. It was stifling hot, and the canvas stank of gas, oil, and dirt.

Ryan listened to the cargo thieves and their enforcer climb into the Ford and slam doors. Whoever sat in the back seat tossed several bags on top of them. Ryan stifled a scream when a bag landed on his delicate ribs.

He lost track of the twists and turns the Explorer made. He shifted the bag off him, so it stopped bouncing on his rib cage and wiggled closer to Gabriella. His shoulders ached from the awkward position Diego had taped his arms, and he couldn't reach the tape on Gabriella's hands.

Each bump jarred and jostled they as they lay beneath the blanket. Ryan's mind drifted to what lay ahead and how they would escape.

CHAPTER FORTY-SEVEN

Ryan woke when a hand grabbed his ankles and dragged him from the SUV. He braced himself to fall to the ground, but they stopped him and sat him up when his legs were out. They did the same with Gabriella.

Despite the moonlight, Ryan had trouble seeing past the amber cone cast by Marcela's flashlight. The all-encompassing darkness seemed to swallow the ambient light. It didn't help that she repeatedly flashed it into his eyes, ruining his night vision.

Diego squatted and sliced away their ankle bonds while Jomar, the man who held the shotgun, kept them covered. With a chuckle, Diego jerked the tape from their bare legs and made them stand.

Marcela led them to a ramshackle house. She snapped on the lights, and they forced Ryan and Gabriella into straight back chairs pulled from the circular table in the kitchen.

"I need to take a leak," Ryan said.

"Go ahead," Jomar taunted.

"Me, too," Gabriella chimed in.

"Piss in your pants," Diego yelled from the kitchen.

"How long will you keep us hostage?" Ryan asked. "Do you want us to smell like piss the whole time?"

Marcela wrinkled her nose. "I don't."

Diego relented. He sliced through Gabriella's bonds while Jomar and Marcela both trained their guns on her. Marcela followed her into the bathroom. When she finished, Marcela marched her to another room. Diego accompanied Ryan into the bathroom. He rolled his neck, shoulders, and wrists to work the kinks out. He peed, then Diego pushed him through the curtain serving as a door and into the room with Marcela. She lay on a stained mattress under a single, barred window. The room stank of mold and urine.

Diego taped Ryan's wrists together, then wrapped his torso and upper arms tightly with more tape. "This will help the ribs."

"I heard you were a Ranger," Ryan said.

Diego smirked. "I got the best of you, squid."

"Yeah, you did," Ryan admitted.

Diego pushed him backward onto the mattress beside Gabriella.

Marcela threw a blanket over them. "Enjoy your night, lovers."

Ryan's mind leaped straight to Joulie. He turned to watch Marcela leave the room. Jomar planted a chair in the doorway and sat, shotgun across his lap.

"Hey," Ryan said.

Jomar looked up.

"Is that a new Remington?"

"The V3," Jomar replied, caressing the semi-auto twelve gauge like it was his lover.

"I'm going to kill you with it."

Their guard burst out laughing.

Ryan lay on his back, the tape's sticky adhesive chafing his skin. Gabriella curled onto her side. The night air was heavy with humidity, and the blanket only served to trap the heat.

"Pull this blanket down," he whispered.

She jerked it off him, uncovering his torso, but the sweat still ran, plastering his shirt to the mattress. His shoulders were on fire. His heartbeat pulsed in the bruised muscles. Each breath felt smaller than the last, like he was slowly suffocating.

Closing his eyes, he concentrated on his breathing. In for a three count, out for four. The breathing exercises, his personal modification of the combat breathing method, usually helped him relax, but it was difficult to breathe with his arms taped to his body. He'd been through worse than this —twenty-foot storm waves he thought would swamp his sailboat, purposely stepping into a field of IEDs to disarm them, getting shot by a Taliban terrorist, and stuck-in-an-MRI-machine claustrophobia. Duct taped on a piss-stained mattress was a new low.

He stared at the ceiling for a long time before Jomar began to snore.

Gabriella sat up and put her arms straight out in front of her. She jerked her elbows back hard, so the tape smacked her breastbone and ripped apart. She quickly pulled the tape from her wrists.

Jomar did not stir. She removed a fingernail file from her pocket and cut Ryan's bonds before pulling the tape away from his chest and arms. His muscles screamed when he moved, but it was heaven to be free.

She kissed him, then they lay side by side, staring into the darkness. Ryan contemplated escaping, but there were heavy bars on the window and three heavily armed people waiting for him to move. Maybe if he felt better or Gabriella could move without crutches then he would try, but for now he had let things play out.

Dawn came in purples, pinks, and yellows, streaming through the window to illuminate the water stains on the ceiling and the spray-painted graffiti on the peeling yellow wall.

Jomar snorted to life when the sun hit his face.

Gabriella interlaced her fingers with Ryan's and squeezed his hand, their eyes conveying the need to stay still. They didn't know how their kidnappers would react when they saw their captives were free. She had pulled the blanket over them at Jomar's first movements.

Their guard stood and stretched, then went to the bathroom. The flimsy walls allowed every sound to echo through the house, and soon, Marcela and Diego were awake. Ryan smelled eggs frying and the wonderful aroma of dripping coffee. His stomach growled. He rolled his tongue around his dry mouth.

Diego appeared, holding a plate of eggs and bread, along with a cup of coffee. With a sadistic leer at Gabriella, he raised the plate to his nose and took a deep breath, then handed the plate and cup to Jomar. Their guard shoveled the food down his throat, before sipping the coffee at a more leisurely pace.

Diego left and came back with a plate of eggs and leaned against the door frame.

Gabriella said, "I could use the bathroom again, and I'm hungry."

"You're a demanding *bicha*."

"What's the plan, Diego?" Ryan asked before Gabriella could scream at him for calling her a bitch.

Waving his fork like a conductor, Diego replied, "We wait for the evening." He pointed the fork at Ryan. "We take you." The fork moved to Gabriella. "We leave her."

"Are you going to kill her?"

"Don't be *loco*," Diego said. "I give her to Jomar. He is

hornier than a two-peckered Billy goat. She'll wish she was dead."

Ryan looked at Jomar, who had a lascivious smile plastered across his egg-smeared face.

"Do you like that?" Diego chuckled. "Two-peckered Billy goat. I got that for an old Ranger buddy of mine from Alabama."

"What do you want from us?" Ryan asked, still angry about allowing themselves to be captured so easily.

"Not her. You, we will sell to your Haitian girlfriend."

"I don't have a Haitian girlfriend."

Diego laughed. "You don't have to lie to have friends, Ryan Weller."

"I'm not lying. We broke up."

Gabriella glared at Ryan.

Diego thoughtfully bounced his fork between his fingers. "We will find out."

"I need to pee," Gabriella whined.

"Take her, Jomar," Diego said. He stood in the doorway and watched as the enforcer stepped to the bed and threw back the tarp.

"What the hell!"

Gabriella held up her hands in surrender. Ryan kept still, arms straight by his sides to protect them from the beating that was sure to come.

Diego walked over and stared down at them. "Leave them. They may have escaped a little duct tape, but they cannot escape a concrete block room." He made eye contact with Ryan. "If you try, I will tenderize your ribs more."

They passed the day confined to the room with bathroom breaks and minimal food. Ryan was thankful Diego did not tape his hands and feet together again. His skin was red from where the tape had ripped his hair out. He hung the blanket over the south-facing window to block the sun, but it did little to stifle the heat. While hanging the curtain, he saw they were on a low hill surrounded by nothing but trees.

What tempered the heat was the ice-cold glare Gabriella gave him from the opposite side of the room. Ryan tried to explain his complicated relationship with Joulie. They were breaking up, and he wasn't sure she'd pay the ransom. Gabriella stuck her fingers in her ears.

Still, he felt responsible for their situation. Her wound dressings needed changed, and she was in pain. Ryan asked Diego for the medication he had removed from his pocket last night. Diego relented and allowed them to have one each.

Ryan took the distribution of pills as a gesture of good will. They wanted the captives to be healthy. Stealing cargo containers was one thing but killing a cop in cold blood would spur a real manhunt. He wondered what Greg was doing, and if he and Vargas were rallying their own search.

At eight p.m., the sun was low in the horizon. Diego entered the room and wrapped the prisoners' hands in duct tape before marching them out of the house. A wind wicked the sweat from Ryan's body, sending a chill through him. He glanced at Gabriella, but she didn't meet his gaze. Diego and Jomar shoved them into the Explorer and tossed the smelly canvas over them again.

An hour later, they stopped. Jomar and Diego dragged Ryan out. Marcela closed the SUV's hatch.

"What about her?" Ryan asked, staring through the Explorer's rear window at Gabriella.

Diego shrugged. "She got loose once; she can do it again."

They had taped her elbows together, making it more difficult to escape, but she still had her nail file tucked into her pocket.

The group walked to a wooden panga. The fisherman waited for them, one hand holding the vessel to the pier with a mooring line. The outboard motor burbled quietly while they climbed aboard.

Once they were seated, he eased away from the pier, steering toward a freighter. Their little craft cut a white wake through the dark blue sea. Ryan stared at the Explorer, vowing to end his captivity quickly and return for Gabriella.

CHAPTER FORTY-EIGHT

Sam Tennison walked to the end of the rebuilt quay. He pulled the stub of a cigar from his lips and rolled it in his fingers. Absently, he stroked his mustache with his other hand. Two men and a woman walked down another pier and climbed into one of the native fishing pangas.

Several weeks ago, his boss, Greg Olsen, had introduced him to one of the men now headed toward a freighter anchored in the harbor. He took a long draw on the cigar, then let the smoke out and turned to find Antonio Rodriguez standing beside him. Antonio was an engineer from the local architect firm the Puerto Rican government insisted DWR have on the job site. He had quickly become Sam's translator and fixer, making problems disappear. He was a good kid who seemed to know everyone in Fajardo.

Sam thrust his chin out. "Who are those people in the boat?"

"The fisherman, he is my cousin Pablo. The others ..." Antonio shrugged.

They watched the boat chug across the water.

"The tall one was with *señor* Olsen."

"Yes, he was, Antonio," Sam said thoughtfully.

What kind of operation was Olsen running? Maybe the big man had found the lost container because he had known where to look. Sam wondered if it had been a show to impress Greg.

While the idea had merit, Sam dismissed it. Over beers one night, Greg had told Sam about his ordeal in Afghanistan and how Ryan had saved his life and the lives of everyone in the convoy. When Sam had looked into Ryan's green eyes, he'd seen no guile. Every man kept secrets, but Sam didn't think Ryan was a cargo thief.

Antonio interrupted his thoughts. "I will ask Pablo who they are when he comes back."

"Good idea," Sam said around his cigar.

They didn't have to wait long. When Pablo returned to the docks after dropping off his passengers, Antonio hurried to help him with the lines. The cousins chatted in the fading evening light.

Sam watched the sun slipping toward the horizon while he waited on Antonio. He was ready to go back to Texas. There were a few things he'd miss, like the friendliness of the people, these fine hand-rolled cigars, the tropical sunsets, and the locally distilled rum.

The freighter had pulled up its anchor. Red and green running lights winked along its flanks as it made the turn toward the open Atlantic.

Antonio hurried back to Sam with Pablo in tow. "*Señor* Tennison, my cousin says the woman, she give the orders. Two of the men carried guns and your friend was most uncomfortable."

Sam pulled the cigar from his mouth. "Did he say anything?"

Antonio asked Pablo in Spanish. Pablo shook his head.

Sam arched his eyebrow, the cigar in his hand hovering near his lips. "*Gracias*, Antonio."

Pablo and Antonio walked off into the twilight. Sam pulled his phone from his pocket and dialed his boss. He remembered when Greg was just the boss's son, running around in short pants, asking a million questions and getting in everyone's way. He'd always been a good kid.

When Greg answered, Sam said, "Do you have time for a story?"

The boss said yes, and Sam told him about the SUV, Pablo's boat ride, and the freighter.

"That explains why he and Gabriella never came back to the marina." Greg gave Sam a recap of events.

Sam cursed. "All that over a few cargo containers."

"Yes, sir," Greg replied. "Did you get the name of the ship?"

"*Island Trader*," Sam replied.

Greg thanked him and said goodbye.

Sam pocketed the phone when the call ended. Using a thumb and forefinger, he repeatedly smoothed the strips of mustache running down his chin. As the sun slid beneath the waves, he was glad he was only a construction foreman.

CHAPTER FORTY-NINE

The Explorer was an oven. Gabriella was thankful it was dark. Even at sundown, the heat had rapidly built inside the metal and glass cage to over ninety-five degrees. Sweat drenched her clothes and plastered her hair to her face and neck.

The inspector forced herself upright and watched as Diego, Marcela, and Jomar marched Ryan to a waiting panga. They climbed aboard and motored away. She screamed into the duct tape covering her mouth, furious at being left bound and gagged in the vehicle. Tears ran unabated down her cheeks and mingled with sweat to drip from her chin.

She kicked the side window. The impact vibrated through her leg. Again, and again, she slammed her feet into the unyielding glass while screaming into the gag. The glass did not break, and it infuriated her. Panic turned to hysteria. Gabriella's sniffles became sobs, which rose to screams as she thrashed against her bonds, struggling to break the duct tape, to loosen her arms or scratch the tape from her lips. She needed to breathe. She needed to be free.

Lying still, Gabriella's chest heaved, the air blocked by

snot streaming from her nose. Despite the seal made by the tape, she tasted it on her lips. Closing her eyes, she willed herself to be calm. *You made it through being shot, you can make it through this.*

Gabriella placed a foot on the window again and pushed. It made her bare heels ache and smeared footprints across the glass.

After a few minutes rest, to catch her breath, she remembered the fingernail file she'd used the night before to cut Ryan's bonds. Gabriella tried to put her hand in the pocket. With her arms taped from wrist to mid-bicep, she couldn't extract the file, but she could reach the hem of her shorts. Lying on her back, she lifted her bottom off the floor and pulled. The material dragged on her damp skin, sticking to her hips. She continued pulling until her fingers found the brass button. When it popped loose, the shorts slid to her knees. She kicked them off and dug out the file.

With it pinned between her knees, she swiped at it with the tape holding her biceps together. The file kept slipping on her sweaty skin and folding over when she applied pressure. After a dozen failed attempts in which she did nothing but scream and swear at the file for not staying put, she snatched it up in both hands. With a maniacal shriek, she spun and jammed it into the rear seat back beside the headrest.

The thick foam and leather held the file long enough for her to start a small tear in the tape. She kept sawing until she'd cut below her elbows. Driving her elbows back against her chest, she broke the duct tape free.

She tore it from her arms and then ripped the gag from her mouth, grimacing as it pulled out her hair. Being able to take deep breaths and shed the tape helped stifle her panic. She unwrapped her ankles and climbed over the seat and out the door.

The whole operation had taken ten minutes, and when

Gabriella tumbled from the Explorer, she looked like she'd just stepped out of the shower. She stood for several minutes, drinking in the cool night air and wondering why she hadn't opened the back hatch instead of trying to kick out a window. She chalked it up to panic.

Diego had parked the SUV across the street from the docks. Faint music drifted out of an apartment window. She spread her arms and let the wind dry her skin and clothes. Then she pulled on her shorts, conscious of standing in public in her panties, even if no one was there to see her.

Her gaze fell on the DWR compound, and the light above the mobile office. Gabriella ran toward it, the sharp stones digging into her bare feet, but she didn't care. She had to get help for Ryan.

CHAPTER FIFTY

Ryan Weller watched the captain nose *Island Trader* into the Atlantic swells. In one corner of the bridge, Marcela Fuentes leaned against the bulkhead, her face a shade of sickly green. Ryan thought she might puke at any moment. Seasickness was the payment Neptune demanded for her sins.

The ship wallowed in the southern swells. Ryan braced his feet. He was at home on the sea. He'd spent two years sailing around the world in a thirty-six-foot sailboat and then ten years in the U.S. Navy on ships both larger and smaller than *Island Trader*. A little wave action didn't bother him. He stepped out to the bridge wing. The woman followed on unsteady legs.

He remembered the tricks sailors played on each other when one of them felt seasick. They would flex up and down on bending knees to exaggerate the ship's roll, and the cooks would serve the greasiest food they could prepare for the first meal underway. He thought about trying to exacerbate Marcela's condition, but she still had a gun.

"Where are we going?" he asked. He knew they wished to

ransom him to Joulie, but he needed more information about their plan to formulate one of his own.

"To see your friend in Haiti," Marcela said. "I heard her conversation with Shawn."

Ryan stared into the darkness. His chances for survival were improving. Taking him to Haiti would be like throwing a rabbit into the briar patch. Joulie was certain to side with him over a two-bit murderer and cargo thief.

Marcela answered an unspoken question. "I need to sell this cargo."

"Don't you have a connection in Miami?"

"We do," Marcela replied, "but it will take too long and there will be people looking for us."

"You need cash to escape," Ryan deduced.

"Yes." Marcela handed a satellite phone to Ryan. "You will call her and make arrangements."

"I don't have her number memorized."

Marcela gave him his cell phone. He unlocked it and pulled up the number. With Marcela watching, he dialed it into her satellite phone's keypad and hit send. He shut off his cell phone to reset the lock screen and returned it to Marcela when she brought up her gun.

Ryan put the satellite phone to his ear. He hoped Joulie wouldn't answer, but he would just have to keep trying until she did. And do it with the muzzle of Marcela's cheap chrome-plated pistol jammed into his ribs. He could snatch the gun from her, but with Diego and Jomar looking on, he was positive they'd shoot first and ask questions later. Plus, he was unsure who else on the ship carried a firearm. This troubleshooting business was becoming more trouble than it was worth, especially when he was the one who might get shot.

When Joulie answered, Ryan spoke in English for his kidnapper's benefit. "It's me."

Her voice softened to a purr, and a shiver ran up his spine.

Despite knowing their time together was over, he still wanted to fall into her arms.

"I have someone who wants to talk to you," he said.

Joulie snapped back to business mode, and Ryan handed the phone to Marcela.

"I have cargo containers for you to buy," Marcela said.

Ryan listened to the discussion. They'd make for Cap-Haïtien, and when they reached the port, Joulie would inspect the freight and determine its worth. Then she would decide if she would purchase them and Ryan's release.

He didn't like how this was shaping up.

Marcela left him leaning on the railing. Talking on the phone seemed to have steadied her nerves. He'd watched her stare at the horizon as she'd talked, the old sailor's trick settling her stomach. Blackness enveloped the ocean. The only sounds were the sighing of the waves against the hull and the thrum of the diesel engines.

He drew in a deep breath of salt air and closed his eyes. This would be over soon.

CHAPTER FIFTY-ONE

With a cruising speed of ten knots, *Island Trader* made the Cap-Haïtien berthing in forty hours. As the captain brought the ship alongside the wharf, Ryan scanned the waterfront for any signs of Greg's Hatteras GT63. He hoped Joulie had called him for backup.

When he didn't see the gleaming sportfisher, he concentrated on Joulie's Toyota RAV4, sitting beside several other vehicles, which contained her security force. Since the riots, she never left the hotel without reinforcements.

She stepped from the RAV4, wearing blue jeans and a white V-neck shirt. Ryan couldn't take his eyes from her. She was beautiful, and she held his life in her hands.

Five men with AK-47s surrounded her. Ryan had tried to convince her that her security detail needed a better rifle than the Soviet 7.62. She'd rebuffed his efforts, saying a gun was a gun; no matter if it was one hundred years old or built an hour ago, they did the same thing: fire bullets and kill people. The AK had worked fine for decades and would continue to provide peace through deterrence as long as she had a say. She chose to spend her money on education and infrastructure.

The sounds of *Island Trader*'s diesels faded as the crew shut them down. Joulie and her entourage approached. Ryan stayed on the bridge with Jomar and Diego. Marcela went to meet the warlord. They spoke for several minutes at the head of the gangway before examining the cargo.

In the few moments alone with Marcela, she'd reminded Ryan of Joulie, ruthless and in charge, a complete opposite from the meek office manager facade she'd presented when they'd first met.

A crane came alongside the cargo vessel and unloaded the containers onto waiting semis. While they worked, the two women mounted the steps to the bridge. Ryan kept his eyes on the warlord, watching her silky black hair play in the wind and the way her body moved as she climbed the stairs. He wanted to wrap her in his arms, but he knew he must stay detached. They could use any sign of weakness as leverage.

Joulie looked him up and down as she stepped onto the bridge. She was a master of her facial expressions and Ryan had experienced the full range of her moods, but he'd never seen her telegraph displeasure like now.

"What is your final offer?" Marcela asked, also sensing Joulie's shifting mood.

Joulie glanced at Ryan, her lips curled in disdain. "How about I leave him with you, and you decide what to do with him?"

Ryan felt the muscles in his neck spasm as the corner of his mouth twitched. He desperately tried to maintain a neutral posture and facial muscles. He hadn't expected the negotiations to be so difficult and doubted Marcela did as well.

"One million dollars," Marcela demanded, growing weary of Joulie's halfhearted negotiations.

Joulie brought her blue eyes up to meet Ryan's. "Yes."

Marcela gave away her glee by bouncing on her toes.

"Stanley will deliver it in one hour." Joulie tossed her hair back as if relieved to be free of the burden. "Goodbye." She walked back to her vehicle. Without looking at the hostage on the bridge wing, she climbed into the RAV4 and drove away.

Something had changed since he'd left. Another relationship had crumbled because of his job and long absences. Just like Emily Hunt, who had also stalked out of his life without a glance over her shoulder, Joulie Lafitte was also disposing of him.

As promised, an hour later, Stanley Lambre arrived with a black duffle bag stuffed with money. Diego and Jomar met him at the gangplank and escorted him to the bridge. Marcela dismissed the skipper and dumped the cash onto the console. She counted one hundred packets containing ten thousand dollars each. Satisfied with the transaction, she stuffed the money back into the duffle.

Diego said, "Now we can leave. This place gives me the creeps."

Marcela swung her little semi-automatic up and pumped two bullets into his chest.

Through a cruel sneer, she said, "Impotent bastard."

He stared dumbly at the blood staining the front of his shirt, then looked up at his wife in disbelief.

Stanley jumped sideways out the hatch.

From the deck below, Jomar shouted and fired at Stanley, the shotgun booming. Ryan took two steps toward Marcela. She swung the little gun in his direction, a vicious smile on her lips.

Ryan chopped her wrist with a bladed hand. Somehow, Marcela maintained her grip on the little pistol. She shrieked and tried to bring the handgun back to bear on Ryan.

Amid the sporadic blasts from Jomar's shotgun, trying to pin Stanley down, Ryan heard the report of a pistol. A red dot appeared on Marcela's shoulder, the impact staggering her. The pistol cracked again, sharp and loud inside the confined steel. Ryan's ears rang. Marcela grasped her throat, her face pale and her eyes wide. Blood gushed through her fingers.

Ryan glanced at Diego, still aiming at his wife. Diego looked up at him, fear and determination mingled with the tears sliding down his face. The thief's head slumped forward, and he dropped the pistol.

Slowly, Marcela's legs gave out. She slumped against the console, then slid down to sit on the floor. Her hands fell away from her throat. The blood had stopped pumping from the severed artery.

Ryan stood rooted to the deck. The absurdity of the situation almost overwhelming.

After a stunned moment, he tossed Diego's pistol to Stanley and picked up Marcela's .380. He slid the magazine out of the Bersa Thunder's grip. Six rounds plus one in the pipe. He slapped it back home and glanced at Stanley.

The bodyguard had moved to the head of the ladder and was shooting at Jomar. He motioned for Ryan to go down the starboard ladder and circle Jomar's position. As Ryan crept down the ladder, he thought of his promise to Jomar.

On the cargo deck, Ryan found the remaining member of the gang hunkered behind the bulkhead, ducking out to fire at Stanley. When he stopped to thread more shells into the Remington's tubular magazine, Ryan stepped out and pointed the Bersa at him.

Ryan shouted, "Put it on the deck."

Jomar glanced up, shell still in his hand. He thrust the gun forward and fired left-handed.

The shot went wide as Ryan dived behind the bulkhead, buckshot pellets pinging off the deck. He pressed his shoulder blades to the sun-warmed steel. The pistol looked like a child's toy in his big paw. It would still spit a deadly projectile, but it was a bedroom gun—beyond fifteen feet, accuracy went out the window. He'd given Diego's more accurate 9mm to Stanley and he hoped the Haitian wouldn't abandon him.

Another blast of buckshot ricocheted off steel. Ryan dropped to his stomach and peered around the edge. Jomar advanced along the deck, his back to the bulkhead, twisting his head left and right to keep both Ryan and Stanley from attacking him. He ran toward Ryan's position.

Ryan squatted into a crouch. He waited, holding his breath and mentally blocking the ringing in his ears to hear Jomar's movements. He heard the scrape of a foot, the snick of a shell being loaded, and felt the vibrations in the steel as Stanley ran down the ladder.

Suddenly, Jomar swung around the corner, the birdshead grip shoved into his hip, left hand holding the muzzle steady.

Rising out of his crouch, Ryan pushed the shotgun up with his left hand and shoved the Bersa's muzzle into the man's gut. He pulled the trigger until the gun clicked empty then pulled it a few more times.

Jomar sagged to his knees, mouth foaming blood.

Ryan tossed the Bersa into the water, then pulled the shotgun from the dead man's grip. He hadn't kept his promise to kill Jomar with his own gun, but he'd keep the Remington.

"We need to go," Stanley said. "I have a crew coming to clean the ship."

"Wait a minute." Ryan turned and ran up to the bridge. He patted Marcela's pockets to find his cell and her sat phone, then moved to Diego to retrieve his Walther and pocketknife. He glanced around for the bag of money, but it had disappeared, along with the captain.

Ryan found the captain in his stateroom.

He leveled Remington. "Where's the cash?"

The captain held his hands away from his body. "Under the bunk."

"Get it." As the man bent, Ryan added, "Nice and slow."

The man retrieved the black duffle bag.

"Set it on the bunk and count it."

With deliberate slowness, the captain unzipped the bag. He reached inside and withdrew the bundles one at a time, setting them on the bed. When he was done, he looked up at Ryan.

"Set ten bundles aside and put the rest in the bag," Ryan said. When the man hesitated, Ryan gestured with the shotgun. "Hurry up. I don't have all day."

Ryan snatched the bag off the bed as the captain finished zipping it closed. He shouldered the strap and backed toward the door; gun still centered on his captive. "Don't do anything stupid. I've left you a gift. Now, forget everything that's happened and get the hell out of Haiti."

The captain smiled and nodded.

Back on deck, two of Stanley's men were bagging the dead bodies. They carried them down the gangplank and tossed them into the bed of a four-door Toyota Hilux. Ryan walked to where Stanley waited beside another Hilux and got into the passenger seat.

Stanley dropped him off at the Hotel Roi Christophe. Ryan shoved the Remington into the duffle and carried it into the lobby.

Emile, the clerk, looked up from the desk and greeted Ryan with his usual gap-toothed smile. "Welcome back, Mesye Ryan."

"Where's mambo Joulie?" Ryan asked.

"In her office."

"Can you tell her I'm here, please?"

Emile picked up the phone. When the old man hung up the receiver, he said, "She is expecting you."

Ryan thanked him and walked through the well-manicured landscape of the ancient-home-turned-hotel. At the small building she had made into an office, Ryan knocked on the door before pushing it open.

Joulie, standing by the window, turned as he came in.

He tossed the bag onto the sofa. "I brought your money back minus a hundred thou. I had to bribe the captain."

"That was your money," Joulie said. "You paid him."

"I thought you invested mine."

"I did, but I pulled it out." Joulie turned to the window again. "How did you think I got my hands on a million dollars in cash so easily?"

Ryan came to stand behind her. She was severing all ties with him.

He saw James playing catch with two other children. He smiled, feeling slightly domestic. A father and mother watching their children play. He slipped his arms around her waist and nestled his face in her neck.

"He's a good kid," Joulie said. "I tracked down his relatives, they were glad for me to take him. I had to pay them a fee, of course."

"I'm glad you chose to become a mother."

"I spent many nights praying about the situation." Sadness filled her voice. "The loa gave me an answer, but they also said we must part ways."

So, this was why he was getting the cold shoulder. The loa had spoken and the loa were never wrong.

Ryan changed the subject. "Did they finish the canal?"

Joulie nodded, then added, "I have gathered your money for you to take. It is best to not have any strings."

It shouldn't have surprised him, but it did. He knew things had changed. He'd discerned that much when she'd been hesitant to lean on Shawn Lindowel. He hadn't expected her to send him packing, investments and all. Outside, James scooped a bouncing ball off the turf and sent it rocketing across the lawn. The kid had a good arm.

Ryan kissed the top of her head.

Trembling, she wiped away tears with her fingertips. She shuddered with a deep sob and spun in his arms. He kissed her hard, pulling her in tight. Joulie pushed him away and stepped back, but he was hungry for more.

She straightened her shirt. "Tomorrow, I have something to show you."

"Why not right now? It a shame to waste this private room."

"That's not what I meant, Ryan. You must get a hotel room."

He waggled his eyebrows. "Will I get any late-night visitors?"

"No." She shook her head and wiped her eyes again. "Please, don't make this harder than it is."

He shouldered the duffle bag and put a little frost in his voice. "Where's the rest of my money?"

"You can take it in cash, or I can wire it to a bank for you."

While it would be nice to have his millions in cash, he said, "We'll send it via wire transfer."

"Give me your information and I will see that it takes place today."

Ryan gave her his bank account information in the Caymans then left the office and started across the grounds to the lobby. James saw him, cried out his name, and came running.

He bent, opening his arms. James's sweat-soaked body smacked into his, and the boy wrapped his arms around Ryan's neck. He squatted there, clutching the boy in a tight embrace, remembering the escape from the tent, the helicopter crash, and the intensity of his talks with Joulie about keeping James. He felt an emotion he'd never experienced with a child: a soaring pride, and a swell of love.

James straightened to look at him. "I knew you'd come back."

"I told you I would," Ryan said, cheeks aching from his smile.

"Play catch with us."

"Let me put this bag in my room." Ryan patted the duffle hanging over his shoulder.

James nodded and ran to rejoin the other boys. Ryan watched him go, sudden thoughts of his own childhood swirling through his mind.

He registered at the front desk, received a heavy brass key, and trudged upstairs. At his suite, he didn't insert the key, but stood on the wide balcony and leaned against the railing. Two lone sunbathers sat at the edge of the pool. They were young, lithe white women whose midwestern accents drifted up to him. Most likely they were missionaries from the U.S., here to make themselves feel good that they were helping the poor before getting on an airplane and flying back to the Land of Plenty. When they were old, they could tell their grandkids about their dangerous trip to Haiti to "help" the natives.

Ryan shook his head. He, too, had ventured to the dangerous country to help the poor natives, but he had made a profit from it.

Inside his room, he sat on the bed and used Marcela's sat phone to call Greg, who asked, "Where are you?"

"First, did you find Gabriella?" Ryan asked.

"Sam Tennison called me. He saw you leaving with Diego and Marcela. Vargas scrambled the cops in Fajardo, but Gabriella had gotten loose and stumbled into our compound before they could get there."

"I'm glad she's okay." Ryan said, and then he explained the chain of events that led him back to Cap-Haïtien and the deaths of Marcela and her husband.

"Vargas told me they found documents at her home showing Diego had a low sperm count," Greg said. "Maybe she shot him because he couldn't get her pregnant. With him dead, she could find someone else to knock her up."

"I don't know why she shot him, just that she called him an impotent bastard," Ryan said, wondering if he, like Diego, suffered from low sperm count due to operating the military's VHF and HF radios.

"Vargas and I mustered an all-island manhunt for you guys when you didn't return from your date. We found her car at the beach and looked at a lot of security cam footage until we saw you following Marcela."

"She led us right into a trap."

"We figured." Greg said. "When are you coming back to PR?"

"I'm not sure when or how I'll get there." He'd neglected to talk to Joulie about his transportation. She wanted to show him something, and he wasn't in a hurry to part with her company.

"Let me know your schedule. Dennis finishes sea trials tomorrow, and I'm sending *Peggy Lynn* to a job. I got you a new diver and a new engineer, too."

"Roger that."

Ryan stashed the money and guns in the cheap hotel safe and splashed water on his face. The safe was redundant. The hotel employees feared mambo Joulie's retribution too much to steal from the guests.

The afternoon sun was low in the western sky as he walked across the grass to the three boys tossing the baseball. Sounds of the city drifted over the high walls, mingling with bird songs and the boys' laughter. It had been a long time since Ryan had played catch. A shout rose from the boys, drawing Ryan's attention. James threw an overhand zinger that stung Ryan's palm when he snagged it from the air. He threw it to the other boy.

The four made a square and tossed the ball until it was too dark to see.

EPILOGUE

It was six a.m. by his watch as Ryan leaned over the sink, shaving the whiskers from his face. The crow's feet were deepening, and his brown hair had begun to recede at his temples. He knocked the razor against white porcelain and let hot water clean the blades. The cheap disposable, provided by the hotel, had dulled with the first pass over his right cheek. He habitually left his mustache for last, and the blunt metal felt like it was dragging the hair out by the roots. Two more passes and he threw the razor into the waste basket, glad to be done.

After splashing water onto his face to remove the shaving cream, he toweled off. His scraped skin burned.

There was a knock at the door, and he pulled on his clean shirt, thankful for the Christophe's laundry service. His clothes had become ripe from forty-eight hours of wear. He'd sent everything down, including his underwear. He had expected a visitor, but she'd never materialized. The delivery person had awakened Ryan when they'd hung the laundry on the door handle at five thirty. He'd risen and showered.

Now, James stood on the balcony, tossing a ball into the

air and catching it in a glove. With a wide grin, he asked, "Want to play catch before I go to school?"

"Yeah, buddy," Ryan said, looking up and down the balcony. His stomach growled. He needed food and coffee. James tossed the ball to him. He caught it one handed against his chest.

Ryan threw the ball back and stepped outside, shivering in the sixty-eight-degree air. His blood had thinned considerably since he'd last lived in North Carolina, where temperatures dipped below freezing and they experienced snow at least once a year.

"Let's get some breakfast."

James nodded and trotted beside the big American as they made their way through the hotel on glossy black-and-white checkered tiles. Ryan paused at one of the large paintings hanging on the wall. "Do you know who that is?"

James shook his head, more interested in tossing his ball than history.

"That's Henri Christophe, the military leader who helped free the Haitians from French rule. He also built this house to use as a summer home."

James seemed unimpressed. "We have to hurry before Esther makes me go to school."

After a hasty breakfast, James raced ahead of him across the lawn, turned, and pounded his glove with his hand. Ryan rocketed the ball to him, ignoring his sore muscles and ribs. It made a satisfying smack when it hit leather.

Esther broke up their game thirty minutes later, scolding James for being late to school. She nodded deferentially to Ryan and shuffled her charge away. Ryan found a seat on the broad veranda and ordered coffee from Henri, the head waiter, who handed him a note from Joulie.

Ryan read the note, then sipped his coffee as he strolled across the hotel grounds. He was both curious as to what the vodou woman had in store for him and apprehensive at the same time.

At the office, a contingent of her guard greeted him, and he waited impatiently on a bench surrounded by the bright red flowers of tall heliconia plants. He was ready to get this over with. As much as he wished to continue his relationship with Joulie, he couldn't date someone who ordered people to their deaths. How long would it be before he became expendable? He didn't want to live like that, and he didn't want to live in a country fraught with turmoil. He had enough headaches in his own life. It was better to move on. This was good for them both, he reasoned.

Whatever righteous anger he'd built in his heart evaporated as she approached. He rose from the bench. "You said you wanted to show me something."

An hour later, they were negotiating the rutted, dirt road curving around Fort-Liberté Bay. Ryan stared out the window at the shacks and huts built along the water. If this were anywhere else in the world, glittering high rises and McMansions would block the waterfront views, but in the poorest country on earth, the hovels had the million-dollar views.

She turned off the main road and brought the SUV to a stop at the edge of the beach. They were staring at the bay and the fishing vessels anchored offshore. Amid them, the sleek white hull of a sailboat bobbed on the sparkling water.

Joulie climbed out and slipped off her sandals. Ryan picked up his duffle bag and followed her to where a man sanded an overturned wooden boat. A slight breeze carried away the flecks of paint and wood. Joulie had to pull her hair from her mouth as she spoke to the fisherman. Ryan watched another old man rasp away at a rotten section.

The fisherman led them to another boat, and after Joulie inspected it, Ryan helped push it into the water. While the fisherman started the outboard, Ryan assisted Joulie aboard.

She instructed the fisherman to take them to the sailboat Ryan had seen earlier. With a glance back at the beach, he could see Stanley standing on the shore with two other men.

When they came alongside the Lafitte 44, Joulie scrambled aboard and Ryan followed. She instructed the fisherman to return to shore.

Ryan stood behind the large wheel, evaluating the boat's sleek lines and well-maintained appearance. Chrome sparkled in the sunlight, the freshly varnished teak gleamed, and the halyards and shrouds appeared new. A custom-built hard dodger sheltered the aft companionway ladder and the row of modern electronics mounted above it. He climbed up on the wide side deck, taking in the four-person emergency life raft between the amidships companionway and the upside-down dinghy on the foredeck.

His eyes traced the lines back to the cockpit, satisfied the previous owner had rigged her to be single-handed. The boat was beautiful, and he could imagine sailing her over the briny deep, leaving behind a white, foamy carpet of wake.

Walking back to Joulie, he saw the sun dodger had curtains to enclose the cockpit. Mounted to the dodger's stainless-steel frame was a wind turbine to generate electricity.

Ryan whistled. "This is some boat."

"It's my present to you," Joulie said, sitting on the lazarette.

"What do you mean?"

"I bought this shortly after you left. I thought we could take day trips together, but it is not to be. So, I'm giving it to you. I have the paperwork here." She fumbled through her bag until she found a thick envelope and a set of keys, which she handed to a stunned Ryan.

He unlocked the aft companionway door and stepped down into the aft stateroom. To port was a large bunk, to starboard, a long settee and bookshelves, and, just forward of that, an aft head separated the space from the main salon. Everything inside was clean and immaculate. Even the cushions had new, blue covers. A modern suite of electronics hung above the chart table. There were more radios and navigation equipment than on a modern freighter.

Joulie joined him in the cabin, and they explored the boat's interior. The knowledge that Joulie would not be coming with him tempered his elation of having a new sailboat to call home. He caught her around the waist and drew her to him. She put her arms around his shoulders.

"Thank you," he whispered, and kissed her.

She pushed him away and told him to get his duffle bag. He brought it into the cabin, and she helped him stash the money in the hidden compartments she'd had a carpenter incorporate into the woodwork. He put the shotgun on top of his cash.

Joulie flopped down on the settee as Ryan closed the hidden panel. "Open the bottle of Clairin in the fridge."

Ryan retrieved the Haitian rum, found an opener in a drawer and glasses in the cabinet. He poured the clear liquid into the cups and served his helper. She gratefully took the drink. Ryan sat beside her and examined the label. It had a sideview of a Haitian woman wearing a traditional blue-and-white *karabela* dress beside the words *Clairin, hand-pressed*.

"It's my design," Joulie commented. "Our people make Clairin by hand-pressing sugar cane. It's made in small batches which I plan to export."

"Another enterprise," Ryan mused, sipping the liquor. She had set her roots deep into the rocky Haitian soil, and he could never pry them loose. So much for running naked on deserted beaches as they sailed around the world.

He let his gaze roam the interior until he spotted the badging above the circuit panel. The plaque listed the builder's name and year of construction. A smile crossed his lips and he laughed.

"What's so funny?" Joulie asked.

"I like how you decided I needed a daily reminder of you."

"How so?" Her voice was teasing. She rested her head on his shoulder and propped her feet on the settee.

"The boat is a Lafitte. You're a Lafitte."

"That worked quite nicely, didn't it?"

Ryan tilted her chin up and kissed her. "I love you," he whispered. "Come away with me. Let's spend our days lounging in the sun and scuba diving. We never have to work again."

Joulie placed her fingers on his cheek. Tears pooled in the corners of her eyes. She kissed his lips. Then she told him what he already knew.

"I can't go with you. My people need me, and my work is here."

Ryan sat back gloomily. "The gods have spoken."

"Yes." She nodded. "I wanted to have both you and my work. I know now that I was being greedy." The tears flowed freely down her cheeks. "I must send you away. But they did not tell me I couldn't give you a proper send off."

They made love in the aft stateroom, Ryan holding her trembling body close, trying to remember her every curve.

———

A STEADY WIND kept the Lafitte heeled over on a port tack. The name on the stern was *Windseeker*, and it fit the boat well. She eagerly turned to the breeze, her bow sniffing the wind. Her master eased the sheets and the main boom drifted outboard. The vessel leveled herself, and he locked the line back in the cam cleat.

The big sailor held the wheel loose in his hands, feeling

the pitch and roll of the sailboat beneath him. She was a living creature, as in tune with the sea as he with her. He set the autopilot and stepped down into the forward cabin. A fresh pot of coffee had brewed while he was topside, and he poured it into a thermos. Single-handed sailing meant long hours in the cockpit, copious amounts of caffeine, and a damn good alarm set to go off every two hours.

He glanced at the alarm clock, checking the time against that on the GPS. They read identically. Another hour on this tack and he'd switch to starboard, beating his way south along the necklace of green gems known the world over as the Lesser Antilles. It had been a long time since he'd last set foot on these islands. Sixteen years, to be exact. Where had the time gone?

After studying the radar and the Furuno chart plotter, he climbed up to the cockpit. As usual, when he came out of the cabin, he stood on the roof and surveyed the ocean in a three-hundred-and-sixty-degree circle. There was nothing but fluffy white clouds, blue skies, and bluer ocean. He braced himself against the two-foot waves as he clambered into the cockpit and poured a cup of coffee. He held it up in a toast to the sun and wind, then took a sip. Just the way he liked it—black like his soul. And it was black, indeed, having sailed away from another relationship.

He had half the equation, a white canvas stretched against a cloudless, blue sky. When would the rest come? He'd met two amazing women in the last year, and he'd lost both. During his brief stop in San Juan to see Greg and get the coordinates for his rendezvous with *Peggy Lynn*, Gabriella had practically thrown herself at him, begging him to take her along while she completed her convalescent leave. He'd considered it, pondering the moments they'd shared, but in the end, she had put a limit on their time together. When her leg was healed, she would return to Puerto Rico and her job with La Uniformada.

In the end, he had sailed off alone. The woman of his dreams was out there, somewhere. Until he found her, he had work to do aboard *Peggy Lynn*.

Ryan reached for the halyard and tightened the sail. Time to get to it.

ABOUT THE AUTHOR

Evan Graver has worked in construction, as a security guard, a motorcycle and car technician, a property manager, and in the scuba industry. He served in the U.S. Navy, where he was an aviation electronics technician until they medically retired him following a motorcycle accident which left him paralyzed. He found other avenues of adventure: riding ATVs, downhill skiing, skydiving, and bungee jumping. His passions are scuba diving and writing. He lives in Hollywood, Florida, with his wife and son.

Visit www.evangraver.com to learn more about Evan and sign up for his newsletter to receive a free short story.

Made in the USA
Monee, IL
25 March 2021